Shrouded in Silence

Other books by Robert Wise

The Son Rises: Resurrecting the Resurrection
Crossing the Threshold of Eternity
The Narrow Door at Colditz
The Bitter Road to Dachau
The Secret Road Home
Be Not Afraid
Crazymakers
Quest for the Soul
Windows of the Soul
Tagged
Wired
Deleted
The Dead Detective
The Empty Coffin
The Tail of the Dragon
The Secret Code
Fear Less for Life
When There Is No Miracle
When the Night Is Too Long
The Third Millennium
The Fourth Millennium
Mega-Millennium
The Dawning
The Exiles
The Fall of Jerusalem

SHROUDED IN SILENCE

Robert L. Wise

Nashville, Tennessee

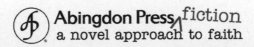

Abingdon Press fiction
a novel approach to faith

Cover design by Anderson Design Group, Nashville, TN

Library of Congress Cataloging-in-Publication Data

Wise, Robert L.
  Shrouded in silence / Robert L. Wise.
    p. cm.
  ISBN 978-1-4267-0868-8 (trade pbk. : alk. paper)
  1. Biblical scholars—Fiction.   I. Title.
  PS3573.1797S57   2011
  813'.54—dc22

2011001592

Printed in the United States of America

2 3 4 5 6 7 8 9 10 / 16 15 14 13 12 11

The author appreciates the reading and responses of Donna
Sisson, who assisted with the final development
of the manuscript.

ACKNOWLEDGMENTS

San Giovanni in Laterano Church does exit in Rome's
Piazza de San Govanni in Laterano with a baptistery adjacent
to the basilica. One can find the *Scala Santa*, the holy staircase, in the church. In addition, Santa Maria della Concezione
sits sedately at Via Vittorio Veneto 27. However, liberties have
been taken with the structure of both churches to facilitate the
story. Special thanks to Stephano Pace, Rome's finest guide,
for leading me through the backside of the amazing sights in
Rome.

The theme of this story reflects months of work in deciphering the original Koine Greek collection of New Testament
Gospels and Epistles in addressing the problem posed by the
missing correct ending to Mark. Multitudes of books and
articles were consulted in researching this project. However,
the names, characters, and incidents are purely the product of
the author's imagination. Any resemblance to actual persons—
living or dead—businesses, or companies is entirely coinciden-
tal. *Shrouded in Silence* is a work of fiction composed for the
reader's enjoyment.

Heartfelt thanks to Barbara Scott and Ramona Richards as well as the publishing team of Abingdon Press for their gracious help in editing the final manuscript. As always, my friend and agent, Greg Johnson, remains the essence of professionalism and the motivation to go the second mile. Thanks Greg.

Prologue

A.D. 68

FOG HUNG IN THE AIR, MAKING THE BLACKNESS OF NIGHT DIFFICULT TO PEN-
etrate. Still, the irregular outline of the Seven Hills of Rome
stood silhouetted against the opaque sky and remained barely
visible. The cold dampness made Plautius Laterani shiver,
but he worried more about fulfilling his assignment. Plautius
trotted briskly down the stone stairs from the legislative assembly and walked toward the soldiers standing at attention by
their horses. It would not be a good night for any of them. His
friend Scipio Livius's hand rested nervously on his sword as he
swiftly walked beside Plautius.

"You've heard the bizarre accounts murmured among sen-
ators gathering on the Palatine and Esquiline hills?" Scipio
Livius asked. "Along Via Sacra, soldiers tell stories, claiming
that the Christianios have a remarkable ability to pray for the
sick and break the spells demons cast on people. These strange
stories of eating flesh and drinking blood circulate among the
Praetorians. You know about these tales?"

Plautius nodded. "I don't spread rumors. The legislators
handle that nonsense. I leave it to them."

But Plautius knew all about the Christianios who kept their
meetings secret while openly sharing their conviction that the

7

Christ had been resurrected from the dead. Plebs chattered that this strange sect believed there was only one god, but of course, such ideas were preposterous. The assembly had just told him the Christianios were compiling a scroll with the full story of this Christ and his teachings and had given Plautius the task of finding the document—not an easy job.

Scipio Livius gripped his sword. "Makes me nervous to hear a new cult has sprung up in Rome. We grow these fanatics like weeds."

Taking all the chitchat with a grain of salt, Plautius still listened with interest. The Laterani family had lost two sons during military incursions in Gaul, and Plautius's mother continued to grieve profoundly over the loss of her children. The reports that Christianios did not fear death and believed they would live beyond this world intrigued him.

"We must ride fast to capitalize on the element of surprise," Plautius told his friend. "No one must lag behind."

"I'll keep the men moving," Scipio said.

The two soldiers marched directly to their horses and mounted. Without uttering a word, Plautius kicked his horse and headed for the gate. The Praetorian guard followed.

"Hurry!" Plautius called to the soldiers riding behind him. "We must attack before anyone discovers we are coming."

The Praetorians raced beyond the Republican Forum, across the Lapis Niger—the black marble pavement—while the moonlight glistened on their metal breastplates and plume-spiked helmets. A surge of cold night air filled his nose with the scent of Rome, and he shivered again.

"Faster!" Plautius shouted. "Stay up with me!"

The twenty-five men riding behind him crowded together and maintained close formation. Their destination lay at the edge of the city where the Circus of Caligula and Nero, the latest national racetrack, stood on the Ager Vaticanus. Spies said the arena had become one of the places where believers hid. It was rumored that one of their leaders called Petros, the Rock, might be there. His assistant John Mark was reported to be in the area writing a mysterious book.

Two days earlier, the emperor had dispatched the army to halt the burning of Rome. Rumors raged that Nero had set the fires, but a few harsh reprisals should end the murmuring of the masses driven from their smoldering homes. To stop the accusations, Nero had dispatched a unit of executioners to catch the arsonists whom he claimed were Christianios.

Plautius knew the Christianios sounded strange even by Roman standards. The great city was already filled with members of every odd group, from bizarre cults to practitioners of the Terebullium, a rite where members walked under the slit throat of a bull to allow the animal's blood to flow over their naked bodies.

But the Christianios were different. These believers followed a crucified Jew whom the Roman army had killed in Jerusalem. Arising before the sun came up, they gathered in catacombs where no decent Roman dared go at night. The reports that they drank blood and ate flesh were answered with whispers that it was only wine and bread, but the stories persisted.

In the darkness before him, Plautius recognized the outline of the stone entrance to the Circus. Huge arches ran across the front of the racetrack joined with houses that stood along the far edge and to the rear. Holding his arm up to stop the soldiers, Plautius turned in the saddle.

"Scipio, a significant number of innocent Roman citizens lives over there. Remember, we only want the Christianios; don't let your troops get blade happy."

Scipio nodded. "Yes, sir."

"Charge onto the racetrack and go immediately to the far back side," Plautius shouted to the soldiers. "Grab everyone and haul them into the arena where we can interrogate them. No indiscriminate killing! Just gather the citizens together." He pulled his sword from its sheath. "Attack!"

With a hard kick, Plautius sent his horse racing through the archway toward the farthest end of the track where the tall Egyptian obelisk towered over them. With a leap, he slid off the stallion and ran up the stone tier that lined the race course. His intent was to be the first into the stone-walled houses and to catch one of these so-called believers.

"Take the men to the left," he called to Scipio. "I'm going straight ahead."

Plautius hustled toward the two-story house just a few feet back from the top of the steps. Out of the corner of his eye, he recognized a small clay marker near the bottom of the door. Two linked half circles made a sign that looked like a fish. Maybe the sign indicated the mark of a fisherman. The house could be important.

Plautius flattened against the side of the front wall and listened. His men were making far too much noise securing the horses and climbing the bleachers. People would be awakened and investigate the racket. Pointing his sword straight ahead, Plautius rushed into a narrow entryway only to discover a short passageway led into an interior garden area with bedrooms situated around the open space. No one stirred in any of the rooms, suggesting it could be a trap. Gossips reported that the believers didn't kill—they were pacifists. Of course, rumors were rumors. Plautius exercised caution.

He bent near the ground to make himself a smaller target. As he drew closer to a doorway, he smelled olive oil. Peeking in, he saw an oil lamp still burning in one corner. The usual low, flat Roman bed with covers thrown back suggested someone had just leaped up and disappeared into the night.

Plautius carefully stepped into the room. A clay pitcher had been tipped over on the floor and cracked. A stylus and ink pot stood next to a wall. The terrazzo tiled floor with geometrical motifs looked normal enough. Then Plautius saw the fragment.

A piece of papyrus with a torn edge lay on the floor near the door. It appeared to be a section of a scroll or part of a writing that had been ripped off when someone dashed out. Moving closer to the flame of the small oil lamp, Plautius recognized the writing as Greek:

> They went out and fled from the tomb; for trembling and astonishment had come upon them; and they said nothing to any one, for they were afraid. But behold Jesus of Nazareth returned on that very night and stood in their midst. The apostles were afraid and retreated from him, but Jesus raised his hand and showed them the wound on his wrist where the soldiers had driven the nail through. "Be not afraid. I bring you peace. Come and see for I have gained the victory over death and prepared for you the path that you might follow me—

Plautius jerked his head up, startled by a racket outside, then looked back down at the document in his hand. Instantly he thought of his two brothers and their mother's grief. This testimonial was not about death but life, and he wasn't about to destroy a writing with such promise. Turning it over to his centurion would be disastrous. There was much more to be read, but other soldiers would soon overtake him. Sweeping aside the *sagum*, his old military cape, he rolled the document and slipped it under his metal breastplate. Hurrying back to the interior patio, he turned and strode to the front of the house.

Although he had no idea what had happened, something had touched him in that bedroom. Maybe these Christianios were just another cult drifting through Rome. Maybe not. He would study this piece of papyrus carefully.

Walking out onto the street, Plautius watched the soldiers rush back and forth from house to house, carrying their torches high and herding citizens to the race track for examination. The locals would be irate at such rough treatment, and they might have a hard time proving they weren't believers. It wasn't fair, but there wasn't much in Rome that was.

Part One
Night Falls

1

September 1, 2008

Murky shadows spread down the streets of Rome and darkened the narrow lanes winding through ancient thoroughfares. A heavyset man in a trench coat trotted down the steps of *La Metropolitana*, the metro system, not far from the *Fontana di Trevi*. When he turned the corner at the bottom of the stairs, the smell of hot pizza offered by a vendor near the metro entrance slowed him, but he didn't stop.

The fountains always attracted a bevy of tourists with cameras flashing like machine guns. They fluttered around the statue of Neptune in his shell-shaped chariot surrounded by a court of seahorses and giant tritons. Cold had already permeated the stone. The stout man walked at a quick clip as if he could distance himself from the chill of the evening. The press of late-night tourists strolling through the quaint streets only helped cover his movements.

A few people milled around the platform, looking indifferent. Leaning against the back wall, oblivious to the crowd, a young man stood locked in an embrace with a black-haired Italian woman. No one looked at them for more than a few seconds.

A rush of air surged out of the murky tunnel and signaled the arrival of the train. The roar of steel wheels clattered against the rails and telegraphed that the speeding vehicle would stop in a matter of moments. Waiting until the last second, the heavyset man jumped into the coach just before the train left the station and settled into a seat at the rear.

At this hour, there weren't many people traveling in his direction—only those who had worked hard all day. The men wore pullover long-sleeved jerseys underneath worn sport coats; tired women in wrinkled dresses paid no attention to him.

A surge of anxiety swept over him when he realized that his hands were sweating. Beads of perspiration popped up on his forehead. Never had he done anything like he planned. His face appeared calm, but his stomach churned. He gnawed at his bottom lip.

All the trains stopped running around 1:30 a.m., but that should give him plenty of time to set up in the tunnel just outside of the *termini* in the Piazza dei Cinquecento. Without moving his head, his eyes roamed around the car to make sure the police hadn't followed him.

He thought about Rome and how it had pushed the present moment into the tiny cracks left from three thousand years of history. It was a tight fit, particularly when the objective was to destroy a portion of the city. He remembered reading a historian who called Rome a palimpsest: a piece of parchment used again and again with the present day squeezed between the lines or written over the top of the faded original. Yet, the city really wasn't so hard to decipher. Central Rome was contained in only two and a half miles from the Basilica de San Pietro to the *termini* station as the crow flies, but for three millennia an entire world had been crammed into the small space.

The train suddenly lurched back and forth, jolting his body. Gingerly, he ran his hand down the side of his coat, feeling with a tender touch. Too much was at stake to risk an inadvertent disaster caused by an erratic train.

"Got a match?" a male voice said.

A worn young man in his late twenties appeared in front of him, wearing a black leather jacket. A cigarette dangled out of the corner of his mouth. It was illegal to smoke on the subway, but this wasn't the time for a lecture or an argument with an Elvis retread.

"No," he said flatly and looked the other way.

With the cigarette still hanging from his lips, the youth walked on up the car, but no one else responded affirmatively either.

The train slowed as it pulled into the next station. Signs along the wall read Piazza dei Cinquecento. Doors opened. The few remaining people filed out, leaving him alone at the rear. The crowd started up the steps toward the exit. He allowed them to move along in front of him before darting into a dim corner next to the wall. Reaching through the slit in his trench coat, he cradled the Glock 9mm pistol strapped in a holster on his hip.

The sound of shoes trudging up the cement steps died out, and in a few moments the platform emptied. Jogging on quiet soles, he rushed to the end of the tunnel as soon as the train left. One last glance around the area revealed he was alone. With a quick hop, he leaped from the platform down to the subway floor and hurried into the tunnel. Not ten feet in, the darkness swallowed him.

From rummaging around in the basement of the public archives, he had found the remnants of the plans for the metro system, which revealed that forty feet down this section of track there had been a storage area in the side of the tunnel. The architectural renderings indicated the area to be the size of a small room that would serve his purposes well. Feeling along the wall next to the steel tracks, he found that the plans were correct. Once inside the chamber, he pulled out a flashlight and made a quick inspection of the space. An old pickax stood against a blackened wall. Small hunks of volcanic rock covered the ground and made a slight crunching sound under his feet. With lights still beaming from the station, he could detect the subway tracks well enough to work quickly.

Settling against the brick wall, he unzipped the lining of his trench coat and pulled out the paper-wrapped briquettes that he set in a row in front of him. The plastic explosives should not detonate until the blasting caps were ignited, but he was no expert, and the narrow clay-like bars made him anxious.

In the dim light, he studied the packages of C-4, the same material terrorists used when they attacked the *U.S.S. Cole* in October 2000 and killed seventeen sailors. In his other pocket, he carried the materials for the detonator that would set off the bomb. Expanding plasma from a small explosion of foil would drive a metal piece called a "slapper" across a gap and a shock would be detonated, exploding the C-4 with a bang about the size of Mount Vesuvius. From what he had learned, it should all go off like clockwork when the next subway coach rolled by in about three hours during the early morning commute.

Lights along the station platform flashed off, plunging the entire area into blackness except for his flashlight. It shouldn't take him long to set the C-4 on the tracks. His hands began to shake, and sweat poured down his face. The detonator mechanism wasn't fragile, but his unsteady hands were a liability. Leaning over the bars of plastic explosive, he took a deep breath and unwrapped the first paper package.

A single, piercing light suddenly appeared on the platform in the darkness, sending a beam down the tunnel. Probably a night watchman, maybe a *polizia*, making a final check for the evening. The stout man clicked off his flashlight and hugged the wall. His glimmer of light might have been spotted from the terminal platform. If so, he was in trouble. Pulling the Glock from his pocket, he dropped to one knee and aimed at the entrance to the tunnel. If whoever had the flashlight entered, one shot in the man's chest would end the threat, but it might also ruin his plans. He caught his breath and waited. The light bobbed his way, and then it stopped.

"Anybody down there?" a man yelled.

He released the safety, ready to kill.

"Anyone in the tunnel?" the voice called again.

A trickle of sweat ran down the side of the terrorist's corpulent face. Yelling down the tunnel was beyond stupid. The guy must be an idiot. If he had to kill a cop, then he would leave the body in the tunnel and hope the stiff went unnoticed until the bomb went off in a few hours. No one would find him in the debris. If the guy walked into the tunnel, he had signed his death warrant.

The flashlight stopped searching the walls of the tunnel and turned back in the other direction. The bomber started to breathe again.

After the light disappeared, he hurried out on the tracks and quickly assembled his bomb next to the rails. Once the detonators were positioned, he hurried out of the tunnel and climbed back on the arrival platform. His calculations suggested that the explosion might collapse the subway entrance and shut down the entire connection at this terminal. If not, the blast would certainly block the tunnel when it destroyed the front portion of the train. Either way, the blast would make a statement that Rome would never forget.

It wasn't that he hated Rome itself; it was the American presence and their constant interference in European commerce that had to stop. Uncle Sam's long, skinny fingers kept dipping into his business, messing up the ice market, fouling his imports, and screwing up Italian politics. The politico big boys wouldn't listen to someone like him, but a few of these explosions around the city, and they wouldn't need a hearing aid to tune him in. He wanted to sting them so badly that they would think twice before doing any more business with the Yanks. Uncle Sam had already gotten away with way, way too much. Now it was time for the Italians to wake up or go down the toilet in one giant flush.

Grabbing his flashlight and a can of white spray paint from his trench coat pocket, he rushed toward the subway wall. Since this was only a first sting, he'd leave a mark to let the police know they were messing with a poisonous snake that would return and bite again. He made a large sweeping arch on the brick wall with the paint. Quick, bold movements designed a wasp's stinger. Standing back with his flashlight, he assessed his artistic creation waiting in the midst of imminent destruction. This design would be his signature for future projects as well.

Once finished, he jumped back down to the tracks and started walking into the opposite tunnel, which would enable him to exit through a manhole cover several miles away. It should cover his tracks. After all, he had all night to reach his destination.

2

September 3, 2008

THE GLARING HEADLINES OF *IL MESSAGGERO* SENT DR. JACK TOWNSEND diving into the newspaper story. The bombing in the subway terminal had disrupted the metro system that brought commuters in underground to avoid Rome's congested streets. Terrorists had set off a bomb just outside the *termini* in Piazza dei Cinquecento, blowing the subway train off the tracks and killing a dozen people while injuring countless others. Because Rome had not been the victim of attacks as London had, the city erupted in an uproar with citizens demanding immediate action.

With close-cropped brown hair and a Matt Damon boyish face, Dr. Jack Townsend didn't fit the usual expectations for an academician. Looking far more like an athlete, the forty-year-old scholar disliked violence of any sort, but particularly feared his wife's reaction to the news. During the time Jack and Michelle finished their PhD studies in biblical research in Tübingen, Germany, he had seen fear in her eyes more than once when terrorists attacked American embassies. He and Michelle had come to Rome to pursue a project that could grab the entire world's attention, but her apprehension about terrorist attacks could derail their work.

When she was five, Michelle's parents had been on a vacation on the coast of Bari, Italy. After a weekend of fun and sun on the beach, the family started back to Rome. They had turned at Cerignola toward Naples and were winding over the mountains when a semitrailer truck bore down the highway out of control and crossed the centerline. Michelle's family ended up in the ditch upside down when the car rolled. The truck exploded in a blast of fire. Since that afternoon collision, she had struggled with an extreme fear of explosions.

Jack read the newspaper story a second time. No one seemed to know who set off the blast, but a group the police dubbed as "The Scorpion" had etched a design on the subway wall that looked like the stinger on one of the dreaded creatures. Reporters had invented the label and as best the journalists could tell, there didn't seem to be any obvious links with international terrorist groups. Local discontents were thought to be behind the attack.

"More coffee?" The bushy haired waiter sailed by holding a large silver pot aloft. The intensely inviting aroma curled around the patrons.

Jack shook his head. "No, Luichi. Thank you. Hard to say no, but I've had enough."

The waiter bowed graciously and hurried off with his white apron flying and the silver coffeepot held high. Luichi fascinated Jack with his artistic flourishes. Jack liked the Dar Poeta sidewalk café partly because of the unpredictable waiters and mostly because of the artichoke dishes like the *alla giudia* cooked in a Roman-Jewish style. The restaurant was not far from the Tiber River and the Amadeo bridge that led into Borgo Santo Spirito street leading him back to the *Piazza San Pietro* of the Vatican where he often worked in the library.

People fascinated Jack Townsend. Curiosity had always been one of his strongest traits, and that's what fueled his passion for researching the Greek Scriptures. But watching the unusual forms bouncing down the street totally hooked his interest. Fat ones. Skinny ones. Voluptuous. Ugly. Gorgeous. They were all out there, and he loved watching them go by. Jack folded the paper and put it under his arm. Leaving a tip on the white tablecloth, he walked out onto the sidewalk.

"Ah, amico!" a familiar voice called out. "Wait!"

Jack turned to discover Tony Mattei waving at him. The heavyset Italian could turn up in the strangest places, and Vicolo del Bologna street was certainly one of them.

"Tony, good morning! What are you doing on this side of Rome?"

"I simply happened to be walking down the street when I saw you. I was concerned you might have been hurt in that awful explosion."

Jack studied the jewelry merchant and diamond broker. Always a flashy dresser with two or three sparkling rings on each hand, Mattei's thick, black hair hung across his forehead like a schoolboy coming in from recess, but this was no naive child. Tony Mattei's eyes constantly shifted back and forth taking in everything in sight. Jack noticed that Mattei's broad smile and his hard probing eyes didn't quite fit together.

"In this city of a billion people you should run into me on the street?" Jack said. "Surprising."

"I am a blessed man." Tony beamed a broad smile. "The gods have smiled on this humble Italian. But my question is about the bombing. Did it frighten you?"

Jack nodded his head. "Sure. I'm appalled. No one wants to be in a city when some terrorist starts killing innocent people."

"But fortunately, not hurt?" Tony turned his head sideways and narrowed his eyes. "I see no signs of injury."

"No. We're all right. Why would you think we were hurt?"

"No reason. No reason. Ah! That is good. Well, my friend, keep your eyes open. We are living in dangerous times."

"You're right about that." Jack waved. "Got to get back to the office." He started walking away. "Take care."

"I will." Tony Mattei waved. "Be careful, my friend."

Jack hurried down the street toward the Amadeo bridge. Strange. Tony Mattei had always been one of those characters who had a way of showing up out of nowhere. When he made one of his appearances at a café, the man drank enough black coffee to float a boat down the Tiber River. He was rumored to drink an equal amount of wine on other occasions. Tony Mattei remained one of those local institutions that made the ancient city of Rome always seem unique and quaint.

He glanced at his watch. Michelle would probably be irritated at him for squandering his time drinking coffee.

"Taxi!" Jack held his hand high in the air. "Taxi!"

The cab driver pulled up in front of Santa Maria della Concezione Church on Via Vittorio Veneto. Jack paused for a long look at the majestic structure of the old church. Somewhat diminished by the construction of Via Veneto, the sixteenth century edifice had originally been part of a Capuchin convent. The relationship to the Capuchin order gave the church an unusual twist. Having walked through the building a hundred times, he couldn't resist another look. The draconian features of the large church captivated his attention.

Capuchins monks had broken from the Franciscan Order in Naples in 1525 in a desire to fulfill St. Francis's original vision of helping the poor and helpless. Taking on a lifestyle of extreme simplicity, the new order set out to minister to the outcasts of society. In time Cardinal Barberini, originally a Capuchin monk, built the structure that also became the cemetery for the order. Jack Townsend opened the heavy front door and started down the dark hall.

A smell of incense and candle wax hung in the air along the narrow corridors that led to rooms with human bones nailed to the walls in patterns of floral designs, arches, triangles, and circles. Even after months of working in a house directly behind the old church, the sights still intrigued him. Jack stopped at the end of the second corridor and glanced up at the large clock composed of vertebrae and foot bones from some long dead monk. Here and there a finger bone filled in a small vacant spot. Only a single hour hand moved on endlessly with no minute hand, signifying that time had no beginning or end. The singular hour hand had turned around thousands of times through the centuries while monks were laid to rest only later to have their bones dug up and used for decoration on the walls.

Far away in the dim, candlelit front of the old church, Jack glanced at the tomb of Cardinal Barberini buried in front of the main altar. *'Hic jacet pulvis, cinis et nihil'* had been chiseled in stone long ago. The entire edifice seemed to sing the same song over and over, 'Here lie dust, ash, and nothing more,' in a myriad of stanzas.

Farther down in the dim crypt, Jack stared at the shadow of a reclining skeleton draped in a brown monk's robe and propped up against a wall lined with femur and arm bones. Not far ahead an indenture in the wall was piled high with boney-white skulls stacked on top of one another and reaching to the ceiling. Jaw bones hung ajar with teeth missing. If the Capuchins intended to say that life was short and all that was left when one's days were over was a stack of skeletons and bones, they'd done a good job getting the message out.

Dr. Townsend sauntered on, thinking how today and the preceding centuries were light years apart and yet so close.

Death had been a constant threat from time immemorial through to the sixteenth and seventeenth centuries when the Capuchins started piling bones, but time didn't stop moving forward. Modern medicine appeared with the age of antibiotics and chemotherapy changing the world. But the advent of terrorism had plunged the thoroughly modern era backward into the time of the monks hammering their brothers' bones to church walls. Like the bombing in the subway terminal, death once more rode supreme through the streets.

"My son, can I help you?" an elderly voice said.

Jack turned around to find Father Raffello standing behind him in the shadows. "Oh! I didn't hear you."

"Jack, I didn't know it was you," the old priest said. "You seemed to be deep in thought."

"I suppose I am. This church always touches a sensitive spot with me." He pointed to the recessed graves in the wall. "I am reminded of how short life is. On the streets I see all kinds of shapes and sizes walk by, but here I am vividly reminded of our common destiny. We don't have much of such retrospection in today's world."

Father Raffello nodded. "So true, but the past remains with us in this church as a constant symbol of the truth that our lives pass away quickly."

Jack nodded. "Afraid so."

"I trust all is well back in your offices?"

"Thank you, Father. We are doing fine."

"Good. Good." The priest started walking away. "Let me know if anything is needed."

"I will. We appreciate having the office space." Jack continued on his way.

Once he reached the side door, Jack exited the church and walked along a narrow cement path leading to the back. Fresh air washed away the scent of candle wax and stale air. The small house at the end of the walkway had once been used by a caretaker before being turned into their offices. Michelle would be waiting for him and she would want to know where he'd been for so long. Telling her that he was sitting outside in front of Dar Poeta drinking coffee and watching the multitudes walk by wouldn't set well. Perhaps, he should come up with some story of doing research on skeletons of long ago departed monks. Nope. That wouldn't fit either. The best he could come up with was that he'd been thinking about this difficult problem they were trying to solve in their search for the conclusion to Mark's Gospel. He could say he was looking for new approaches. Thinking.

Would that work as an answer? No, but it was probably as good of an answer as any he'd come up with.

3

Jack tried to shut the office's front door without making a sound. Instantly, he caught Michelle's eye, but her surprise was quickly replaced by a hint of scolding for his tardiness. "Ah, Jack!" Michelle Townsend said in a professional tone. "We have someone here who's *been waiting* to meet you."

Sitting across the desk from her, a small middle-aged man held a notebook in hand and gazed at him with anticipation in his eyes. The man's eager smile suggested that he'd been waiting for some time.

"A . . . a . . . yes," Jack mumbled. "Sorry for being late."

At the back of the office, a tanned young man sat poring over a large manuscript. Dov Sharon glanced up from his desk, nodded, and then went back to the codex he had been studying. It took a bomb about the size of what hit the subway to stop the Jewish student when he was deciphering a manuscript.

Jack nodded and smiled. "Be with you in just a moment." His Italian wife with her sparkling black hair pulled back in a pony tail and flashing brown eyes had a flair for creating the right impression that he sometimes messed up. Behind Michelle's heart-shaped face and alluring mouth, a magnificent mind never stopped working. Contoured in an artistic arch, her dark eyebrows framed eyes that always carried magnetism. The flush of pink in her cheeks gave her dark skin a striking contrast but didn't mellow the warmth Jack always noticed. "Need to put several items in order."

Because Michelle's grandfather had been a scholar at Viterbo's Museo Archeologico Nazionale before her parents immigrated to America, she had grown up speaking Italian like a native which also gave her a natural facility for languages. Entering the graduate school at Tübingen, Germany, with four years of completed Greek study pushed her to the top of the class in graduate studies in ancient manuscripts. Mostly, though, Jack simply thought she was the most beautiful woman he would ever see in his entire life.

"I want you to meet Mario Corsini, a reporter for *Il Messaggero*," Michelle said. "I told him that you often read his newspaper." She looked at Jack with that penetrating stare that meant 'play this one straight or else.' "Signor Corsini speaks excellent English and arrived unexpectedly some time ago. I was expecting you *earlier*."

"I got delayed down the street and—"

"Let's not even go there," Michelle said with a flatness that meant business.

"Unfortunately, Rome is in turmoil this morning," Jack said. "I read the story in your newspaper today, Signor Corsini."

"Yes, I was telling your wife the details just as you arrived," the reporter said.

Jack glanced at his wife's face and saw her jaw tighten. In any case, she already knew, but the sudden distant glaze over her eyes meant she wasn't any less frightened.

"As you Americans have a way of saying," Corsini said, "this story really sucks."

Jack studied the man sitting before him in a wrinkled blue shirt with no tie. Corsini's coat appeared to have been worn night and day for a number of years and his black hair looked as rumpled as his blue jeans. A pair of reading glasses sat halfway down his nose, and yet, Corsini's black eyes radiated intelligence. Jack could see he was not a dull man.

"I'm sure you didn't come to talk with us about the bombing," Jack began. "Mr. Corsini, please tell me what we can do for you."

"Perhaps, it will sound strange to you," the reporter said. "But I have been following your work for some time. Since I am a rather typical Italian Roman Catholic, I never read the Bible until I stumbled across a book describing the issues of textual and form criticism, which reported your work with the Scriptures. I found myself hooked on the problems of correctly translating Scripture. I have been following the subject ever since."

"Well, Mr. Corsini," Jack said. "Many Christians don't even know this area of debate exists among scholars, but it has long-range consequences."

"Please, call me Mario. I am honored to be here talking with you." He smiled modestly. "I was taken with how ancient Greek was originally written in one continual line with no break between the words and scholars must deem what is appropriate to pull apart in figuring out the true meaning." He picked up a pencil and wrote GODISNOWHERE on his notepad. "This is an example of what caught my attention because it can be broken apart into 'God is no where' or 'God is now here'. Your job is to come up with the correct translation."

"Very good," Michelle said. "These are the types of issues that Jack and I deal with."

"I read the book the two of you wrote titled *An Answer to the Cynics*. You certainly answered some of the hard questions raised by people who doubt the Bible."

"I am impressed with your reading, Mario," Jack said. "Michelle and I worked on a number of these problems during our time in Tübingen. We felt it was important to study with some of the harshest critics if we were going to defend the faith as we believe it should be upheld."

"Yes," Mario said. "You certainly have a strong confidence in the Scripture. I understand that you are working on a new project. I came today to see if there might be a story for my newspaper."

"I am flattered," Jack said. Out of the corner of his eye, he noticed Dov Sharon had stopped working on the codex and was listening. Corsini's visit had grabbed his attention and that was unusual. "In our own way, Michelle and I are dealing with the problems asserted by some scholars who say that modern humanity can't really believe in Jesus. The discipline called *formgeschichte*, or form criticism, in many cases has attacked the veracity of the Scriptures, and we are hoping to answer these charges."

Mario Corsini leaned forward and picked up his pen. "In what way, Dr. Townsend, are you at work on such problems? I sense that I might have a story I can write about Americans in Rome solving ancient biblical problems. I can't imagine a better place to think about the past than to have offices next to Santa Maria Church. The edifice is the most amazing collection of bones that I've ever seen. Good heavens! You are working on top of an open cemetery. Something important ought to be down there somewhere." He held his pen ready to write.

Jack chuckled. "Well, I think Michelle and I can be candid about our current project. Have you ever noticed that the average Bible has three possible endings for the Gospel of Mark?"

Corsini blinked several times. "What?"

"Yes," Jack said. "You might find this interesting to check out for yourself. Take a Revised Standard Version for instance.

31

It will clearly distinguish these three possible conclusions and lay them before you for your choice."

"I didn't know that," Mario Corsini said.

"Yes, my friend, and what makes this fascinating is the internal evidence in the actual Greek text. The eighth verse ends with the Greek preposition γαρ or 'for' and is an incomplete sentence, which would indicate that the original ending of the Gospel had been torn away. My hunch is that the other two optional endings were added later by scribes to make the Gospel feel more comfortable and complete for readers. I base this on the fact that I studied the oldest entire manuscripts of the Bible in existence. One is kept in the Vatican Library. Codex Vaticanus agrees with this position as does Tischendorf's Codex Sinaiticus taken from St. Catherine's monastery at the foot of Mount Sinai in the desert of the Holy Land. These manuscripts extend at least back to the Emperor Constantine and possibly beyond."

"That is amazing!" Corsini kept scribbling on his notepad.

"My wife and I have an unusual contention, Mario. We believe that during the early persecution of the church, the original ending was torn off. From our reading of the earliest Church Fathers, we believe the first ending of Mark's manuscript is hidden here in Rome, and we are trying to find it."

"Absolutely astonishing! Yes, I knew you'd have a story for me. Excellent. Do you know where this fragment of the manuscript is?"

Jack winked at his wife. "Can't talk about that today. I can only say that we are currently looking. How about my letting you know when we turn up something?"

Mario Corsini leaped to his feet. "Excellent! Yes, my newspaper would be most delighted to obtain such a story." He fumbled through his coat pockets looking for a card. "I want you to call me immediately. I am your humble servant. Don't worry. My paper would love the story." He thrust his calling card into Jack's hand.

"Wonderful, my friend." Jack put his arm around the man's shoulders. "Mario, we will let you know when we are ready to have the story published."

"Excellent!" Corsini made a slight bow in Michelle's direction and started toward the door. "I will stay in touch."

Following him out, Jack closed the door behind Michelle and himself. Both waved as Corsini walked away.

"We'll be watching the newspaper," Jack said and turned to his wife. "Well, we've had a busy little morning thus far."

"Do you think you should have told him what we're after, Jack?"

"Why not? A little publicity won't damage our work. Having a few cardinals read that story in the *Il Messaggero* won't hurt us in having continuing access to the Vatican Library." Jack pulled his wife closer. "By the way, I haven't given you a mid-day I-love-you kiss yet."

Jack kissed his wife passionately, and she put her arm around his neck. He whispered in her ear, "I haven't smelled any fragrance this good since the roses budded out."

Michelle grinned. "Aren't you the lover boy?"

"I try to be."

Michelle stepped back and shook her head. "I don't know. Something about all of this business with Corsini bothers me. Maybe it was the conversation about the bombing that really upsets me."

"I was afraid you'd react to the terrorist attack."

Michelle stiffened. "You didn't tell me about that explosion, Jack. Were you keeping the story from me because I become so frightened?"

"I truly didn't know the details until I saw the paper when I stopped at the Dar Poeta café for coffee this morning," Jack flinched, realizing what he had just said.

"Dar Poeta! So that's where you were!" Michelle planted both hands on her hips. "That's why you were late!"

Jack grimaced. "Actually, I was."

"Drinking coffee and watching people walk by," Michelle cut him off. "I swear! She looked at him fiercely, but grinned. "You're worse than a child." Michelle laughed. "But you and your taste for artichokes are certainly predictable."

"Maybe you'll have to punish me tonight." Jack grinned. "Think so?"

"Honestly!" Michelle opened the door and they walked back inside.

Dov Sharon got up from his desk and limped over to Michelle and Jack's conversation. "I couldn't help overhearing what the reporter said. We still don't actually know where the ending to Mark's Gospel is hidden." He raised an eyebrow. "Do we? I mean isn't our work something of a secret?"

"Yes and no," Jack said. "We don't go around sharing all our insights, but it won't hurt for us to pick up a little free publicity. We are funded by a foundation in America, and they'll be glad to learn that the press is following us, but we're still in the speculative phase. We don't want to talk about our hunches or about where we might eventually dig."

"That makes sense," Dov said. "Just checking. I think I'll run down the street and grab something to eat. I missed breakfast this morning."

"Sure," Jack said. "We'll be here."

Dov closed the door behind and Jack could see him walking away from their offices.

"Do you think Dov is really on the up and up?" Michelle whispered.

"Why do you ask?

"I don't know, Michelle's voice trailed away. "Sometimes he seems so distant like he's not telling everything he knows."

Jack looked at her with a puzzled frown. "I don't know what to say. I really like the man."

"I certainly don't dislike Dov. It's just that something bothers me about him."

4

Uncertainty and fear rumbled down the ancient streets of Rome. The police had not found significant clues to identify the perpetrators of the terrorist crime during the three days following the bombing in the subway. With the police stymied, the citizens of Rome became more agitated over what might happen next. Yet, the furious speed of cars on the narrow boulevards and overcrowded thoroughfares did not diminish. The press of Rome's always urgent business of merchants and tourism continued to hammer out a daily tempo that never slackened. Constantly studying the social terrain through glasses thick enough to be prisms, Dr. Albert Stein understood these facts well.

Stein had moved to Rome from Munich, Germany, a few months before and had taken up residence in a flat on Via del Gracchi not far from Vatican City. Having studied at and departed from Tübingen five years before the Townsends arrived, the short, thick professor had completed his PhD studies at Stuttgart and then gone on for more detailed work in biblical form criticism at Oxford, England, before coming to Rome. He had selected the small residence on Via del Gracchi because it was not ostentatious and the location gave him close access to the Vatican's vast library. A harsh critic of Scripture, Albert Stein had been smitten with the desert discoveries near the village of Nag Hammadi in Egypt. Studying the *Gospel of Thomas* as well as *The Gospel of Judas* had captivated his interest. Subsequent ancient tracts like *The Gospel of Truth* and *The Gospel of the Egyptians* pulled Stein into Gnosticism. Brilliant, Stein remained equally caustic and acrimonious. Hoping to become a renowned household name with worldwide recognition, his lack of notable achievement had left him frustrated.

As the recovery of the automobile business climbed after World War II, money had poured into the Stein family coffers more by good fortune than by design. Having been part of the Nazi war machine, their manufacturing industry fell with the state. The Steins expected harsh reprisals from the Allies, but the Americans needed the Stein factories for the rebuilding of Germany, and out of the ashes a new promise had risen. With the private fortune of the Stein family's holdings in Germany's automobile industry behind him, Albert Stein had the resources to pursue his private interest in any direction he chose. Nevertheless, the Stein family maintained an irrational hatred for all things American. Six decades later, Albert Stein still carried an abiding disdain for anyone from the United States.

Albert knew that a streak of cruelty ran through his personality. In sharp contrast to his academic achievements, a hidden malevolent urge could erupt when he became highly agitated. For years he had tried to control these outbursts, but when the surge of rage overpowered him, he was capable of murderous responses. With time he had written off the problem with the quip "everybody has their problems."

The loud honking of a car in the street below his balcony interrupted his reading. Stein looked at his watch and walked to the window. Another tie-up in traffic had shut the street down, but he needed to take a break from his work to keep an appointment he had made earlier. Putting out the cigarette he had been smoking, he reached for the files on his desk and pulled out a manila folder marked "Klaus Burchel." Satisfied after making a quick survey of the contents, he grabbed a sport jacket and stopped in front of the mirror beside the front door, which he always did to make sure his appearance was proper.

Albert could see that his blond hair and the unusually thick lenses in his glasses made him look somewhat older than forty-eight, but he had an Aryan face for which the Germans maintained pride. His high forehead fit the aristocratic background he liked to claim. Albert picked up the black fedora he habitually pulled low over his eyes to cover his face. The reflection always told the same story of man with a well-defined nose that suggested a forceful personality. Because of his disposition that could explode in violent behavior, Albert knew he needed the appearance of the elite to cover this flaw in his character. Even with his financial resources, beating someone with a cane could turn into an enormous problem. His elegant dress attempted to add to the appearance of a patrician. The mirror seemed to say he looked dapper and was ready for a stroll down to the restaurant.

The explosive side of his personality seemed to have developed out of nowhere. Of course, his father had a nasty habit of beating the children, but the savage tendency had been fed by his conflicts with Albert's older brother Rune. Whatever superiority that age gave Rune, Albert had learned that ferocity could equalize. Time and repetition had ingrained these tendencies. Obviously, few PhD's had a disposition for cruelty, but he did. Forget it. Life had to go on as it was.

Albert paused and glanced around his small living room at the strange assembly of electrical equipment he had accumulated for his secret project. Mix-and-match surveillance camera equipment sat next to weatherproof security cameras. Infrared light sources had been stacked in one corner with splitters and audio recovery monitors. A digital video recorder stood on a small antique table. Boxes with small microphones were pushed together. Wires and cables lay strung out on the floor. Albert smiled, knowing he was prepared for serious espionage.

Closing the door behind him, he hurried down the stairs and out onto the street, walking toward Ristorante Il Matriciano. The family-run establishment specialized in uncomplicated country fare, which Stein always enjoyed. Their classic *bucatini alla matriciana,* richly flavored with bacon, tomatoes, and basil, remained one of his favorites. Albert intended to arrive early before his contact showed and take time to glance at a newspaper. He increased his pace and quickly found an outdoor table to his liking. Sitting down, he snapped his fingers at a man selling papers and signaled for him to bring one over.

"A Signor!" The vendor hurried over. The old cap pulled down over his head modestly shielded his eyes. "A newspaper?"

Stein nodded, and the man handed him the paper. Albert placed one euro in his hand then brushed him away. The man tipped his hat and humbly returned to his stand.

The headlines remained the same, shouting their reports on the subway tragedy. Albert scanned the big stories and quickly turned the page. After reading about a blast in a subway, he pressed on. Suddenly he stopped. The smaller headline read, "Americans Track Lost Scripture." Stein lunged forward and caught his breath. It was a story about Jack and Michelle Townsend doing research in Rome. With a hard thrust of his fist, Stein pounded the table.

If there was anyone that Albert Stein despised, it was Jack Townsend. He had been a stumbling block for Stein's research for the last several years. Constantly posing questions that made Stein's insights seem shallow, Townsend inevitably kept Albert from the recognition he thought his work deserved. Albert had printed a book contending that during the period of oral tradition immediately following Jesus' death, the actual story of his life had been fabricated and twisted by his followers. It was not possible to know anything Jesus actually said from the Gospels that were written a generation later at the earliest. Stein would place their creation in the second century, although this was contested by many scholars. Townsend had countered that the words of Jesus were inseparable from his person. Jesus and his teaching were not like the oral transmission of the scribes because he always remained present in his words. That argument had cost Stein and created in him a hatred for Townsend that simmered to this very moment.

One of the reasons Stein had come to Rome was to get the jump on Jack and Michelle Townsend. When he learned they were headed for Rome, Albert immediately anticipated arriving in the city ahead of them and spying on what they were researching. While he had other work to do, he had to beat them to the punch, particularly with such a project as described in the *Il Messaggero* newspaper. Now this article splashed the Townsends' enterprise all over the world! Stein's endeavors deserved such headlines, not these upstart Americans.

The edges of the newspaper curled up in Albert's hands and his fists tightened. How could it be that Jack Townsend had gotten ahead of him again? It was the exact thing he hated. The Townsends were not only scholars at the opposite end of the theological scale, they were Americans, which made the injury a double insult. The denazification program that followed Germany's World War II defeat had been an affront that lay buried in Stein's soul. Nothing about these arrogant Americans sat right with him. The story in the newspaper only inflamed an already chronic wound.

Albert abruptly crushed the paper in his hands with a loud crackling noise. Other customers turned to see what caused the sound, but Albert threw the newspaper on the sidewalk. The vendor who had sold him the newspaper looked up in surprise. Stein returned a hostile glance, knowing that his thick glasses made his anger appear even more intense.

Albert crossed his arms over his chest and cursed under his breath. This was the last thing he expected. He glanced at his watch; his appointment should be showing up. If there was ever a time when he needed an assistant, it was now.

Albert visually scoured each person walking down the sidewalks, looking for the man. Ambling down the street in a slow shiftless pace, Albert could see a skinny young man who looked to be around thirty, shuffling along in worn tennis shoes and torn blue jeans. From his right eye the remnants of a nasty scar ran down the side of his cheek. The injury made him easy to identify, but it also meant he had been a risk taker and Stein needed a daredevil more than an invisible man. As he drew closer, Albert could see that his shaved head added to a sinister appearance, but time or a wig could erase the lack of hair. The young man had large, strong looking hands with calloused sides that supported his claim to skill in Karate. He looked exactly like the surveillance report said he would. Albert raised his hand to signal Klaus Burchel to come in his direction.

The German nodded that he understood, but his leisurely shuffle didn't pick up the pace. Klaus Burchel swung into the eating area and eased down opposite Stein.

"Hey man, you must be Dr. Albert Stein," the young man said casually.

"And you are Klaus Burchel?" Stein said in a flat voice with no movement in his face.

"You got it, dude." Burchel jutted his lower lip out arrogantly. "At your service."

Stein studied him for a moment. He looked like one of the despicable pack of displaced students wandering around Rome with weird haircuts and drug-induced mentalities. Albert watched the man's eyes and guessed there was much more here than a brain fried from popping pills. Burchel might look like a punk, but he had more between his ears even though he was keeping the fact concealed. Stein already knew far more about the young man than Burchel would have dreamed possible.

"Then, let us begin at the beginning and proceed. You will always call me Dr. Stein and never allude to me by my first name or any asides such as 'man,' or 'dude,' and I intend that you do the same in private. Is that understood?"

Burchel blinked several times. "Sure, yeah."

"I don't want to hear 'yeah' either. Your answers will be 'yes' and 'no,' and I expect you to be candid and straightforward. No jive talk. No drug lingo. Understood?"

"Whatever."

"One more of those cute replies and you're finished."

Burchel's eyes narrowed, and his mouth dropped slightly, but he said nothing.

"If you are going to work for me, our relationship will be on a professional basis with you doing *exactly* as you are told." Stein leaned forward so he could stare straight into Burchel's eyes. I will always refer to you by the name of Klaus Burchel although I know your real name and who your grandfather was."

Klaus Burchel jerked and the breath seemed to leave him. A defeated look swept over his face and all swagger vanished. "You do?"

"I know you are financially overextended and need the work," Stein continued. "You are in Italy because you needed to get out of Germany for legal reasons as well as a few financial problems. If you perform as you are capable, I will reward you significantly. I am hiring you to be my bodyguard and driver. You will be asked to do a number of things that are illegal. You've done such in the past, so those jobs should not be a problem for you. As your service to me increases, so will your pay. If you don't, you will be instantly terminated. I know that you can become difficult and resistant. I also know you were raised to be conforming. I expect instant obedience. Understood?"

Burchel swallowed hard. "Yes . . . yes. I agree."

"Can I take it you are willing to work on this basis?"

"Absolutely. Yes. I do need the money, but how did you find out about . . . my grandfather?"

"I made a complete check of your background because I have the resources to do so." Stein bounced his long thin fingers together. "I know all about you. For example, I know that you hate Jews and Americans."

Burchel's mouth dropped.

Stein reached in his pocket and pulled out a roll of bills. "I am giving you a thousand euros to buy new clothes. Get rid of those despicable tennis shoes and worn pants. Throw them away and start dressing like a competent human being. When I see you again I want you in a suit. Any problem with that?

"No sir!" Klaus Burchel stuck out his hand for the money.

Stein kept the bills in his hand. "Once you take this cash you are working for me and I expect absolute fidelity. You will be at my beck and call twenty-four hours a day. I expect to reach you by cell phone at a moment's notice. Is that clear?"

Burchel's mouth dropped slightly as he nodded his head.

"How long you been snorting coke?"

Burchel caught his breath and reeled back in his chair. He bit his lip. "Too long. I will quit doing drugs."

"You will, indeed," Stein said. "And don't renege on me if you want to keep this job?"

"Yes, sir."

"All right," Albert Stein said and handed him the money. "You can leave. Get yourself cleaned up and report to my apartment by 9 a.m. tomorrow." He shoved a card across the table. "The address and phone number."

"My phone number is—"

"I already have it, " Stein cut him off. "Now get on your way."

Klaus Burchel stood up. All signs of arrogant indifference had disappeared. His head kept bobbing as he backed away. Finally, he turned and walked swiftly down the street.

Through his thick glasses, Albert Stein watched him disappear intp the crowded thoroughfare. As usual, he had started the relationship by putting himself in firm control. He had no question in his mind but that Burchel would do as he had been told. He needed the money. Whether Burchel liked it or not, following orders was simply part of the German militaristic disposition that flowed in his bloodstream as it had with his grandfather, Richard Baer, who Albert still admired. He would make that inclination work for his interests.

Klaus Burchel blended into the crowd and disappeared down the stairway running into the subway system. At the bottom, he stopped to count the euros again. A thought floated through his mind. He could take the money and run. What a plum gig he could throw! A thousand euros would buy several nights of premium highs. On the other hand, the old freak could turn up information like a magician making canaries appear out of thin air. Running might end up with getting his head smashed. The old man even knew about his grandfather and Klaus's true name.

Burchel needed the money badly. Rome was expensive, and it cost even to bed down in flop houses. He'd gotten his butt hung out to dry once too often. In the shadows of the subway, Klaus Burchel made a decision. No matter how much he hated this arrogant jerk's demands, he'd buckle under. If Stein could gather the information that he had, he might be useful if a possible run-in with the police bubbled up. But most of all, Klaus simply needed the money. He'd keep his mouth shut and, to keep the cash flowing, kiss the old man's backside as faithfully as a guard dog welcoming the master home.

5

THE AROMA OF PASTA COOKED IN GARLIC, BUTTER, AND CHEESE DRIFTED through the café while a man with an accordion walked among the tables, playing familiar Italian tunes and occasionally bursting into singing. Off in the distance, the busy sounds of the Piazza Campo dei Fiori added a touch of local color from one of Rome's most picturesque squares and markets. Craftsmen displayed their leather products in stalls next to a multitude of tiny shops selling everything from roses to eggplants. The chatter and clatter drifting in only added to the atmosphere of Der Pallaro restaurant.

Michelle set her fork down and looked around the expansive room. "Jack, I'm surprised we came here tonight. It's not inexpensive. We've never been to this café before."

"I thought you'd like a change of pace and the food has an excellent reputation. They serve some of everything they are making in any given day, and their portions are generous. I'd always heard we should drop in. Today seemed like a good time." His smile appeared tense. "I bought you that new Bisou Bisou tunic because I like the large red flowers against the black design, and you look chic in those leggings as well.

When I saw them on the rack in the window, I knew I had to get it for you."

Michelle looked at the fettuccine on a plate painted with flourishes of a meandering colorful design. "Yes," she said hesitantly. "I love the new clothes and your thoughtfulness, but we don't often eat out at such expensive bistros."

"A breath of fresh air always invigorates," Jack said. "Puts more zip in your step." He chuckled. "Maybe, a little filet will strike a note of romance in your heart tonight. Hmm?" He forced a chuckle again.

Michelle thought his laugh to be a bit nervous. He hadn't bought such beautiful clothing just on a whim. Some unexplained situation was unfolding, and he clearly didn't want to tell her what it was. Not that romance wasn't in the air, but more was going on than Jack had explained. He didn't generally hide things from her, but she intuitively sensed when more was going on. He hadn't picked out this festive restaurant because perfume floated through the air.

"Look, dear," Michelle used the most thoughtful and kind voice she had, "I think we're here because something more than a full moon is out tonight." She leaned over the table. "Did you get a speeding ticket?"

"Oh, no! No. No. Nothing like that."

"Then level with me. Why are we *really* out on the town tonight."

Jack took a deep breath. "Well . . . I . . . I . . . just thought you might have been bothered because of the bombing in the subway system." He rubbed his chin nervously. "I was concerned because I know how upset these incidences make you."

His answer hit all of her panic buttons. It wasn't what she had expected. Suddenly, Michelle couldn't catch her breath, and her head felt extremely light. An uncontrollable urge surged up from within and her heart started to pound. His explanation completely flipped her.

"I know that fear is bumping around these streets like a runaway motorbike. Everywhere I turn, I hear people talking about the terrorist attack, and I know that has to be highly upsetting to you."

Michelle tried not to respond, but her hands had started to shake, and she immediately pulled them under the table.

"Maybe you don't want to talk about the incident," Jack said. "I only want you to know that I'm willing to listen if you're struggling with the impact."

"You certainly outflanked me," she sputtered and cleared her throat. "Yes, you certainly did."

Jack was intensely studying her face. Not a good sign.

"You're getting a little pale, dear. Are you all right?"

"Jack, just because I get nervous when bombs go off doesn't make me into a freak." Her voice raised a notch. "Sure, I was only a child when that awful event happened to my family, but I'm OK. Don't worry so much." She could feel her hands becoming wet. "Really."

"I just don't want you to get overanxious," Jack said.

Michelle could feel her knees becoming wobbly and knew she must get out of the chair quickly. "Honestly, I'm fine, Jack. If you'll excuse me for a moment, I'll be right back."

"You're not OK," Jack said. "Let me call—"

"I'm fine," Michelle said more dogmatically than she intended. "I'll be right back."

Her first steps away from the table felt so uncertain than she feared she might fall, but the bathroom wasn't that far away. Michelle stared at the door and knew she had to get inside that small room before she exploded. Once inside the bathroom, she dropped the toilet lid and sat down. The room began to whirl around her.

Jack had been more than right. The subway incident had triggered terrible emotions she had to fight. In the middle of the night she had tried to pour her anxiety into a secret container she tried to store deep in her unconscious. Although she had partially succeeded, Michelle knew a confrontational stimulus could pop the cork. For reasons she couldn't grasp, that had happened tonight.

Michelle watched her fingers start to shrink and her hands change into the shape of a five-year-old child's. The wall, only feet in front of her face, was becoming a window. In the background, she could see the city of Cerignola and the road sloping up toward the rolling mountains. Her sharp-pointed shoes disappeared and shiny, black-patent leather, little-girl shoes took their place. The wall vanished and Michelle could see the back of her father's head in the front seat ahead of her.

"Thank you for a wonderful weekend," her father told her mother.

"Of course, my love," Maria said back and smiled.

Their car kept moving steadily up the incline, and little Michelle could see the mountains getting larger and beginning to loom over them. She could still almost smell the sea air as it washed in along the coast of Bari where they'd spent their vacation. The water had been warm, and she loved playing in the sand. Little red crabs always scurried along the shoreline. Michelle loved her father's trips forever.

Ahead, around the curve, a large gasoline truck barreled down the road on the wrong side of the divider. Michelle looked again. The truck appeared to be coming right at them.

"Watch out!" father screamed and pointed.

Far from slowing, the driver didn't even look at them. Michelle saw his eyes when the man finally realized his huge semi was coming straight at their car. The man's face contorted into a grimace of terror, and he jerked the wheel violently to the left just as Michelle's father yanked their vehicle in the opposite direction.

Michelle felt her side of the car rising off the pavement as the vehicle careened into the ditch next to the side of the mountain. The car kept lifting and started to tip over. The truck's cab twisted violently and the trailer behind swung toward their car. Before she had time to grab the door, the backseat, anything. Michelle felt herself turning upside down. She bounced off the top of the car just as the back end of the trailer caught their front fender and spun their car like a top. The backseat cushion broke loose and tumbled on top of her. The car turned upright again only to bounce over once more. Broken glass flew in all directions. She hit the ceiling again before the car smashed against the massive rock jutting out of the side of the mountain. Michelle tumbled onto the crumpled top of their car. Pain pushed through her body like a rampant fever, and she hurt all over. The smell of gasoline rushed through the scattered windows before an explosion sent a ball of fire straight up into the sky. Smoke and searing heat surged through the car.

"Get her out!" Michelle's mother screamed. "Jack! Michelle's in the back seat."

A strong arm locked around her waist and lifted her into the front seat before pushing her through where the front windshield had been. For the first time, Michelle realized she couldn't make her left leg move and that it hung at a strange angle. Only then did she see her father's face covered with blood running down his cheeks. A grotesque gash had been slashed across his forehead. Her mother was sitting on the ground with the side of her blouse ripped open and blood running down her arm.

A second explosion filled the air with such a deafening roar that Michelle's ears went blank and her father fell to the ground. No sounds filled her ears, but chaos roared through her mind. She grabbed her head and curled up in a ball next to her father's bloody shirt. The pain had become more than she could bear.

Slowly the picture faded and the bathroom wall took its place. The ball of fire turned into a streak of paint on the smudged dirty wall, the silence replaced by the sounds of people walking down the hall outside the bathroom door. With a trembling hand, Michelle reached up and felt the side of her face. Tears filled her eyes and sweat had started running down her cheeks. Her face felt clammy and flushed. She tried to catch her breath, but it wasn't easy to do so. Michelle hung her head and braced her body against the wall.

Ten minutes later someone beat on the bathroom door, and a woman's voice said, "Are you all right? You speak English?

"Yes, yes," Michelle mumbled. "I speak English. I'll be out in just a moment?"

"You are sick?"

"No. No. Just a moment."

Michelle forced herself to stand up and staggered to the mirror. The color had washed out of her face and she looked bedraggled. How could it have happened so quickly? Heaving in and out, her breath began to stabilize even though her knees continued to feel wobbly. How could she ever tell Jack about how deeply her problem affected her? It was the one secret she had kept from him all of these years. Fortunately, it seldom came up like it had tonight. The terrorist explosion had been so close to them that it had far more than unnerved her. Talk of the blast was everywhere and kept descending on her like an ever darkening cloud. Tonight, Jack had reintroduced the problem in a way that slid more deeply into her past than usual, and the childhood experience had erupted like a volcano. Nevertheless, he must not know about her condition. That resolve had been her pledge to herself from their beginning together. It must forever stay in her yesterdays. She would not tell him about the seriousness of her post-traumatic stress disorder.

6

ALTHOUGH FOUR DAYS HAD PASSED SINCE THE SUBWAY BOMBING, POLICE remained everywhere with rifles in hand, and Michelle continued to feel apprehensive. With the coolness of early morning still hanging in the air, Jack and Michelle Townsend unlocked their office door and walked in. The sun had already come up and cars buzzed down the streets of Rome with their usual ferocity. Carrying a cardboard container with three cups of steaming coffee, Michelle placed the holder on her desk. They didn't often arrive before 8:00, but they had come to a turning point in their work and needed to review what they had discovered before going further. An early morning conference was needed before the next phase started. Michelle sat down at her desk and glanced at her watch.

"Dov should be here momentarily," she said.

Jack nodded. "We begin as soon as he comes through the door."

"Oh, let's start now." Michelle got up from her desk and threw her arms around Jack's neck. "Why must you be so enticing?" She kissed him forcefully.

"What?" Jack sputtered. "What was that for?"

"Maybe, just because you're my husband and I like kissing you in spite of all your shortcomings." She kissed him again.

"That's certainly the right way to start the day," Jack said.

Michelle giggled and returned to her desk. She glanced around their front office filled with four desks. Three of the staff occupied the largest desks and the old rolltop held piles of books. Even the two large bookshelves were crowded with worn copies of ancient volumes with rows of books piled up across the top. Stacks of files and papers stood around the edge of the floor. The walls had been painted literally a hundred years ago and streaks of dirt and discoloration ran down the sides. Jack claimed they lent character and the fathers in the Santa Maria Church had told them not to paint the walls anyway. Michelle hated the appearance but couldn't change it. Through the open door, Michelle could see an old conference table in what must have once been a bedroom. Five chairs had been placed helter-skelter around the worn table. A couple of old oil paintings hung on the walls when they moved in and had been left in place. She couldn't decide if the oils were worthless or masterpieces lingering from a couple of centuries back. Unable to decide, she left them alone. The worst fact about the house was no central heating system. In the winter, they had to build a fire and wear coats to keep from freezing. Not a good situation.

"Here comes Dov," Jack said. "I hear his cane thumping on the walk outside."

"Good. We can start the discussion."

The door opened and Dov Sharon walked in. "Boker tov," he said in Hebrew. "Shalom to all."

Michelle studied Dov, a small man. Jack had first met him while working in the Armenian Library in Jerusalem. With wiry black hair that stuck out in every direction, Dov's intense, penetrating, dark-brown eyes fit well with his handsome long, narrow face. Dov didn't say much and seemed to constantly glance around the room or shoot a look out the window. He acted like a man who remained suspicious of some undefined entity.

The Sharon family had migrated to Israel after his grandparents barely escaped execution in the Auschwitz concentration camp in southwest Poland. Their time in a kibbutz had been difficult. Dov had been a *sabra*, a native-born Israeli. Jack had greatly admired the tenacity of the Sharon family, and when he discovered Dov's exceptional ability to translate ancient Hebrew, he signed him up for their team. The choice proved valuable, but Michelle remained unsure.

"I brought you a cup of coffee," Michelle said and handed it to Dov. "It will warm your heart."

"Toda raba," Dov thanked her in Hebrew. "You have started my engine running."

Jack pointed to the other room. "Let's go in and sit around the conference table. Bring any papers or documents you need. We'll be updating our work."

Michelle picked up her coffee and a file. "I'm ready."

She paused and watched her husband for a moment. A gentle sort of man who could forget the time of day while walking down the street, he was actually on the shy side. Michelle had learned early in their relationship that weight lifting had helped him overcome much of his childhood bashfulness. Under Jack's short-sleeved shirt, she couldn't help noticing his strong, muscular arms. His unusual strength remained one of the paradoxes in this man's life. Although brilliant, he got lost watching people walk by or gazing at some strange sight. But no matter how often he disappeared in his thoughts, she loved him because he was such a kind man and generous to a fault.

"I'm ready as well," Dov walked behind her.

Jack sat down at the head of the table. "Dov, you've been working on a Hebrew translation of the *Sarajevo Haggadah* I noticed."

"All week. Been checking some of the literary style of this ancient manuscript to sharpen my awareness of any possible shifts in Hebrew during recent times. There are a few unusual pictures as the manuscript came from a time when Jews considered figurative art to be a violation of the commandments. It's rather straightforward. I'm more than ready to shift to your project."

"Michelle, tell Dov where we are," Jack said. "Let him know how we got to this point in our work. Give him a brief summary."

Michelle nodded. "Let's start here." She picked up a Bible and opened it to the end of Mark's Gospel. "The King James Version ends by including verses nine to twenty as genuine while the Revised Standard Version puts these same verses in footnotes. For interpreters of the Bible these variations pose a problem. If the Scripture is inspired, how can we make sense out of these differences?"

"I understand," Dov said. "Such problems make people anxious."

"Exactly," Michelle said. "There is also a shorter ending that virtually everyone fairly well agrees was tacked on. Even conservative scholars dismiss it."

"The longer ending is found in some significant manuscripts like Codex Ephraemi and Codex Alexandrinus as well as a number of fragments," Jack added. "Of course, the original ending would have been on papyrus. Because some Church Fathers in the earliest centuries used this ending, Jerome put verses nine through twenty in his Latin Vulgate. That's essentially how it wound up in the King James Version."

"I see," Dov said thoughtfully.

"We found an interesting aspect of the longer ending while studying in Jerusalem," Michelle continued. "In three of the oldest Armenian manuscripts, these verses are present, but a fourth manuscript attributed them to a presbyter named Ariston."

"Fascinating," Dov said. "What about the earliest Church Fathers? How do they stack up?"

"We found that Clement, Origen, and Eusebius used the shortest ending concluding in 16:8," Jack said. "That adds to our conclusion that the verse eight ending with the Greek word γαρ or, in English, 'for' indicates we have strong evidence that the first ending to the verse was torn off. I believe we are almost ready to start hunting for where the fragment might be hidden here in Rome."

"You've concluded that there's no question but that the first ending is around Rome somewhere?" Dov sipped his coffee. "You ready for me to bring my shovel to work tomorrow?"

"Not quite," Michelle said. "We've got to do some cross-checking and more research. I'm concerned that we don't really have enough clues to know where to start looking for the papyrus yet. We've got to dig much deeper in the Vatican Library."

"And that's what you'd like me to do?" Dov said. "Trudge down to those dark halls and wander through the dusty stacks?"

"I think so," Michelle said hesitantly. "What about you, Jack?"

"I agree," Jack said and rubbed his chin thoughtfully. "I believe we've got to search for clues about what might have happened in the first century to Mark's conclusion to his Gospel. We're going to need to dig farther into sections of the Vatican Library where no one usually looks. You can use one of our passes to get you in. It's not easy to get permission to wander around in those ancient corridors."

"I think you're going to need to try to get behind the time of Irenaeus, and that won't be easy," Michelle said. "Irenaeus was a disciple of Polycarp, and that will be hard to find if it's even there. We have the writings of Clement, and we believe he was with Paul in Phillipi in A.D. 57. We need to research behind Clement, and that's a real toughie."

"I suspect that there might be materials in the Vatican Library that may be hidden because they were lost from sight," Jack said. "Who knows what's buried in that pile of ancient documents. I want you to bring an intellectual shovel and start digging deep, Dov."

Dov grinned. "You know that I'm not particularly comfortable wandering around in the world of Rome's Catholic Church, but I can't think of anything I'd rather do than try to turn up the writing of somebody like Linus or Cletus who might have perished in the persecutions of Nero. Then there was that guy called Laterani. Maybe I can find something new. Sure; I'll hit the stacks."

"Good," Jack said. "I think that's an important place for you to go today. I understand your reluctance. Many Jews don't exactly trust what the Roman hierarchy did in the past, but you won't have any problems today. You can start going through the archives in Vatican City immediately."

Dov smiled. "My, my; amazing how times can change. OK, give me your entry documents and I'll tool on down to St. Pete's palace to see what I can rummage out of their garbage pile of old valuables."

"That's what I like," Jack said. "A devout attitude."

"We do our best." Dov slowly pushed himself up out of his chair. "The Vatican is not particularly considered a friend of the Jewish people. I'll need that pass to get by the boys who guard the door." He stood up and stretched before walking toward the front office area. "OK, I'm on my way."

"You are going to seek entry into the Archivum Secretum Apostalicum Vaticanum," Jack said. "The Vatican Secret Archives."

"Secret Archives!" Dov raised an eyebrow. "Are you kidding me?"

"Not secret in the sense of hidden," Jack explained. "Secret means the archives are the pope's own private documents, not those of a department of the Curia. It's been estimated that the archives contain fifty-two miles of shelving with more than thirty-five thousand volumes in the selective catalog alone. Who know how much is actually down there?"

"You want me to cruise through thirty-five thousand books like a kid going around the block on a skateboard?"

Jack laughed. "Not quite. There's everything down there from the marriage annulment of Henry VIII of England to correspondence with Michelangelo. You'll find the rooms to be elegant almost beyond belief. The ceilings have been painted in a manner similar to the Sistine Chapel. You'll be dazzled."

"Wow. You're talking big time for a little Jewish boy from the sticks in Israel."

"Yes," Michelle said. "It's a scholar's paradise. I know that some documents go back to at least the eighth century with an almost uninterrupted documentation from 1198 forward. You're going to dig way behind those dates."

"What we're after is far behind the eighth century," Jack said. "There's also an Apostolic Penitentiary that has ancient documents with everything from excommunications to the issuance of indulgences. Rather astonishing manuscripts floating around in there as well."

"I guess so," Dov rubbed his chin thoughtfully. "I got a hunch that I can see where this is going."

"The Secret Archives started back with the pontificate of Paul V Borghese. A cardinal suggested they start the archives in the rooms called Paoline, next to the Sistine Chapel. From there it's gone on and on. I want you to see if you can get way below the surface. I believe there is a library underneath these vestiges of the past and it's probably on the bottom floor down there where they do archeological digging on the first-century level under the Vatican. I want you to find the ultimate basement."

"The entry pass is on my desk," Michelle said. "That'll get you by the priest-guard at the door. From there on, you're on your own, Dov."

"Don't worry. I'll carry a stun gun and whack anyone who tries to slow me down. As American tourists say, "See ya." Dov waved and shut the door behind him.

Michelle watched him through the window for several moments as he hurried down the sidewalk that led to the street.

Michelle said, "Dov worries me. Does anyone really know anything about his history?"

Jack shook his head. "I know what his family told me. I just thought he was extremely good with ancient Hebrew and was obviously a bright guy. I didn't actually do any research on him."

"You should have. After all, you could have run into him by accident in that library in Jerusalem, or he might have been there waiting for you."

"Come on, Michelle. We're only biblical scholars, not terrorists looking for nuclear weapons. Why would anyone want to intrude on our work?"

"Have you forgotten about that Albert Stein, that belligerent German scholar? Your book flattened his attack on Christianity and made him angry enough to want to kill us."

"I think you're overstating the case," Jack said.

"Oh really? Listen, when we ran into him at the Translation Seminar at The Hague, I thought it would take a team of bouncers to keep him from attacking you with a chair."

Jack shrugged. "The guys reactionary with a short fuse. I didn't take him seriously."

"Obviously. Just like you didn't take Dov that seriously."

Jack rubbed his forehead and slid his hand over his face. "Maybe, I should have checked Dov out more carefully, but I still think Dov's exactly what his parents said he was."

"You have a brilliant mind with a few snags. One of them is that you tend to be too trusting. All I am saying is that we need to be careful. There may be people out there who don't like us tinkering around with how the Gospel of Mark is supposed to end."

Jack shrugged. "I suppose you're right, but I guess it's a little late to be running an investigation on Dov. I don't think the National Security Agency or the Central Intelligence Agency would be interested in getting in on the problem."

"Now you're blowing me off," Michelle said.

"You know that I always take you seriously."

She poked a finger in his face. "Then pay attention to our boy, Dov. Watch him closely. Understand?"

Jack nodded. "I'll give it some thought."

Michelle shook her head. "I bet you will."

A HUSH HAD SETTLED OVER DR. ALBERT STEIN'S OFFICE WITH KLAUS SITTING at the opposite end of the room saying nothing. Periodically, Stein glanced through his thick glasses at his new chauffeur and body guard sitting stoically in the corner. Burchel had shed his shabby street look and shown up in a three-button brown wool suit of finely woven quality. Ties were definitely optional and occasional at best in Rome, but added the finishing touch. The dark purple shirt with a striped bluish tie reflected the best taste of a clothier with a good eye. Even with his head shaved, Burchel had taken on the look of a young business executive wearing tasseled leather shoes of the Bristol style. Out of the corner of his eye, Stein watched Burchel's stiff, erect posture, which appeared to be a sign of paying rigid attention.

Dr. Stein's small office didn't compare well with the spacious chambers he was accustomed to in the family estate in Germany. Yet, the space proved sufficient because he liked having books around at arm's length. One entire wall had disappeared behind a vast bookcase that movers had hauled in. The shelves now contained old, worn books and manuscripts that filled the shelves to the ceiling. Dusty, ancient curtains hung from the top of the window to the floor, imparting a morose atmosphere. The rug had fulfilled its purpose more than a decade earlier, but the dilapidated carpeting with a few holes here and there still stood over the worn wooden floor. The antiquity of the office matched Stein's preoccupation with archaeology.

Turning the pages slowly, Stein continued reading for another twenty minutes. Glancing at the clock on the wall, he concluded that Klaus had been sitting in the straight-back wooden chair for more than forty-five minutes without moving. Not bad for an undisciplined punk from the gutter. The man had passed his first test.

"Your grandfather would have been proud of you," Stein said and turned his book over. "I know you hate sitting there doing nothing but what I commanded you to do."

Klaus flinched, but said nothing.

"See! You can control yourself if you put your mind to it. Such control is important for the business at hand. Do you understand?"

Klaus nodded. "Yes, sir."

"Ah! Excellent responses. Your style has been acting out like a madman on a drunken spree. I am teaching you again how to restrain yourself just as your parents tried to do."

Burchel flinched. "Might I ask a question?"

"You are reflecting the good family background that you came from when your parents attempted to train you correctly as a child. The whole story is in your file. Yes, requesting to ask a question is exactly what I expect."

"May I ask what you are studying?"

Albert lit a cigarette and blew smoke into the air. "Have you heard of the Nag Hammadi texts?"

Klaus shook his head. "No, sir."

"In 1945 in Upper Egypt in the village of Nag Hammadi, a peasant discovered a collection of twelve leather-bound papyrus books that provided a major breakthrough for modern scholarship. These writings dated back to the second century and gave us new insight into Gnosticism. I believe they reflect the influence of Gnosticism on early Christianity. Unfortunately, the importance of these manuscripts has not been fully appreciated by the Church. I am trying to remedy that problem."

"Gnosticism?" Klaus frowned. "What is that?"

"It comes from the Greek word for 'knowing' or 'knowledge.' Gnosticism is fundamentally a religious system that takes the believer into a realm of mystical thoughts and imparts hidden insights."

Burchel frowned. "I know nothing of what you are saying. Sounds sort of like Zen."

"Not bad." Klaus smiled. "The word *Zen* would make sense to many of your contemporaries. However, the issues from the Nag Hammadi library are far more consequential than Oriental mysticism. We know the first Church Fathers were opposed to the Gnostics, and the texts that I am studying might prove the Church Fathers were incorrect rather than the Gnostics."

Klaus blinked several times. "Wouldn't that destroy the Church as we know it?"

"You are a bright boy, Burchel. It is one of the reasons that I hired you. Underneath that drug-stuffed skull of yours is a brain that will work if you allow it to do so. You have the capacity to draw quick and insightful conclusions." Albert smiled. "Yes, if my ideas are right, the contemporary church would be destroyed."

Klaus rubbed his head and pursed his lips. "Why would you want to destroy the Church?"

"Because it is filled with error and deception! I believe the ancient Gnostics to have been more honest and forthright. Building on a corrupt Jewish heritage, the Church went flying off into the sky pursuing political ideas that finally landed them in control of the government of the Middle Ages and produced an oppressive world order run by a pope. See where I am going?"

Burchel nodded his head several times. "Yes. Yes. Germany suffered under such controls. I see the possibilities, but what are you reading that gives you these ideas?"

Albert held up a book. "This is *The Gospel of Judas*. I also have *The Gospel of Thomas* and *The Apocalypse of Adam*. Other such books await my scrutiny."

Klaus scooted to the edge of his chair. "Can you tell me some of what you are discovering? Some of the ideas?"

Stein shrugged. "For example, some of the texts suggest that Jesus believed in two messiahs. These messiahs' objective would not be some eschatological end-time return but the founding of an earthly kingdom."

"That's wild," Klaus said. "Never heard of such a thing."

"I fascinate you?" Stein smiled. "Yes, Burchel, I can fill your empty head with many ideas that will give you a new perspective. You are working with a man who can pay with much more than just money."

Klaus rubbed his chin. "Do you believe anything in the Bible?"

"I find passages that fit with these Gnostic gospels and I accept them because I find meaning that other scholars have missed."

"Interesting." Klaus kept nodding his head. "Can you give me an example of a passage that you believe is true?"

Stein flipped his cigarette into the ashtray. "Try this one. 'The kingdom of God must be taken by force.'"

"By *force*?"

"Yes, by the use of physical strength!" Albert slammed his fist onto the desk with such abruptness that Klaus jumped slightly. "I am following the path of truth when I exert my personal power. The Nazis understood this principle well." Albert jabbed his finger at Klaus. "Force is essential. I can teach you how to walk down this same route if you are inclined to learn."

Stein watched Burchel's eyes carefully. The young man appeared bewildered and mystified. Albert could tell he was wrestling with what he had heard. Like a hypnotist dragging a victim under his spell, Albert could see Klaus sinking deeper and deeper into the sphere of his total control. In addition, to securing a new employee, Albert was gaining psychological superiority. His plan was working.

"I must think about these matters," Klaus said with uncharacteristic maturity. "At this point, it sounds as if we are on the same page."

Stein smiled. "I hope so. It is to your advantage that our thoughts stay as one." He stood up and leaned back on the desk. "If you are ready to practice taking the kingdom by force, your first assignment now awaits you." Motioning for Klaus to stand, he pushed across his desk a Smith & Wesson 459 pistol. The young man immediately sprang to his feet.

"I want you to find where a couple lives and the address of their offices. If you get caught for some inane reason you must not indicate any relationship to me *whatsoever*." Stein shifted back into a hard, authoritarian voice. "Understand?"

Klaus nodded.

Stein handed him a piece of paper. "The names of the Drs. Jack and Michelle Townsend with there last address are here. That's all I have at this moment. It may take you some time, but there was a story on the Townsends in *Il Messaggero* several days ago. That should give you a lead. I want to know where they are and how to make contact should I choose to do so. Any questions?"

Klaus shook his head.

"Call me the moment you have uncovered them. I will be expecting a prompt response."

To Stein's surprise, Klaus abruptly saluted with military precision like a soldier responding to a military officer. The young man turned on his heels and marched out of the room. Albert Stein watched in consternation, concluding that he had made far more of an impact than he would have anticipated.

Klaus hurried down the stairs, patting the gun hidden in his suit coat. He knew Stein had been testing him by making him sit immobile, and he didn't like the strain. But Stein was no fool. Obviously, the man was brilliant and understood power. Not just because his grandfather had been an SS officer, Klaus had always admired the military for its precision and order. In contrast to his slovenly lifestyle in Rome, underneath it all, Klaus respected the saluting and heel clicking that had long been part of the German military. Today Stein was sending him off on a task that counted, and it felt good to be doing something responsible with a gun in hand. Yes. He could work for this strange scholar regardless of where the tide turned.

8

JACK TOWNSEND STEPPED INTO THE OFFICE AND GLANCED AROUND THE room. Even though the clock hands had just turned a couple of minutes past 8:00 a.m., Dov Sharon had already arrived and was at work. Sitting hunched over his desk, he appeared to be studying a manuscript. Strange that he would be at work so early.

"Hey, you're beating the clock this morning," Jack said.

Dov looked up. "Didn't sleep well last night, so I showed up a tad early. No big deal."

"That's what I call high-dollar positive motivation," Jack said. "I'd guess the last two days you've been working in the Vatican Secret Archives. We haven't seen hide nor hair of you. Anything turn up?"

Dov pushed the manuscript away. "Mainly, I've been trying to identify what might have been overlooked in the past. Somebody up there at the top of the Vatican personnel chain likes you or I'd never have made it inside those forbidden chambers. I thought I would never get through their security. Obviously, they don't let many people down there in that pile of dust and deteriorating manuscripts.

"You're right, Dov. The really ancient materials are extremely hard to find. After all, they bear witness to an archaic world that's long gone."

"I thought one of those bulldog priests was going to make me strip to get in and out of the dungeon hidden down there under that library. They take their security big-time seriously."

"Got to give 'em credit, Dov. They don't allow any slipups with priceless documents. Those boys keep a critical eye on everything. Did you come up with any specific material we can use?"

"I found a box of manuscript fragments in a depository that's been sitting there unexamined for a long time. No one had worked through the basket of materials, and they aren't sure exactly where it originated, though they do know it was discovered during street work in Rome. So far I've found only business receipts, lists of transactions, materials of that variety from the first century, but I keep looking. Never can tell what's at the bottom of the heap."

"You got it, " Jack said. "Some of the most important archaeological discoveries have occurred more by accident than intention. I'm sure you're looking in the right place regardless of what you haven't found."

"I'll keep after it," Dov said.

"What are you looking at this morning?"

"I'm back on my study of the *Sarajevo Haggadah*," Dov said. "The copy I obtained fascinates me."

"I'm acquainted with the name and know it's Jewish, but I'm afraid I don't know much more. Can you fill me in on a few details?"

"In addition to its antiquity, the *Haggadah* is an important witness to our European Jewish heritage. The manuscript has survived as harrowing a journey as the Jews have trudged through during the last seven centuries."

"Really?" Jack pulled a chair closer to Dov's desk. "Tell me more."

"I believe the original *Haggadah*, the Passover ritual, was written in Seville, Spain, somewhere around 1480. That positions its origins in the late medieval period. That's a good starter for why it's important. Any material than reflects how that period operated is significant."

"That's for sure," Jack said. "Did I understand correctly that the Nazis tried to steal the document?"

"Absolutely. In 1941, Nazi General Johann Hans Fortner tried to grab the *Haggadah*, but a renowned Islamic scholar named Dervis Korkut smuggled the document out of the museum right under the general's nose. Korkut hid it in a mosque in the mountains around Sarajevo. Can you believe that? A Muslim saved a Jewish treasure?"

Jack nodded his head. "Remarkable."

"Along the way, the *Haggadah* was placed in a container with elegant silver clasps. Over the centuries many people have contributed to preserving the present condition."

"The *Haggadah*'s been around so long, it must have been with the Jews when they were expelled from Spain in 1492." Jack said. "Am I right?"

"It's a complicated history, but around 1516 the first Jews settled in Venice. They came as loan bankers, and those who followed them were faced with social restrictions. Of course, King Ferdinand and Queen Isabella of Spain issued their edict in 1492, expelling all Jews in a matter of days. I believe the *Haggadah* left Tarragona, Spain, at that time and was taken to Venice. At least, that's what the trail suggests. As our people were forced out of Spain, a book as important as this one had to have left with them."

"It would be fascinating to get back inside that story and discover what pops up," Jack said.

"Equally interesting would be the story of how the silver clasps on the manuscript were added as well as the bright colored illuminations. The broken old black clasps had originally been high-grade silver. To be able to put gold and silver leaf inside the *Haggadah* would have required a high level of affluence. Of course, no one knows who made the illuminations, which actually make the *Haggadah* look more like a Christian prayer book. Obviously, this document has a complex history."

"My kind of stuff," Jack said. " I started pursuing research because it's like trying to solve a mystery. The data is often a puzzle wrapped in enigmas. I love the pursuit."

"And often the chase has been deadly," Dov said. "In Venice, only the intervention of a priest named Vistorini in 1609 saved the book from being burned in one of the pope's Inquisitions. The more recent attempts of the Nazis to destroy the document still runs shivers down my spine. Hitler's pack of wolves would have stopped at nothing to destroy everything Jewish."

The door to the office suddenly opened and Michelle hurried in. "Jack, I'm concerned."

"Concerned? What's going on?"

"There's a man standing across the street with a camera shooting pictures of our office building back here behind Santa Maria Church. He's crouched behind a light pole wedged at an angle that allows him to photograph between the church and the adjacent building. He particularly aimed at me."

"Come on, Michelle. I think you're still in an overreactionary mode due to that bombing in the subway. Why would anyone want to take pictures of this house?"

"Possibly the camera man read Corsini's story in the newspaper and it touched a nerve," Michelle said.

"And what nerve would that be?" Dov smirked.

"Stop it!" Michelle protested. "You guys aren't giving me the time of day on this problem. I'm telling you that the man took my picture several times."

Jack rubbed his chin. "OK. OK. What did he look like?"

"That's the strange thing. The guy didn't look like a tourist. He had on a brown business suit and a flashy purple shirt. He wasn't like the usual stroller shooting pictures."

"Notice anything else about him?" Jack said.

"Yeah. The man had a scar on his cheek and was completely bald."

9

Acting on Michelle's prompting, Jack Townsend walked up and down the street in front of the Santa Maria Church but saw nothing unusual. A few tourists slowed to look at the church, but no one appeared suspicious. No one seemed to be taking pictures. Certainly, no man in a brown suit with a bald head. Finally, he returned to their offices behind the church.

"I didn't see anyone out there who looks like the man you described," Jack said. "Sorry the purple shirt floated away."

"You're suggesting I'm having hallucinations?" Michelle barked.

"No, no. Probably the guy drifted on. I'm only saying he was probably a tourist interested in the church edifice and you . . . well . . . maybe just overreacted and—"

"And nothing!" Michelle bristled. "I know what I saw, and I think we need to pay attention if that creep shows up again."

"Sure," Jack said. "All agreed?"

Dov held up his hand. "I vote yes. I'll hit him with my stun gun if he gets any closer to our building."

Michelle glared, but only shook her head.

"Let's get back to work as usual," Jack suggested. "Dov, you're going back to the Vatican Library today. Right?"

Dov glanced at his watch. "They'll be open in thirty minutes, and I'll go over there to start digging into that heap of fragments I was working on yesterday. They've left everything in place for me to start in where I left off."

The office door swung open and a man in a clergy collar popped in. "Are we having fun yet, children?" he boomed in a resounding voice that roared through the house.

"Father Donald Blake!" Jack said. "What's an American Roman Catholic priest doing roaming in our secluded offices at this early morning hour?"

"I'm making sure you're genuinely working and not just trying to fake out your financial supporters," Father Blake said. "I know how you academic types operate. It's that old trickster's act with smoke and mirrors."

With only a fringe of hair around the edges, the priest's bald head mirrored his protruding stomach. Short and heavy, Father Blake's broad smile reflected a merry soul who walked on the sunny side of the street as often as possible. Around fifty, he appeared to be a man who accepted anyone regardless of their convictions, although his intense, probing eyes seemed to constantly search for inconsistency.

Michelle laughed. "You are full of it, you old fraud. I know how you priests operate. You float around all morning trying to sniff out a free cup of coffee. You don't fool me."

Blake laughed. "Hmm. I'm afraid I don't smell any coffee in here. You were expecting me and hid it in the back room?"

"You've shown up before we've got the pot on the burner," Jack said. "Everyone's up early this morning and—"

"Let's not dilly dally," Father Blake broke in. "How can I get that free cup if this woman doesn't put her mind to the task at hand?"

"I think I'm getting the message," Michelle said. "You're hounding me to get the pot fired up. The one that's sitting over there in the corner *by you*. I swear you can't even allow me time to sit down."

Blake grinned a sly smile. "You know what they say about a woman's work."

"You male chauvinist pig!" Michelle joked. "You never give up."

"I can't let the world go to rack and ruin because women keep trying to change the rules."

"Oink! Oink!" Michelle shook her finger at him. "Look. You and Jack go sit in the conference room, and I'll bring the coffee in when it's done."

"Ah, no finer words were spoken at this early hour," Father Blake said.

The two men sauntered into the adjacent room that had once been a bedroom. In the center a ramshackle old table made a center for discussion. Jack sat down at one end and Father Blake slipped in across from him.

"A fine morning," Blake said. "One of those days that makes me remember why I came to Rome."

"To make calls on people like me?" Jack laughed. "Come on. I see you wandering around St. Peter's and down the streets. What in the heck do you really do?"

"Why, I listen to people; hear their hurts and share a word of kindness. I can't imagine any more satisfying work."

"But you are a priest and I've never heard you say to what church you are attached."

Blake smiled broadly. "I don't want to work in one congregation. The whole world is my parish."

"Sounds vaguely like a Protestant preacher named John Wesley."

"I'm friends with all of them, saints and sinners alike." Father Blake leaned back in the chair and placed his hands over his round stomach. "Never object to being identified with anyone who counted, my boy." The priest began drumming on the table with his fingertips as if the questions made him nervous.

"Here you are, gentlemen." Michelle stepped into the room with a tray filled with two cups of coffee, a pitcher of cream, and a bowl of sugar with two spoons. "Nothing's better than freshly brewed coffee."

"I must take back the harsh comments I made when I came in," the priest said. "Your wife has redeemed herself by treating us with the honor due our status."

"Don't push your luck," Michelle said. "You're on the edge as it is."

"Ah!" Blake rolled his eyes and beat his chest. "How sad for me. Always living on the jumping-off point into the precipice."

"My heart bleeds." Michelle grinned and walked away.

"Well, Jack, how is your research coming along?"

Townsend shrugged. "You know how it is. I work for weeks and nothing happens. Then, one day I make a big breakthrough. Right now I'm only in the digging stage of investigation."

"I saw the article on you in *Il Messaggero* several days ago. Quite impressive."

"We thought it gave our work a nice boast. Can't buy advertising like that you know."

Father Blake took a sip of coffee. "If there's any paper that everyone in Rome reads, it's that one. No telling how many people got a glimpse into your work." The priest stopped and looked intensely into Jack's eyes.

Jack started to speak and then stopped. Blake's instant shift from being a jovial soul to becoming a probing interrogator had to be a signal of some sort. Something was going on. Jack set his coffee cup down on the table.

"Father," Jack said slowly. "Everyone knows that you're the happy priest who walks up and down the streets of Rome sharing a friendly word with everyone from waiters in the street corner café to the policeman directing traffic. You know all the officials processing people in and out of the Vatican. The smiling face of Padre Don is a symbol of good cheer." Jack took a deep breath. "I sense something else is at work this morning. You sound like you know more than you are telling me."

The priest pursed his lips thoughtfully. "You must remember that I listen to a wide range of voices and hear many rumors. And rumors are often no more than street gossip. However, you are right. I hear many things. Some of the banter does raise concerns."

"And you are here today because you've heard some chatter that bothered you?" Jack said.

Blake looked out the window. "We all know about that horrible bombing a few days ago that killed a number of people and destroyed the terminal station. The newspaper reports have been clear that the police haven't been able to identify what group was behind the blast." Blake drummed on the old conference table with his fingertips. "That doesn't mean they don't have some clues."

Jack chuckled. "What in the world would that have to do with us? We're innocuous scholars who are accused of living in the past. In fact, when it comes to the politics of Italy, I'm about as apolitical as you get."

"Unfortunately, none of that has any bearing on my concern. The problem is that you are an American."

"American? That's a problem?" Jack shook his head. "You've got to be kidding."

"Afraid not. One portion of the untold story about this bombing is that some evidence suggests that the terrorists were anti-American activists. Being a Yank who gets his story in the paper labels you as a possible target."

"Oh, come now, Father. You've got to be stretching the rubber band rather far to squeeze us into that picture."

"I'm only sharing information with a friend," the priest said. "However, I wouldn't discount anything that I am telling you." He crossed his arms over his rotund stomach and leaned back. "Have you seen anything unusual around here lately."

"No. No. Of course not." Jack stopped. "Well, this morning Michelle thought she saw a man across the street taking a picture of our facility, but I didn't—"

"Stop!" The priest bounded forward in his chair. "That's exactly what I'm talking about. Someone taking a picture of this building is cause for alarm."

"Michelle could have been completely wrong. When I went outside and looked around I didn't see anyone. This bomb explosion made Michelle a little hyper."

"And well it should!" Blake leaned closer. "All of this kidding about chauvinism aside, your wife is a brilliant woman, and I highly respect her. You can't write off what she thought she saw as hysteria. Listen to me, Jack. You need to take her concern seriously."

"I must say, Father, I didn't expect a warning to pay closer attention to what's going on around us this morning. Maybe, I should have reacted more quickly to Michelle."

"When you live behind a church that's famous for being a bone collection, I'd think you'd do well to pay attention to your own carcass, my boy. Life is short enough as it is. We don't want you to wind up down there in the basement with your skeleton on display like the monks from the sixteenth century. That's the word for today from your ol' buddy on the street."

"You're saying that just because we're Americans someone might be interested in giving us the same shock treatment the subway got?"

The priest leaned across the table and pointed his finger. "You've got it! Remember what I've told you."

Jack pulled at his lips apprehensively. "Hmm. Sure. We'll keep our eyes open." He rubbed the side of his face. "One newspaper article could set all of this off?"

"Whoever did this bombing hates Americans. Getting your story plastered across Italy's number one newspaper casts a spotlight on the fact that you're from aboard. Yes, that could make you a target." The priest abruptly stood up. "Think it over, Jack. It's worth the time." With a simple wave of the hand, Father Blake bounded out of the room, walking passed Michelle standing by the door.

Jack could hear him bidding Michelle and Dov good-bye, but Jack stayed by the table. Could this good natured soul be right? Of course, Blake always meant well, but he sounded like he might be only repeating gossip. Nothing reported in the newspapers substantiated his claims of Americans being the actual target of the bombing. Why blast a Roman subway if the terrorists hated Americans? Something just didn't fit right with Blake's story.

Michelle stuck her head in the door. "What'd the good priest have on his mind this morning?"

"Oh, nothing," Jack said. "Nothing at all." He kept staring out the window.

10

Dr. Albert Stein muttered to himself and kept examining through his thick glasses the photographs scattered across his desk. "Most interesting." He held one photograph closer to the lamp. "Yes, indeed."

Klaus Burchel stood beside him with a camera, looking, watching, and saying nothing.

Stein held a magnifying glass over one picture, studying it more closely. "Most significant."

Burchel continued to look, making no comment.

"You took this picture directly across the street from the Santa Maria Church?" Stein asked. "Right?"

"Yes, sir."

"And the address on this piece of paper is the apartment the Townsends occupy?"

"Yes, sir."

Stein laid the magnifying glass aside and leaned back in his chair. "More than interesting. How did you find all these details so quickly?"

"Through the newspaper story. I went to the office of *Il Messaggero* and ran down some reporter named Mario Corsini. I told him I was a biblical scholar and wanted to chat with the

Townsends. The man gave me their address without asking a question. I tried the same thing at the Santa Maria Church except that I told them I had an appointment with Jack Townsend at his apartment but lost the address. They wrote out the street location without hesitation. Not bad, huh?"

Stein nodded his head. "Indeed. I know quite well what Michelle Townsend looks like, and this is unquestionably her. Most interesting is that they have offices behind a Catholic church. Townsend must have worked out some agreement with the local fathers to obtain the space."

"I didn't make any inquiries," Klaus said.

Stein reached in his shirt pocket and pulled out a pack of cigarettes. Flipping a small golden lighter, he took a big drag. For a moment, he held the smoke in, then blew a puff overhead. Lost in thought, he tapped his fingers rapidly on his desk.

"You did exactly what I told you to do and nothing more," he said to Klaus. "This is what I always expect. If you had done anything else, someone might have identified you later. We couldn't have that. The newspaper only left a few clues about what the Townsends are up to, but I must learn much, much more."

"Yes, sir."

"Go buy some black pants, a black sweatshirt, and a face mask. I already have the electronic equipment you'll need. Pick up the clothing immediately. You will need to work tonight."

The young man scratched his head. "I'm not sure where you're going with this, but I'll get the clothes at once."

Stein tossed one hundred euros on the desk. "That ought to cover it. Get back here immediately."

Klaus grabbed the money. "At once, sir."

The absence of moonlight deepened the blackness of night, enveloping the ramshackle buildings standing up and down Via Vittorio Veneto. Santa Maria Church had locked its doors much earlier and the towering church had taken on an imposing appearance. Klaus Burchel stood across the street inside a narrow alley and watched the empty street for more than an hour. His relationship with Stein crossed his mind. As long as he remained the obedient servant, Stein humored him. Returning to the "yes, sirs," and "no, sirs," hadn't been easy, but in a couple of days Stein's more pleasant reactions signaled it was working. Stein paid on time, and the money was excellent. Klaus periodically craved a hit and thought about seeking out a snort or two. Of course, Stein could have someone watching him so he shelved the idea, although the desire still switched within him.

Black sweats and an old stocking cap made it impossible for him to be seen. Periodically, a taxi or small car rambled down the street, but by 3:00 a.m., no one was strolling down the sidewalk. The empty street proved that he could cross without observation.

Pulling his black coat collar up around his neck, Klaus darted across the pavement and into the shadows alongside of the church. For several minutes, he stood against the stone block wall and listened. The sounds of his running faded, and he heard nothing. No one seemed to be out at this late hour of the night. He waited another five minutes before pulling the black face mask out of his backpack. With a couple of quick jerks, he tugged the covering over his head. Klaus scooted silently along the side of the church until he reached the front door of the house behind the large edifice.

He had learned to pick a lock long ago and figured the advancing age of the house should make it easy to break in. As anticipated, he found the front door secured with a warded lock. The L-shaped warded intrusion tool he carried in his pocket made quick work of the security lock.

Stein had warned him that once he was inside the house, his work had to be done fast. Get in; get out; open and shut. Even though it was the middle of the night, there were no guarantees that a surprise visit couldn't happen. Quickly pulling the old MicroPower WM-1 transmitter from his backpack, he straightened the red and green wires before sliding under the closest desk and beginning to install the device into the telephone line. Once the transmitter had been hooked in, he took out the test receiver from the backpack to make sure the connections were secure. The tone and volume of sound were excellent.

Pulling the desk drawer out, he fastened the MicroPower unit against the inside of the back of the desk behind the last drawer where no one could see it. At that moment a cracking noise echoed from the adjacent dark room.

Klaus froze. The scraping sound came again. Crawling back out from under the desk, Klaus stood perfectly still and listened to make sure no night watchman was creeping around in the dark. Another faint sound reverberated from the same room. Klaus's heart pounded. Could he have stepped into a trap? It sounded like someone was waiting to ambush him from just a few feet away. Ducking beneath the desk, he pulled a small flashlight from his pocket. Taking the Smith & Wesson 459 pistol Stein had given him from his side pocket, he flipped off the safety and turned on the small narrow beam, aiming it at the black hole in front of him. A rat the size of a kitten stared back with its red eyes reflecting the light.

Behind the ugly creature, Klaus could see a long table in a conference room. Klaus cursed under his breath and started to throw the flashlight but thought better of the idea. The rodent blinked and scurried away. Satisfied that he was still secure,

Klaus went back to work. After surveying the other desks, he concluded only one telephone line came in and went out of the office. With the bugging device in position, he could leave but knew the sending range of the device might be an issue. If the reception proved too limited, Stein would have to station him down the street with a recording device to pick up talking.

Carefully closing the front door and making sure it was locked, Burchel inched his way back down the cement walkway until he reached the edge of the shadows beyond which the street lights glowed. Once confident no one was watching, he pulled off the black mask and started his trek out of the neighborhood.

11

Rome's street traffic remained at the usual feverish pitch and pace.
Cars honked incessantly, and buses plowed ahead regardless of
who got in the way. Wiggling through the jam-ups meant taking your life in your hands. Jack Townsend often darted in and
out through the lanes of cars but knew the risks. Jaywalking
had turned into an art that remained on the iffy side even
during late September when the tourist numbers started to
dwindle.

Michelle believed he was going to the Vatican Library
and that wasn't untrue, but he had taken the subway exit
that brought him up at a different point. The Tiber River and
Amadeo bridge that allowed him to walk to Borgo Santo
Spirito and end up at the Vatican wasn't far away, but his
actual destination lay directly in front of him. The Dar Poeta
sidewalk café with the artichokes he dearly loved stood just
a few feet ahead. Jack hadn't told Michelle about this little
detour because she might worry, having the terminal bombing
still weighing on her mind. That was the excuse he gave himself before entering the subway station near their offices and
being whisked away. When he walked into the sidewalk café,

the bushy-haired waiter immediately recognized him and came rushing forward with his large silver pot held above his head.

"Ah, Signor Townsend, I have your favorite blend today that I know will send a thrill through your heart." Luichi filled the porcelain cup sitting in front of Jack. "Drink and may the gods bless you with joy!" Luichi hurried on to the next table.

Jack found the coffee to be a tad stale and hardly a heart-warming treat, but it was OK. Luichi always overstated the menu like an enthusiastic salesman closing in on the finish of a sale, but after all didn't most Italians? After a second sip, Jack began watching the multitudes drifting by. A young woman in a form-fitting red jersey came twisting down the sidewalk with large circular earrings swinging back and forth. He pretended not to look but followed her until she disappeared into a store up the street. A stylish looking man in a brown tweed sport coat wearing high dollar Giorgio Brutini shoes hung on to a metal chain for dear life while an excited furry pup pulled him forward. The sights of strange people walking determinedly forward in pursuit of who knows what gripped his imagination.

"A little something to eat, Signor?" Luichi asked.

"I was just thinking about the artichokes *alla giudia* cooked in a Roman-Jewish style. Yes?"

"Ah, you always know what is best," Luichi said. "The most excellent selection of all." The waiter patted Jack on the shoulder and hurried away. No matter what he would have ordered, Luichi would have declared it to be the most elegant possibility.

A heavy-set man wearing a plaid English vest came leisurely strolling by with a huge Great Dane at his side. With his outlandishly oversized dog, he looked more like a character in a movie than the average Roman citizen. The unusual sight kept Jack's eyes glued to the street. A Lamborghini sports car swirled through the thick traffic and came to an abrupt stop in front of the restaurant. The driver's dark complexion and his long black hair swirling in the wind gave him an appearance of a movie actor roaring through the city.

Movies seemed to be on Jack's mind. The scene felt like a clip from some classic movie made on Rome's streets. In the far distance, he could still see the spires of St. Peter's Basilica. So much history had unfolded in this small area that any portion of the scenery grabbed the imagination and inspired fantasies of all shapes and sizes.

"Il mio amico!" some voice called out. "Friend!"

Jack looked around. Walking up the street with his arm waving in the air, overweight Tony Mattei hustled along like a tourist rushing to get on a bus before it left him on the street.

"Ah, my friend!" Tony Mattei hurried in and plopped down across the small table from Jack. As usual, Tony's black hair hung over his forehead, making him look like he had just been in a wrestling match. With a brilliant red handkerchief sticking out from his black silk coat pocket, Mattei consistently showed up with the countenance of a walking billboard. On each hand he had two sparkling diamond rings Jack had never seen on his hands before. Tony Mattei looked like a Mardi Gras parade marching through town.

"My friend, Tony," Jack said. "We always seem to run into each other at the Dar Poeta.

"It is because the gods smile on me everyday that I am in this neighborhood. They bring my dear friend from America across my path so that my dreams and hopes may be encouraged."

Jack chuckled. "You been drinking wine already this morning?"

"Oh, no!" Tony shook his head. "I speak the truth from a humble and sincere heart."

"Would you drink a cup of coffee with me instead, Tony?"

"Of course! Yes! I would be delighted."

Jack raised his hand in the air and snapped his finger. "Luichi! A cup of coffee for my friend." The Italian immediately picked up an empty white cup and started toward them.

"The last time we were here the terrible bombing had just occurred," Tony said. "Then in the next moment I pick up the newspaper and read this amazing story about you and your writing. I said to myself, 'These Americans are everywhere!' Is that not so?"

"That story was nice, but it didn't change anything in the world. Just a few lines about our research. That's all."

"But I can see how prominent you have become now. To be featured in *Il Messaggero* says that the entire nation of Italy knows that you are a person of great esteem and fame."

"Come on, Tony. The reporter simply found our work to be interesting and thought it would make a story. Really. The bottom line is that our approach to an archaeological problem fascinated the reporter. That's all."

"Hmm." Tony tilted his head and pursed his lips. "I think there is more here."

"Your coffee, my friend." Luichi set the cup and saucer on the table and hurried away.

"The diamond business is going well this morning?" Jack asked. "No?"

Mattei shrugged. "Well, we are into the fall now and there are not as many tourists. Business slows under these circumstances."

"Rome is always filled with visitors," Jack said. "My hunch is that you are doing well on this nice warm autumn day. I bet your stores are doing fine."

"We try," Tony said defensively. "That is all we can do. Let me shift the subject." He squinted and shook his head. "If memory serves me correctly, at sometime or the other, you mentioned that your wife was frightened by explosions. Did the subway bombing bother her?"

"Michelle struggles with any incident of that order," Jack said. "She tries not to mention the explosion, but I know it is upsetting."

"Yes, yes. And you, Jack? How are you feeling about this terrorist act today?" He shifted nervously and crossed his arms over his broad chest.

"All forms of violence are repugnant to me. In addition, it was a cowardly deed done in the darkness. No, I don't like any aspect of such a gruesome and panic-mongering attack. Don't most Italians feel the same way?"

"I hope so." Tony raised one eyebrow.

"Now, I have a question for you. Why do you think this group of terrorists set off the bomb?"

Tony rolled his eyes. "How would I know? The newspapers don't seem to link this action with any international terrorist organization. Possibly, the terrorist made a mistake by not being clearer about his reasons for setting off the explosion."

"That's putting it mildly. The terrorists made a huge mistake doing *anything*."

"Yes. Yes. Of course." Tony smiled. "Perhaps, we should move on to a more comfortable topic. Is the American economy doing any better?"

The shift in the conversations seemed strained as if Tony wanted something out of him that wasn't yet clear. Possibly the man was only on the flustered side, but he sounded nervous and was jumping around like a toad on hot cement. Instead of coffee, maybe he should have stayed with those large volumes of winc hc was reported to drink all the time.

Tony kept expounding his ideas about why the Italian economy suffered due to the intemperate unregulated actions of the British and American importers. Jack listened and said little. When Tony got started, the man rolled on and on like a runaway freight train, and this morning the engine kept going down the track.

12

THE AFTERNOON HAD NEARLY FADED WHEN JACK AND MICHELLE TOWNSEND gathered around the conference table in the side room in their offices. The door had been left open to hear anyone coming through the front door entry. Papers and manila folders lay strewn across the old table as well as a few books.

"Let's begin by bringing each of us up-to-date on what we've discovered so far," Jack said. "Michelle, what's coming up as you sit in there hour after hour and pound on that computer?"

"I'm not having much luck," she said. "I've been trying to access The Royal or Ancient Library of Alexandria via the Internet to find some ancient documents, but I don't get much beyond mention of its existence. I've tried a number of angles but the doors just aren't opening for me."

"Hmm," Jack mused. "Not surprised. What we're looking for is simply going to be much more secluded. Dov, what'd you come up with?"

The young man shrugged. "Most of what I've turned up is rather pedestrian. My guess is that while a street was being repaired, the workmen broke through the top of an ancient storage room where documents had been stored by the Roman government centuries ago. I'm not sure it's worth much more rummaging, but that's not the big news."

"Don't sit there grinning," Jack said. "Lay the heavy stuff on us."

"You were right to tell me to keep probing. I found the basement under the basement," Dov said. "When I started looking into this material, I realized it was far too dusty and dirty to be sitting around in those gorgeous Secret Archives rooms. Poking around in the storage area led to the discovery of secluded stairs that wound down to an entirely different level underneath. I found the area where the Vatican stores the ancient material that has never been cataloged. There's also a large space in the back where they are doing archaeological digging in a first-century landscape. Far out or what?

"You've found the goldmine!" Michelle exclaimed.

"Dov, you've made a breakthrough," Jack said. "Yes, this is highly important. I didn't even know that a hidden area existed below the library. You're discovery is significant. Earlier, I didn't find anything that offered a significant lead on where to look for the first-century clues, but finding the hidden basement means we're certainly searching in the right area."

Albert Stein twisted the dials for a moment, cursed, and slammed his fist against the inside wall of the large van parked only two blocks from the Santa Maria Church. "I can't pick up enough volume," he screamed at Klaus Bruchel. "I'm missing important parts of what they are saying." He glanced around at the reception devices and batteries that filled the back portion of the van, giving it the look of a make-shift electronics laboratory. "Where did you hook up that MicroPower transmitter?"

Burchel shrugged. "It's on the underside of one of the desks," the young man said. "I think they must be sitting in another room. Probably the conference room. That's the best that I can tell you."

Stein cursed again. "You should have thought of that possibility, you fool." He turned up the volume again and put the earphone back over his head. A low hum made the sound somewhat distorted. He listened more intently.

A few words filtered in. "And Dov continues to work on the *Sarajevo Haggadah*," Jack Townsend said. "Finding any —— there, Dov?"

The microphone popped and Stein missed half of the sentence. "—— comparing the Hebrew forms," Dov Sharon answered. "—— not getting much, but I find it more than interesting. Because Bosnia was under the control of the Austro-Hungarian Empire when the book surfaced in 1894, it was natural that it be sent to Vienna because the city was the hub of critical scholarship in those days. Unfortunately —— mishandled the rebinding of the *Haggadah*."

Stein jerked off the earphones. "It's makes no sense that they are fooling around with that ridiculous Jewish Passover book." The man muttered under his breath. "Their interest has to be elsewhere. Makes Townsend sound like he's lost his mind. Good God! They're not a bunch of idiots! Stein put the earphones back on his head.

"I'd suggest we stay on our original track," Jack Townsend said. "Dov, —— stay with your research and we'll look —— of the library. Michelle, I want you to concentrate on Irenaeus. Since he was a disciple of Polycarp, that Church Father —— in touch with. —— Maybe, you can come up with a lead —— in the past."

"OK," Michelle said. A sudden burst of static knocked out much of what she said. "—— shift to a new area easily

93

I will ——" The static knocked out her response. "—— later —— return to —— was."

"Good," Townsend said. "We'll start tomorrow."

Stein cursed. "Sounds like they are sitting around a table. I can only pick up enough to make matters worse." He pointed his finger at Burchel. "You've got to get back in that house and wire up that additional space. You must do this work tonight. They are obviously pursuing some venue of importance. Get back in there and wire up that space."

Klaus Burchel nodded. "Do you see any dangers in returning so soon?"

"Of course! That's why you'd better do it right this time."

13

AN UNEXPECTED FALL RAIN DUMPED A RAPID DOWNPOUR ACROSS ROME in the late evening. Standing outside in the black pants and coat he had worn the first time he broke into the Townsend's offices, Klaus Burchel huddled against a building across the street from Santa Maria Church and watched the church's guttering pour the night's runoff into the street. Lightening crackled and lit up the dark sky; thunder pounded on his eardrums. Burchel's umbrella kept the splattering rain out of his face, but the thunderstorm proved too fierce to keep him from getting wet in the cold rain.

If he could get inside the church and hide until the middle of the night, the cloudburst might pass over. Klaus glanced at his watch. Even though it was only 10:00, the church doors appeared to still be open. Couldn't be many people in there at this hour. Stein wouldn't like it, but the demanding jerk didn't have to stand out in the rain with a backpack on either. Enough of the fall weather had already arrived that the coldness had started to cut to the bone. Shifting his weight back and forth on his damp feet, he finally decided it was worth the effort to get inside the church. Turning the collar on his coat up, Klaus made a mad dash across the street and up the steps of the church. With a hard yank, he pulled the massive front door open and slipped inside.

Since night had fallen, light inside the church had become dim. The high altar hovered in the dimness of candlelight, leaving the nave filled with shadows. For a moment, Klaus considered ducking under a pew until he dried out, but someone might still be around and could see him. Big trouble would erupt from getting caught looking like a curled-up dog hiding in a corner. In fact, he needed to quickly find a room to hide in. Only then did he notice the dark entrance to his left and the stairs leading down into the blackness. Without further thought, he bounded down the ancient stone steps.

Only at the bottom of the stairs did he realize that he had stumbled into the crypt that ran under the entire church. A brass plaque on the wall explained that the Capuchin monks had once used the building as a monastery and more than four thousand monks had been buried there between 1528 and 1870. The graves situated around him were considerably more than he bargained for. Klaus shuttered. Barely making a sound, he crept forward into the funerary.

Klaus realized that his bravado and swagger on Rome's streets had been an attempt to cover his extreme superstitiousness. Growing up in Germany in a time of economic and social upheaval, he had worried that monsters hid in his closet at night, waiting to devour him as soon as he went to sleep. The blackness of the unseen in the dark always appeared filled with creatures of death ready to flay him with razors. The craziness of those childhood fears arose again in the shadowy gloom of the ancient cemetery surrounding him.

Pressing against the stone wall, he turned a dim corner and came face-to–face with a skeleton shrouded in a deteriorating brown robe tucked in a recess in the basement wall. The boney jaw hung at a skewed angle as if it were about to drop from the face at any moment while the bones of the hand dangled from under the brown robe. The obscure darkness of the skeletal eyes seemed to stare directly at him. Klaus's mouth went dry, and he leaped backward nearly falling on the rock floor. His heart roared like a drilling rig pounding on solid rock. He started to run, but saw nothing opening before him accept more murkiness. Backing up against the granite wall, he tried to catch his breath and fight off the certainty that death was stalking him down these corridors. Reaching around to his backpack, Klaus rummaged through the contents until he found a large hunting knife in a leather sheath. Pulling it out, he tucked the blade in his belt where he could grab it at a moments notice.

Surely, no one came down into these crypts at night. At least, he couldn't imagine such a thing. Probably the candlelights of the crypt were kept lit day and night so a person wouldn't have to worry about being left alone in the total darkness. All he could do was suck it up and stay crouched in the shadows. It was either that or go back out in the cold rain.

Klaus pulled the knife out of his belt and crawled back in a black corner with the blade pointed at anyone that might show up unexpectedly. Even though he had the gun Stein had given him, he knew that the sound of a gun firing would bring the police. Klaus couldn't have that. There was no choice but to fight off the fear that kept boiling up inside of him. For a moment, he thought about this stinking job he'd taken with Stein and cursed the fact he'd ever gotten into it. Then, again, he needed the money and the opportunity to disappear before the police caught him. What a stupid mess he'd gotten himself into.

Father Raffello awoke with a sudden jerk and nearly fell out of his chair. He blinked several times before staring at his wristwatch. It was 2:25 in the morning! How had he done such a thing? Fallen asleep on the job! The priest couldn't believe his slovenly behavior. He must have drifted off somewhere around 10:00 in the evening and left the front door of the church unlocked. Good heavens! How could he have done such a thing? Never, never had he drifted off in sleep like that before! Who knows what in the world could have happened with the edifice remaining wide open. Even though he was eighty, Father Raffello prided himself on running Santa Maria with skill and precision. How had he done such a thing? Terrible. Terrible.

Slipping off the chair he was sitting on in the confessional booth, he stood up and then abruptly stopped. He hadn't simply awakened; something had awakened him. A noise. A sound. Something unexpected. Pushing the curtain aside, he peered out into the nave. The creaking noise came again. Someone was coming into the church at 2:30 in the night? No, someone was going out.

Father Raffello took a deep breath. No person could have been walking around in the church all this time and not be up to no good. He shot a glance at the altar to make sure they hadn't tried to carry off the great golden candlesticks, but there they were in position with candles burning as always. But what about the poor box? A thief could have grabbed the money for the poor.

The old priest rushed up the center aisle and into the narthex. In a second, he could see that the lock remained secure and jerking the box he determined the coins had stayed inside. Yet, he thought it worthwhile to check out every aspect of the entryway, but nothing was missing. Father Raffello still wasn't satisfied. A nagging suspicion haunted him, and the old man always found his intuitions to be important to follow up on until he was completely satisfied everything was in order.

Some kids might have come in and could be stealing a few bones from downstairs under the church. Yes, that was it. Every now and then, teenagers showed up for just such a prank. Grabbing a candle, the priest hurried down the stone steps into the crypt. He had been down there so many times that he could quickly recognize any loss. Hurrying up and down the long corridors, he found nothing amiss, but as he turned to leave, Father Raffello noticed muddy footprints on the floor. Decades earlier, dirt from the Holy Land had been sprinkled on the floor of the crypts and never removed. Someone had been walking around that evening leaving muddy footprints in the loose dirt. Kneeling on the floor, the priest could tell the footprints were much larger than the usual size of teenagers. No question about it! He had heard that person leaving and that was what woke him up. Father Raffello rushed back up the steps.

If nothing was amiss in the church proper, possibly the intruder might have gone around to the back and was working on the Townsends' offices behind the church. If nothing else, it was worth a look. Father Raffello pushed the large front door open and peered out. The rain storm had passed and the heavy clouds moved on so he could walk around the building without an umbrella, but the night air felt brisk. Quickly, the priest returned inside and unlocked a closet at the side of the narthex. Pulling out a black cloak, he fastened it over his robe and pulled the hood over his head. Undoubtedly slinking through the early morning hours, he looked as scary as the dead monks propped up against the stone walls in the crypts below.

As quietly as possible, the priest found his way along the side of the tall church and started down the cement path. Just as he reached the back of the church, a tiny light flashed on in one of the rooms. Father Raffello froze. He looked again. No light. Possibly, he had made a mistake. The windows were filled with darkness. Yes, he had only imagined the light. Breathing a sigh of relief, he tucked his hands in his robe and thought of returning to the church.

A small light flipped on again.

Father Raffello caught his breath. No question about it! Someone was walking around in those offices. He should run back in the church and call the police, but if he did the thief might leave and he'd miss seeing who it was. If nothing else, he could stand there and get a good view of the crook so he could identify the thief at the police station. That might prove to be the most useful thing to be done. Just wait. Then again, that was certainly a dangerous path to take.

The door knob turned. The man was coming out. No time to run. Just watch.

The figure quickly shut the door behind him and turned as if doing something to the lock. In a matter of seconds, the black figure turned back around and started to leave the porch. Only then did Father Raffello realize the man had a black mask over his face.

"Stop!" the priest demanded.

The man's scream echoed off the stone walls of the expansive church before he launched forward with a vicious thrust.

Father Raffello felt the excruciating pain of a knife blade plunging into his stomach. The torment was so severe that he couldn't scream. All the strength went out of his body and the priest crumpled to his knees. He felt the blade pulled out only to come again at his upper chest. Blackness instantly swallowed the priest.

14

Even though it was an early morning in late September, the temperature felt unusually warm. Jack and Michelle Townsend pulled their small Fiat into their reserved parking space behind their offices. Michelle noticed Jack kept glancing at her out of the corner of his eye and was studying her composure.

"You satisfied yet?" she said.

"Satisfied?" Jack frowned. "I don't understand."

"Yes, you do. You're checking me out to make sure I've got my head together."

"No!" Jack protested.

"Our little dinner the other night at Der Pallaro was about my stability. You're checking me out again this morning."

Jack stiffened. "That's not fair."

Michelle laughed. "I want you to know that I am hunky-dory, as my little mother use to say, just fine. You can relax."

Jack squirmed. "Of course. Sure you are."

Michelle giggled. "You are one funny man, Jack Townsend. I know you worry about me all the time." She squeezed his hand. "I want you to know that's no problem. Your love keeps me going. OK?"

Jack leaned over and gave her a kiss. "You bet. Let's go."

Slamming the car doors shut, the couple started up the walkway holding hands, teasing, laughing while swinging briefcases at their sides. Jack pointed ahead. "Looks like a crowd of people milling around our front door."

"What would anybody be doing out here at this early hour?" Michelle ask. "Aren't a couple of guys bending over something in the grass?"

"I-I don't know." Jack stopped. "Good heavens! Someone is on the ground!"

Michelle dropped her briefcase. "God forbid! That's a man lying in the grass!"

"Stay here until I see what's going on," Jack said forcefully. "I mean it. Stay exactly where you are. I'll be back."

Michelle felt her anxieties starting to build. A black form sprawled in the grass looked like a priest from the church. Her heart started to pound and fear began grabbing at her throat.

Jack broke into a trot to get to the front of the white house.

Dov Sharon and Father Donald Blake stood behind a group of men gathered around the porch. Several policemen were kneeling over the figure lying on the ground. Only then did Jack discover a pool of blood spreading from beneath the body.

"It's Father Raffello," Dov said. "I found his body when I arrived this morning. I immediately called the police."

"Stabbed," Father Blake added. "I just happened to be in this area when the story broke. "I got here shortly after the police arrived. Nasty business."

Jack covered his mouth and groaned. "No! It can't be. How could anyone kill such a kind old priest of the church?"

"We're not sure," Father Blake said. "My hunch is that he caught a thief breaking into your offices. A struggle resulted and the assailant killed the priest. Rigor mortis has already set in, so the stabbing must have occurred in the middle of the night."

Jack looked back at Michelle and motioned for her to stay put. "Lord, help us! We don't have anything of value in that office that a thief would kill for. Books and manuscripts. Some work lying around. But nothing a common thief could trade in for much return and certainly not for a human life."

The priest put his arm around Jack's shoulder and pulled him farther to the back. "We've got to think this assault through carefully. I told you the other day that the publicity in the paper had problems. Now the bubble's burst. I'm sure this murder is tied to what happened in the subway explosion. You're underestimating your standing with someone who hates Americans. My hunch is that this is another example of hostility toward Yanks. I think poor Father Raffello simply got caught in the backlash of an attack. It's hard to say, but think again. What have you got in there that's worth stealing?"

Jack ran his hands through his hair. "We've been doing research at the Vatican Library but haven't made any breakthroughs. Dov's been working on a copy of the *Sarajevo Haggadah*, but his research is not worth much money either. I just don't know. I'm left completely mystified."

"Hmm," Father Blake stroked his chin. "Of course, no one would know what you've got in those offices, but they'd probably guess a great deal. Most of the folks around here assume that Americans keep bucket loads of money under their beds at night. See what I mean? You're vulnerable. Even though we don't know for sure, it still doesn't negate my hunch. You've got to be careful, Jack. I believe these people will come after you."

"Hey, what's going on?" Heavy-set Tony Mattei hurried up the walkway. "I heard that there was a killing over here."

"Yes," Jack said. "The priest in charge of the church was killed last night.

"Heaven help us!" Mattei rolled his eyes. "Serious business indeed."

Father Blake eyed him suspiciously. "How'd you find out?"

"When a priest is down?" Mattei puckered his lips and looked like the question was nonsense. "This is Rome! You think the report of a murdered priest doesn't spread like a flooding river? Of course, I heard! The word is everywhere."

A detective standing over the body got up and came over to the three men. "I'm Alfredo Pino with the police. As best we can determine, the murder happened outside of your offices, and the doors remained locked. No evidence of a forced entry. We don't see any problem with you going back, but you will need to use the back door and stay away from the entry as well as out of this front area. An ambulance will be here shortly to pick up the body, and our investigation will be going on all day. If you find anything amiss inside, we want to know at once."

"Of course," Jack said. "We will call you immediately if anything turns up."

"Excellent." Alfredo Pino walked away.

"Looks like we can get in," Jack said to Father Blake and Tony Mattei. "See you gentlemen later."

Jack led Michelle and Dov to the back of the house, but getting inside proved to be arduous. Small tables, chairs, and boxes had been stored in the kitchen, and no one ever came in the back way. Dov Sharon pushed on the door while Michelle stared silently at the ground. Once the door had been pried open, Jack cleared a path through the junk into their working area.

"Come on in," he called out. "I think we can get our house in order."

For several minutes no one spoke while they turned on lights and cleared their desks. Watching Michelle out of the corner of his eye, Jack could clearly see that she was deeply disturbed, but didn't want to talk about it as usual. Periodically, he peered out the window to follow the progress of the police. Eventually, medics rolled in a gurney and hauled Father Raffello away. Only then did he break the silence hovering over their offices.

"Let's meet in the conference room and consider where our work has taken us this morning," he said. "I know it's going to be difficult to function normally."

Michelle and Dov walked mechanically into the adjacent room and laid their notepads on the gnarled old table without saying a word. No one spoke for what felt like an eternity.

"I know working is nearly impossible under the circumstances, but I believe the best thing we can do is to continue," Jack said. "Activity will help us emotionally stay on track."

"Just a minute," Michelle interrupted him. "Dov, you're saying the man was dead when you arrived? You found him?"

Dov Sharon nodded his head.

Michelle stared intensely at the young man. "You didn't have any disagreements with Father Raffello? No problems?"

Dov's eyes narrowed. "None."

"OK," Jack interrupted the exchange. "Enough of questioning what happened. That's up to the police. Let's begin by reviewing what we found at the library yesterday. Dov?"

"Rosh Hashana begins tomorrow," Dov said. "So, I put in extra time yesterday and stumbled upon a most surprising find. During the first centuries of the Christian era, a Laterani family was involved with a number of important documents that the public doesn't know about. Their connection to the early church remains highly important, but the Roman Catholic Church is rather defensive about the materials attributed to the Lateranis. Behind these stories, I discovered that there's supposedly a book of some sort that the priests judiciously keep hidden in the Vatican Library. I don't know if this has any connection to what we are seeking, but it's an intriguing lead."

"Where's this hidden book located?" Jack asked.

"That's part of the riddle. Only a couple of their priests seem to know where it is, and believe me, they're not talking. I'm not even sure the pope knows about this story. It's that secret."

"How'd you find out?" Michelle asked.

"You aren't going to believe this," Dov said. "I was making my inquiries when I noticed that a peculiar old priest seemed particularly agitated about my requests for information. He got out of his chair and went hobbling back into the stacks. Because my questions bothered him, I followed the priest, staying on the other side of the rack of materials. Near the end of a long row of documents, another elderly priest was waiting for this guy. No one else was around so I simply eavesdropped. That's when I got the larger story."

"Fascinating," Jack said. "Any road signs we can follow?"

"Yes," Dov said. "Once Rosh Hashana is passed, I will give you a guided tour of that end of the library. By now, I imagine the old priest has my tag number and will be leery when I show up."

"Well!" Jack rubbed his hands together. "For a morning that has started out so badly, we are making important progress."

Dr. Albert Stein pulled the earphones from his head and readjusted his thick glasses. The transmitters that Burchel had installed the night before had worked even better than he had hoped. Equipped for reception, the van remained parked near to Santa Maria Church. Their conversation came through as clearly as if the three people had been sitting in the next room. While it had not answered many of his questions, it had been more than worth the trouble and expense. He now knew the name of the Laterani family. In fact, Laterani property had been part of building the first church in Rome, and in some way that he couldn't quite remember, a portion of the land had ended up in the estate of Constantine. It was exactly the sort of information he had hoped for.

Stein looked at his watch. Klaus Burchel still hadn't show up. Where was he? Burchel should have been here long before now. The young man had done well in installing the second MicroPower WM-1 transmitter, but not getting back to him in proper time signaled trouble. Could he be snorting cocaine again? Definitely. Whatever he was up to, Burchel would be in big trouble for his tardiness.

Stein looked around the van. His intention had been that Burchel would spend the day running a recorder to pick up the conversations. Since Klaus wasn't there, Stein had no choice but to stay in the stuffy van and listen. It was the kind of research that he never wanted to do.

With their early morning conference concluded, Dov Sharon gathered his papers and pushed them into a briefcase. "I'm going back to the Vatican Library to see what else I can find." He turned toward the door. "I hope to be back late this afternoon." Not looking at Michelle, Dov hurried out the door but said nothing else.

"I suppose you've got a good reason for offending our colleague?" Jack said in a flat unemotional voice that barely concealed his anger.

"I know you don't agree with me," Michelle said. "But I find it interesting that the person who found poor Father Raffello was Dov Sharon. I've told you before that I have suspicions about him."

"I think you're pushing the envelope, Michelle. There's not one shred of evidence that Dov has ever done anything wrong. He's simply a quiet studious type. OK?"

Michelle pushed back from the table, said nothing, and silently walked back to her desk.

Part Two
Night Darkens

15

THE CONSISTENT CLATTER OF THE TRAIN'S WHEELS AGAINST THE TRACKS irritated the young German. The beat of steel against steel resounded like the echo of a judge's gavel pounding out judgment, condemning Klaus to torture and perdition.

It came again and again. No escape. No escape. No escape. No escape.

The clamor wouldn't stop.

Killing a Roman Catholic priest in Italy had to be the worst crime of the century, but even worse, the death had never been his intention. How in God's name could he have done such a thing? The mess started in that diabolical church crypt where they propped up horrid skeletons with bones sticking out like party favors to entice ghouls showing up in the middle of the night. The Capuchin monks surely had draconian intentions when they started placing those skulls around like Halloween decorations to terrify children.

Sure he was superstitious, but Klaus Burchel hadn't dreamed the ghostly sights could scramble his brains. Skeletal fingers dangling from a rotting brown robe like dirty icicles made his blood run cold. The black, empty eyes of those yellowing skulls had peered into his soul and found it as empty as were those

ancient craniums. Every inch of that basement had been a horror show that left him terror-crazed.

And when that priest showed up in front of the house with
a hood over his head, the padre had looked like death creeping after Klaus. The shock of a ghastly, shrouded apparition
shot the knife forward more by reflex than by design. He had
stabbed the Holy Joe basically because the bum shocked him.
Good God! Who wouldn't? Having a ghost confront you in
the middle of the night would send anyone running for a meat
cleaver! The killing had been purely an accident brought on by
that old fool appearing out of the darkness. But, it was done.
Finished. Over.

The constant rumble of the train felt like a runaway drill
pounding in his head. It made him want to jump up and leap
off the coach at the next terminal, but he couldn't. Once Stein
found out about the killing, he'd probably turn him in just to
save Stein's own hide. The worthless man had the money to
cover his problems, but certainly not Klaus's. The only alternative that he could see was to flee the country, even if the police
in Germany might still be after him.

At the German border they would check his passport,
and then again, they might not. Smearing some makeup over
the scar on his cheek should cover that aspect of his identity.
They'd gotten somewhat lax last time he went through, but one
could never tell. Changing to the Euro hadn't affected many
aspects of crossing borders. Being able to have his passport
changed in Italy from Klaus Baer to the name Klaus Burchel
had taken the pressure off, but one could never tell about how
these matters would turn out. The German government didn't
take any crime lightly, and when it had political ramifications,
the police turned into fierce watchdogs.

Klaus could almost hear the voice of neo-Nazi–leader
Heinrich Bruno telling him that an attack on the municipal

offices in Munich would make him a hero of the people. His family had the background that would resonate with the grumbling masses. Too many people were struggling financially not to listen to a new voice calling for a redress of their grievances. After all, Hitler had begun this way. Why couldn't he? Bruno had been convinced it was the right moment for the neo-Nazis to rise up again. It had all seemed so right.

Break in. Destroy files. Leave their mark behind. Attack. Be fearless!

It sounded promising, until a police car pulled up in the front windows in the middle of the night and sent Heinrich Bruno running. All hell broke loose when one of the other men had foolishly shot at a policeman and hit him in the shoulder. Only by a quirk of fate had Klaus found a side door and escaped down a narrow alley before the police came around the building.

Far from thinking him a hero, Klaus's parents had hustled him onto a train and out of the country. Only after he arrived in Rome had he been able to work out a new passport with a different name, but it had cost a bundle. How had Stein figured out enough of this problem to discover his true identity? The scum bag obviously had connections up to the very top of the German government. It was even more staggering that Stein had discovered the name of his grandfather.

The train slowed to a stop for crossing the border into Switzerland. The Swiss always took the border entries more seriously than the Germans, and Klaus knew they would make a check of his passport, so he pulled it out and stood up to get in line for the control. Out the window, he could see the snow-covered mountains and the towering peaks. The sight impressed him and momentarily took his mind off what the passport control might say about him. With makeup over the scar on his cheek, he pulled his hat low, hoping to further cover the area. Stepping out into the cold mountain air on the station platform, he hurried inside the small building where it was warm. Only three people were ahead of him in line and he quickly passed to the front. Even at this hour, the passport officer looked bored and didn't hesitate to stamp his passport. Klaus quickly got back to this seat on the train. The coach started moving again, and they were on their way.

The train began winding its way down the mountain tracks that would eventually carry him through Switzerland and into Germany. At Bern, he would change to a train that would take him to Zurich and then on toward Munich. Of course, his parents would be surprised and pleased to see him, but he had given them no hint of returning. Possibly the confrontation at the Munich City Hall had blown over; possibly not. He couldn't chance a mistake.

If there was an explosion, it would be because his family name would ignite the fuse. The name Baer could blow holes in walls. Many people in Germany were named Baer, but none had the connection that he did to Richard Baer. After the war, his grandfather had gone into hiding and worked as a woodsman in the Hamburg area for a number of years. Then someone who didn't like the Nazis turned him in, and the new government captured him in December 1960. Three years later, Grandfather Baer died in prison. By that time, the Baer name had become onerous in Germany history.

Klaus both admired what his grandfather had done and felt apprehension about what could follow from those actions. After all, killing Jews no longer had the popularity it once did. It wasn't easy being the grandson of the last *SS-Sturmbannfuhrer*, the commandant, of Auschwitz Concentration Camp.

16

From the doorway, Jack Townsend watched Dov Sharon walk through the back door into the kitchen and stumble around the boxes and furniture cluttering the room. Pushing a box aside, Dov trudged into the living room where the desks stood.

"You feel OK today?" Jack asked.

"Yesterday's excitement threw my system out of whack," Dov said. "Having a priest murdered in your front yard tends to leave you stuck in low gear." He plopped down in his desk chair. "A little on the macabre side, wouldn't you say?"

Michelle looked up from her desk. "That's putting it mildly. The police haven't been back inside so I guess they've settled on the idea that the killer caught Father Raffello in front of our building."

Dov said nothing.

"Well, the police certainly got right on it," Jack said. "I thought it strange they let us back in the building so quickly."

"Yes," Dov said. "I noticed that they're not out there working this morning."

"They must have gotten everything they needed yesterday," Jack said. "All that's left is yellow plastic tape sealing off the area as a crime sight. I'm sure they'll let us know when we can come in the front way again."

"Dov," Michelle said, "we never did get back to what you found in the Vatican Archives. You hinted that the priests keep something hidden. I'd like to hear more about what you're on to."

Dov nodded. "Sure nobody's listening?" He looked around. "The matter's sensitive and must be kept in the highest confidence."

"Sure," Jack said. "That's a given."

"Yesterday afternoon while the police investigation was going on, I went back to the bottom basement of the Vatican Archives and did some intense nosing around. In the far back, they have several rooms where no one's admitted, even with a pass. I had a hunch that the material we're looking for might be in there."

"What's in there?" Michelle ask.

"Like Codex Vaticanus and Codex Sinaiticus, there are a stack of sheets of papyrus lying on top of one another. Of course, these texts are all hermetically sealed to protect them from contamination because of the air. The manuscripts are not large and may only be a few pages. The scuttlebutt I picked up is that there is a text in there from the first century. That alone makes the manuscripts of a priceless value."

"Wow!" Jack said. "That is big time."

"I found one old priest down there in that dungeon who liked me," Dov continued. "When I got to talking about my Jewish background and what happened to my grandparents during World War II, his lights came on. Apparently, he'd had some connections with smuggling Jews out of Italy during the Holocaust. My stories unlocked the conversation and we were on. I took Father Donnello out for coffee and filled him up with cream and strawberries. The strawberries really hit his button. Somewhere in the conversation the priest told me that they refer to the materials as 'The Brown Book.' He whispered that the actual name is *The Prologue of James*. Father Donnello wouldn't talk about what it contained but was convinced that the authorship was apostolic."

"My, my!" Jack exclaimed. "Highly significant. This is exactly what I was hoping for. It could be that you are right on target. What a discovery! That name's intriguing. *The Prologue of James*! You've made a major breakthrough, Dov."

"Father Donnello tossed the title out during our conversation, but if it's not what we're looking for, we have to be close to our target. The problem is going to be getting a good look at this brown book. I'm sure we would never receive official permission to nose around in those dark, musty stacks."

Jack rubbed his chin thoughtfully. "Yes, that's going to be a real problem. We've got to think this over carefully. Dov, could you go back today and pump that elderly priest for a little more information? Possibly, he knows more about what's inside that brown book, as he called it. It's a long shot but worth a try."

"Jack, why don't you go with me. You've got a reputation, and he might have heard of your book. You could ask better questions. I think you could make progress down there in that dank old basement."

"Excellent idea! Why don't we leave now and we can—"

"Can stop at Dar Poeta and munch on their goodies," Michelle interjected. "Who are you kidding?"

"I can't believe that you'd accuse me of such a thing," Jack said. "Really! Nothing but insensitivity."

"You think I don't know what goes on when you go sneaking out the door?" Michelle grinned. "I know all about where you're going. Just make it after you've been to the library. You boys keep your collective noses clean."

Almost unable to believe his ears, Albert Stein settled back on the footstool and stared at the receiving unit attached to the inner side of the van. "*The Prologue of James?* So, this is what the Townsends are after."

The title was unknown to him, but no question that the Americans were on to something that was important, but this time he was ahead of them. It was almost too good to be true. He had a title and a location. It would take some doing, but he was looking at the challenge of a lifetime to beat them in finding that manuscript.

"What could be in that parchment?" Stein mumbled to himself. "What have they stumbled on to?"

Because Klaus Burchel hadn't shown, he had been in the van long enough for his bones to feel like it had been forever. More than an entire day had passed since Burchel had disappeared. It made no sense that the man had simply walked away unless he'd gotten himself in real trouble and that remained a significant possibility. Such a problem could put Stein in an even more difficult position. His initial anger began turning to concern. Where was Burchel, and what was he doing?

The farther down the ancient stone steps Jack walked, the more aware he became of descending into the lowest level underneath the Vatican. Dov walked ahead of him, holding tightly to the railing while Jack followed.

"You're having fun," Dov said. "Following me has to be the highlight of your day so far."

"I'm easily pleased," Jack quipped. "What could be more meaningful than tickling your elbow?"

"Just about anything," Dov said.

When they reached the bottom of the stairs, Jack glanced across the vast room with an archaeological dig going on at the far side. "That's one big area," he said. "We must be on the ground level of what was once first-century Rome."

"We are," Dov said. "I discovered that this portion once was part of the Circus of Caligula and Nero. They tell me excavations have revealed that citizens once lived over there in those ruins from twenty centuries ago. Can you imagine the Romans racing chariots around this exact area?"

"Stretches the minds," Jack said. "Fascinating to imagine what once went around that ancient racetrack."

"Yeah, and if we find anything today from the ancient first century, it will really twitch your wires."

"You bet. Where do we find this Father Donnello?"

Dov pointed toward a small office with a closed door near the center of the area. "He's usually in there working on some document. The man's a genius with languages. You'll like him. Let's take a look."

Dov trudged across the stone floor toward the door. The sound of a chair scrapping across rock signaled that the priest was inside. The door opened slightly and a bearded face peered around the corner.

"Aha!" Father Donnello beamed. "It's my little Jewish friend. Come in and rest a spell." The skinny priest swung the door wide open, revealing the brown habit of a Franciscan. A beard hung down to the end of his neck. "I see you brought a friend today."

"You'll like him," Dov said and walked in. "This guy's a big-time scholar."

Father Donnello stroked his long, grey beard. "Interesting. What does he study?"

"Scripture," Dov said. "Please meet Dr. Jack Townsend."

"Townsend? Not the Townsend who wrote *An Answer to the Cynics?*"

"The same," Dov said.

Then Father Donnello extended his hands. "Saints preserve us! I've read your book three times and devoured it. Brilliant answers to the hostile critics of Scripture."

"Actually my wife, Michelle, and I wrote it together," Jack said. "Credit goes to her as well."

"Certainly," the priest said. "Sit down. I am honored by having you two come to see me. Most of the time I am down here virtually alone except for the archaeologists working over there in the ruins, and they're a silent bunch anyway."

Jack smiled. "I understand. "We're here because we take the Scriptures seriously."

"Ah," Father Donnello exclaimed, "Excellent." He picked up a small coffeepot sitting on top of a single-coil electric heater. "Can I fix you some coffee or maybe hot tea?"

"Thank you," Jack said, "but we'll pass for the moment. We came to talk to you about a particular document."

"Oh?" The priest smiled. "I am delighted to share whatever I can."

"Can you tell me more about what is called *The Prologue of James?*"

Father Donnello stopped and immediately set the coffeepot down. "We never speak of such a matter."

17

KLAUS BURCHEL SAT HUNCHED OVER A TABLE IN THE *HOFBRAUHAUS* BEER hall just off of the main square in the center of Munich. A small German band with a boisterous tuba player tried to chase away the coldness of the fall afternoon with their strident folk songs. In their lederhosen and Bavarian hats with feathers sticking out the side, the potbellied ensemble kept pounding out loud drinking songs. The two-story pub amounted to a huge beer hall with women in native costumes flying around the rooms holding large steins of beer in their hands to keep the patrons happy and drinking.

"Mein herr." The buxom barmaid in the Bavarian dress whirled in front of Klaus's table holding three mammoth glass steins overflowing with beer. "What'll it be, pretty face?"

"Lager," Klaus said.

"Coming up." the woman swirled away almost as if she was dancing to the um-pa-pa the tuba kept hammering away underneath the melody line of the song.

Klaus had started using his family name again because it felt more comfortable in Germany to be known as a Baer, but it had its problem. The surname problem was only a part of what depressed him. He had returned to the *Hofbrauhaus* hoping

121

the raucous beer hall might offer encouragement. In the basement, Adolf Hitler had held some of his first rallies to gather support for his fledgling movement. Beneath this very floor, Hitler and Nazi Party members had stormed an official political meeting and declared that the revolution in Germany had begun. On November 8, 1923, the Beer Hall Putsch had set off a fire storm that resulted in Hitler landing in prison where he wrote *Mein Kampf.* Yet, it was this exact disaster that set the stage for his rise to power. Klaus could take comfort that the emergence of the Third Reich came out of the ashes of the Putsch. Even though sixteen Nazis and four policemen had been killed, the struggle had been worth the confrontation. That tidbit of history encouraged him to consider continuing even after killing the priest in Rome. What counted was the struggle, the continuation of the battle.

His parents had been alarmed when he showed up on their doorstep. It had been a considerable walk from the train station, but no one had stopped him for questioning. It seemed that the police had allowed his past felonies to slide and weren't interested in catching him. However, his parents weren't so sure. In the opinion of some, the name Baer and his grandfather Richard Baer's death in prison kept a cloud hanging over their house. The return of a son in trouble with the law wasn't positive. At best, they had no clue that he had killed a priest in Rome.

"Here you be," the barmaid said and slid a tall mug in front of him.

"Thank you," Klaus said and looked away.

Sipping his beer, he thought about what he'd found in Munich so far. His parents were glad to see him but didn't want him lingering for long. Besides the fact that the police could be watching, he had a disposition for getting into trouble. The Baer family had certainly had enough problems without another explosion caused by his misguided behavior. His stay would have to be brief, but where would he go next? At every turn, his path seemed blocked. Perhaps, he should go back to Italy. Then again, the police might be on to him. He couldn't remember leaving any clues behind so maybe they weren't on his trail. Possibly, he had a week; maybe a few days. Regardless, he would have to move on soon.

The face of Albert Stein drifted across his mind. Stein could be looking for him and that caused concern. With time, he'd found Stein's demands to be bearable. Because he never gave the ol' man any static, their relationship had become more durable. Still, Klaus didn't like the man. Stein remained the most arrogant person Klaus had ever known.

Klaus took a long sip and watched the band. Nothing made much sense. Possibly another three or four more steins and he'd be more insightful.

18

Jack Townsend hurried through the back door into the office and found Michelle calmly typing away at her computer. Dropping his briefcase on the desk, he glanced at the stick-on notes Michelle had fixed across the top.

"A guy's showing up for an appointment at any moment?" Jack said. "Really?"

"Yeah, he called while you were gone and sounded urgent. I have no idea who the man is. By the way, you can enter through the front door now. The police released the crime scene."

"Good. The front entry is much easier to manage."

"What about Dov?" Michelle asked. "Think he's doing any good over in the Secret Archives this morning?"

"Hope so," Jack said. "Today's conversations are important. He's meeting with Father Donnello, the priest with the secret information." He looked at the small yellow notes a second time.

"Who in the world is Guido Valentino? Never heard of him before."

"Beats me," Michelle said.

"Hmm, I hope he's got something worthwhile on his mind because time is of the essence today. I'm expecting Dov to come back with a significant progress report on what's inside this so-called brown book. If so, we will need a long conversation. I'm safeguarding our time for that possibility."

"You bet. For sure I want to hear what he has to say." Michelle turned around. "Jack, I've not been trying to make you upset about how I see Dov. Maybe I'm wrong. It's just that I level with you about everything. And . . . and I have a few doubts."

"Don't worry," Jack said. "We'll get passed it."

The front door opened and a man in a business suit walked in. Looking to be in his mid-thirties, his dark skin and black hair signaled he probably was a local Italian. Tall with a stocky build and muscular shoulders, his penetrating eyes and thick eyebrows gave him the look of a person with a significant mentality. Unusually well-dressed, the man appeared affluent and dapper. He obviously knew how to make a good impression.

"Can I help you?" Michelle ask.

"*Buongiorno.* I am Guido Valentino," he said with a heavy Italian accent. "I have an appointment with Dr. Jack Townsend."

"Oh, yes," Jack said. "I am Dr. Townsend."

Guido Valentino bowed at the waist. "The pleasure is mine."

"Come in and sit down," Jack said. "Please meet my wife, Michelle."

"Ah! The woman I spoke with. Madam, thank you for making the arrangements." Valentino bowed again. "Thank you."

"We share all our experiences and research," Jack explained. "It is no problem for Michelle to listen. Tell me how I can help you."

"I want to *help you*, sir," Valentino sat down. "I read the story on your work in the newspaper and found it to be highly encouraging. I am interested in the same subject."

"The original ending to the Gospel of Mark?"

Valentino nodded his head. "I have studied Koine New Testament Greek for a number of years and have been involved in translating ancient manuscripts at the Musei Capitolini, Rome's oldest museum collection in the world. I know how to conduct the research that you are pursuing."

Jack held up his hand to stop Guido. "I'm sorry, but before we go any further, I must tell you that we have no funds to hire another staff person. We simply don't have the money."

Guido smiled. "Please, I have not come for a salary. I have sufficient funds to cover all of my own expenses. I am here as a volunteer to be of assistance to you."

Jack leaned back in his chair. "You are serious?"

"Dr. Townsend, my family has been in Rome for centuries. I know this city like the back of my hand. My time has been spent doing the work of a scholar. Because of this background, I am more than interested in your current project. It is exactly what I have been hoping for, and that is why I have come."

Jack glanced at Michelle sitting there with her mouth slightly open. Obviously, she was surprised.

"Perhaps, it would be best if I came to work for a month and you could see if my language skills are adequate. Should I not meet your needs, I would withdraw with no questions asked. However, if I am able to work, then I would be ready to be a major part of your project."

Jack studied Valentino carefully. If this man was deceptive, it certainly didn't show. Everything about his straightforwardness suggested he could be trusted, and he had a goodness about him. Moreover, this Italian manifested a humbleness that suggested he would be easy to work with.

"I have a statement describing my studies." Valentino pulled several sheets of paper from inside his coat. "I think this will answer any questions about my background."

Jack glanced through the resume. "Impressive. When could you start work with us?"

"How about tomorrow morning?"

Albert Stein took off the earphones and stared out the windshield of the van. He had heard enough. It was time for a decision, but he had to think first. The windshield mirrored his hard, set eyes and thick glasses. His blonde hair looked like a scrambled mess from having spent endless hours in the van and sleeping on the floor. His bloodshot eyes left a sinister appearance. Albert's older brother had once described him as having eyes that only his mother could love. The quip hung in Stein's memory like a splinter under his fingernail. He occasionally thought he should have killed his brother for that remark rather than only beat him with their father's leather whip. Lack of sleep in a comfortable bed always brought out the violence forever lurking in a hidden corner of his mind.

Clearly, the Townsends weren't wasting any opportunity, and the addition of a new translator to their staff limited the amount of time he had left to act on the situation. The more he thought about the matter, the clearer it became that he must act at once and that meant he needed Klaus Burchel back on the job. Regardless of what the man had done, his services would help complete the task at hand. The immediate order of business was to run him down and get Klaus working again. Then, the rest of his plan would follow.

Stein picked up his cell phone and started to dial. Only then did he notice the newsstand and the vendor hawking newspapers only a few feet away. He had been living in the stinking vehicle for days and had lost contact with what was going on in the outside world. For the first time, it struck him how bizarre his actions had become since Burchel disappeared. Crawling out the side door, he stepped onto the street.

Stretching felt good, and the air smelled fresh. He had been so intent on electronic eavesdropping that he hadn't bathed in days. No question about it: he had to find Burchel so he could return to his normal lifestyle. Listening day and night to the outside world through a headset was madness and it had to stop.

Stein noticed the vendor gazing at him and supposed his clothes must look like they had been pulled out of a dirty clothes hamper. Walking over to the old man, he grabbed a newspaper off the top of the pile. Without shifting from a hard stare, Stein slapped money on the stack of magazines. The vendor looked away but reached for the coins.

Stein leaned against an office building and started glancing through *Il Messaggero* to discover what he'd missed in the last several days. A story on the third page leaped off the page at him. He held it closer to his eyes.

PRIEST MURDERED

Police continue to search for clues in the murder of Father Raul Raffello, rector of Santa Maria della Concezione Church. Found behind the basilica with stabs wounds in the chest, the priest apparently was killed in the middle of the night. Police are not releasing information but continue to believe the priest interrupted an intruder and was killed by the assailant.

Albert Stein slowly lowered the newspaper and stared at the building in front of him.

"So that's what happened to Burchel!" he muttered to himself. "Klaus Burchel must have killed that priest. That's why he's disappeared. Burchel's on the run."

Afternoon had fallen by the time Jack Townsend glanced out the window and saw Dov Sharon walking up the sidewalk. He laid down his pencil and immediately stood up. "Hey, here comes our boy! Get ready for an update."

Michelle looked up. "My, my. I wonder what our hero has brought home."

Dov pushed the door open. "Oy vey! A reception committee just waiting for me to wander in. You'd think I had something important to say. My, my. How enchanting."

"Don't give us that Jewish country-boy lingo," Jack said. "We want to know what you've come up with immediately."

"Come up with?" Dov frowned. "Was I suppose to find out something today?" He plopped down in the chair and scratched his head. "Seems like there was something you wanted me to do, but I'm afraid it's slipped my mind."

"Come on!" Michelle insisted. "Cut the nonsense. You know we're dying to know what Father Donnello told you."

Dov grinned. "As a matter of fact, the gentleman and I became old-fashioned pals. We cozied up to each other like camping buddies. Once you get the good Father talking, it's hard to get him to stop."

"Let's get specific," Jack said.

Dov leaned over his desk and the grin disappeared. "The so-called 'brown book' is slang for a parchment that apparently was written in the first century. A member of the Sanhedrin named Alphaeus had apparently inquired about an opinion from a highly significant person who became a big-time player in the earliest church. The man was James, the brother of Jesus."

"*The brother of Jesus!*" Michelle shrieked.

"That's what I got from Father Donnello. They have a document in which the brother of Jesus is commenting on who he thinks Jesus of Nazareth was."

Jack dropped down in his chair. "You've got to be kidding."

"The official name of this little masterpiece is *The Prologue of James.* Apparently what we have is an opening into the mind of James where he lets his hair down about the family secrets."

"I've never heard of it," Jack almost whispered.

"That's the point. Late in the twentieth century, the manuscript was found during an excavation of the Convent of the Sisters of Zion in Jerusalem. Water kept seeping up through the floor of the chapel and workmen tried to fix the problem. By tradition, Jesus was dragged through the Ecce Homo arch that was supposed to be beneath this convent. Eventually, they unearthed the Lithostrotos, a piece of the original pavement with a game scratched on it that the Romans played to make someone a mock king. The archaeological discovery made headlines at the time. But what no one let leak out was the fact that they had turned up this document. The codex was whisked off to Rome and never saw the light of day. Are you beginning to get the picture?"

"You're implying that this manuscript contained some highly controversial ideas?" Michelle ask. "That's why we never heard of it?"

Dov grinned sardonically. "You think the church would hide such a thing?"

"They have before," Jack said. "What you've found is an amazing discovery."

"Yeah," Dov said. "Think about how the brother of Jesus might have reflected on his sibling growing up and claiming to be the messiah. We get hints in the Gospels that family members might have thought Jesus was on the deluded side some of the time. What if James recorded some information that blows the problem wide open?"

Jack rubbed his mouth nervously. "We are sitting on a keg of dynamite."

19

THE DAYS OF EARLY OCTOBER HAD BEGUN TO LEAVE AN UNUSUAL BITE IN the air. Cold weather hadn't turned to snow, but Munich felt like the white stuff wasn't far away. An early winter might be coming. Walking across the *Marketplatz*, Klaus realized he had overstayed his welcome. A week ago he had expected to be gone by the end of that week. Saturday and Sunday slipped by, and he had stayed in his old room. The civility of his parents had begun to wear thin by the next Monday. Now four more days had passed, and he was still sleeping in that cozy old room he'd grown up in as a boy.

Before long his mother and father would start their own investigation into why he had suddenly turned up. Although the Baer name was considered a problem by some of the right-wingers, there were many who still remembered that his family had been in authority many years ago during the terrible war. *SS-Sturmbannfuhrer* Richard Baer had been so tightly linked with the government that strands of his influence still existed sixty-four years later. By running down one of those connections to the current government, his parents could begin to put some kind of story together that might be uncomfortably close to the truth. He couldn't have them turning up what had occurred in Rome. They'd boot him down the stairs for sure and send him flying out the door. The issues were simply too tense.

The wind picked up and blew across the *Marketplatz*, sending bits of paper and debris swirling through the air. Klaus turned up the collar on his coat and slowed his pace. Even with the wind whistling, he didn't have anywhere to go and was walking aimlessly. He had to think about what he should do next. That was the pressing issue that had to be solved quickly.

A tall man in a brown overcoat with a small black hat pulled down over his eyes passed him. Out of the corner of his eye, Klaus saw the man slow. Klaus picked up his pace. The man could be with the police and had possibly picked up information on his return to Munich. Not a good sign. At the curb, he stopped and whirled around, expecting to catch the brown overcoat trailing him. Nothing. Klaus looked again. No one in sight. He hurried across the street and down a narrow alley. No one showed up.

Feeling reassured, he started walking again. After two blocks, he spotted a small café, which would serve hot rolls and coffee. Perhaps, a little internal warmth would help clear his thinking. Picking up the pace, he walked in and stopped at the counter. Choosing a nice warm cinnamon roll and a paper cup of coffee, he sat to the back of the restaurant.

He immediately noticed a newspaper had been left on the table. Possibly the paper would give him some important information about what was happening across the country that might have some bearing on where he should go. Quickly scanning the headlines, he found the stories mainly described murder and mayhem happening around Munich. A brief story from Augsburg reported a car wreck on the autobahn, but the change of governments in Berlin didn't interest him and he certainly didn't want to read about the Trade Fair in Mannheim. He started to fold the paper when a man sat down in the chair immediately across the table.

Klaus stared. The brown overcoat and hat-covered face had been following him all the time!

"*Hallo*," the man said. "Greetings from Albert Stein."

Klaus gasped. "W-w-hat's going on?"

"You left rather abruptly without expressing any appreciation for what Dr. Stein had done for you. His recompense and care were inadequate?"

"Oh, n-no. N-not at all. I had an emergency that took me away."

"Really?" The man removed his hat and set it on the table. Dark-set eyes and a thin face with a narrow moustache left a foreboding appearance. "I wonder what that emergency might be." He leaned across the table and pointed his long, narrow finger as if he was about to reach out and stab Klaus in the throat. "Family problems? Care to share with me?"

"Who are you?" Klaus had caught his breath as his shock had turned to alarm. The man obviously had been sent by Stein, and that could mean anything. Probably, he had a death assignment. "Don't jack me around."

"Oh, the tough-guy routine. Stein said you might try that with me. Let me warn you that I am an expert in the martial arts, and I doubt that you want to end up on the floor before I drag you out of here by the legs." He suddenly smiled. "I don't think you want to wrestle with me."

Klaus bit his lip. The man was positioned to block him if he bolted for the front door. He might be bluffing, but then again, he probably wasn't. Stein had the ability to use who-knows-what means to get anything he wanted. There was little point in resisting. He might as well go with the flow.

"It wasn't hard finding you," the man began. "I figured you'd run for home. Your age and background pointed in the direction of Munich."

"Look," Klaus said more softly. "Level with me. Who are you?"

"Let's just call me a detective with excellent connections. In fact, I had access to the fact that you crossed the border by train into Switzerland. When you came into Germany with an Italian passport under the name Burchel, it wasn't difficult to pick up the trail."

Klaus studied the hardness in the man's eyes and smelled the scent of a killer. Probably, he had come to finish him off. A cold chill rippled through Klaus's body. No matter what he did, this guy could drop him and be gone out of the café before the employees even knew what had happened. He was cornered.

"Y-you've come to kill me?" Klaus ask.

"You are a lucky man," the detective said. "If I were going to finish you off, I'd have done it back there in the *Marketplatz*. No, the gods of eternity, have smiled on you, Klaus Baer. Today is not the time for your funeral if you play your cards right." His voice dropped into a threatening growl.

"Stein wants his money back?"

"No, Klaus. He wants *you* back."

Klaus felt his jaw drop slightly. "Your kidding."

"Dr. Stein knows all about what you've done. Your problem is not that little deed you performed out behind the church in the middle of the night. It's the fact that you ran and did not come back to him. That's the big problem to be considered."

"I-I d-didn't want to expose him to the danger," Klaus said in a pleading voice.

"Well, that's for Dr. Stein to decide," the man said. "I'll leave it with him. In the meantime, you are going to return to Rome to finish the work you began."

"To Rome!" Klaus exclaimed.

"Your friend Stein has been doing your job. Even now, he is having to do the task that you should have completed. However, leaving immediately may set better with him."

"Immediately?" Klaus's voice raised slightly.

"You are not to go back to your parent's home. We are going to the airport, and I will fly with you to the Rome International Airport. I have your ticket in my pocket even as I speak. You will simply disappear just as unexpectedly as you came here. Perhaps, a nice thank-you letter to your parents will explain your leaving suddenly. However, when we walk out of this hole-in-the-wall you will ride with me to the airport, and we will leave.

"Don't I have any choice in the matter?" Klaus said defensively.

"Oh, yes," the man said. "You can decide to stay here. You do so by declining to leave with me. In that case, you will be dead within the hour." He slipped his hand under his coat as if to reach into a shoulder holster. "You have a choice. You have thirty seconds to make it."

Klaus kept watching his eyes. Total indifference settled across his face. This dude would just as well kill him as fly him back to Rome. Life or death hung in the balance and the issue rested on his shoulders. The matter was simply that simple.

"I understand," Klaus said. "Let's go to Rome."

20

THE WINDING STEPS WOULD HAVE BEEN STEEPED IN DARKNESS EXCEPT FOR a few electric lights stationed along the way. Even though the descending stairway was stone, the steps had been used for centuries and portions had worn slick. Dov Sharon grasped the handrail as firmly as possible. A slip and fall on the cold granite would do him considerable harm. Since stumbling across the existence of this concealed staircase, he had been in the archaeological dig and archives beneath the Vatican Secret Library every day. His relationship with Father Donello had grown considerably, and the old man seemed to particularly enjoy his company. He was also starting to share personal accounts with him.

When Dov reached the bottom step, he made sure his feet were firmly planted on the rock floor before he took another step forward. Once certain that he could walk without tipping, he started toward the priest's office. He had barely gotten halfway across the floor when the office door flew open.

"Ah! Dov, my boy," the priest exclaimed. "Come in! Haven't talked to anyone all day."

"Good to see you, Father Donnello. You're looking well."

"You're kidding. I sit down here day after day in this dark hole while my skin turns whiter by the moment and my arms increasingly shrivel. I must look like a dried mushroom."

"Not at all," Dov said. "After all, don't you say Mass in some of the chapels upstairs?"

"Once a day, but that's inside stained-glass windows. No reprieve there."

Dov laughed. "You're trying to make yourself look bad."

"No, no, it's all the truth," the priest said. "Come in and have a cup of tea. I just heated the water a few moments ago."

"Good," Dov said. "I could warm myself with a nice brew."

The priest ushered him inside the small office and pointed to a small stool. Hustling around in his meager supplies, he pulled out a small bowl of sugar and a stained cup that probably didn't need to be washed but looked like it wouldn't hurt.

"As I remember, you always take a little sweetener?"

Dov smiled. "It softens my hard heart."

The priest laughed. "I know of no other way to crack the shell of a Jewish boy than with a little sugar or a big glass of whiskey." He shook his finger in the air like a teacher and laughed again. "Only kidding you my fine young man."

Dov took the cup and sniffed the fragrance. "Smells like herbal tea."

"Oh, it is. It is. I don't touch any of that caffeinated junk because it would keep me up at night."

"Can't have a priest wandering around in the dark, now can we?" Dov smiled. "You are one funny man, Father Donnello."

"Funny! Don't be absurd. I'm an old piece of toast left over from a stale breakfast. No humor there."

Dov set the cup on the table. "Tell me, Father. Why is it that you've been so kind to this little Jewish boy? You've treated me like a family member."

The priest shrugged. "I don't know," he mumbled and turned away. "It's my goodness bubbling over," he teased.

"Come now. I think there is more than you've told me."

The priest looked slowly over his shoulder. "I'm not down here in this dark cell because I enjoy a lonely life. Many, many years ago, I made my bishop angry when the Nazis swarmed across Italy. Mussolini was on his way out then, but they hadn't hung him upside down yet. I could see that the Germans were out to wipe out the Jews, so I had to help. It was the fact that I sheltered so many Jews from harm that angered the bishop. He thought I had endangered the church. The old crank was nothing but an anti-Semitic hate monger parading around as a clergyman."

"The bishop sent you down here?"

"Yes." The priest wrung his hands. "Even when it's unjust, we have a system of authority that operates with its own logic. I imagine someday they will find me down here deader than a worn out boot." He shook his head. "You see I do know a little something about the inequities that the Jewish people have faced." The priest chuckled. "So, Mr. Dov, I find your journey particularly interesting."

"I am honored you have invited me into your private lair. Talking with you is fascinating."

"Yes, and you don't think that I recognize when you are pumping me to find the location of that special little gem, the brown book, *The Prologue of James*. I know that's where your eyes are fastened."

"Come now," Dov said. "I think you're intriguing even if you never speak a word about the document. I enjoy our conversations."

The priest rubbed his chin for a moment and scrutinized the young man. "I've given a considerable amount of thought to your interests, young Dov. Why would a nice young scholar with unusual skills in the Hebrew language give any attention to this rather strange document?"

"Is it in Hebrew?" Dov asked casually.

"Ah! There you go again! You're trying to trap me into telling you insider's information about this work."

Dov smiled. "If it's in Hebrew, wouldn't that be of extraordinary interest to me?"

"Well, it's not!" the priest said dogmatically. "Like about everything else of value from this period, it's in Greek."

"Just as I suspected," Dov said casually.

The priest laughed. "You are a sly one, Dov. Now let's get serious. Why are you so interested in this hidden manuscript?"

"The Jewish people have been victims of misinterpretation and misunderstanding forever. Persecution has gone on through the length of our history. Not only the Romans but the Christians heaped coals of fire upon the heads of our people. We weren't out there wandering across every continent because we were trying to find a good motel for the night. History has made it clear that there was no room in the inn for us. The Nazis were only the latest and worst in a long story of persecution. Perhaps, there is something in this *Prologue* that might shed light on who we truly are and would result in increased understanding."

"Interesting." The priest rubbed his chin. "Hmm. But why do you think this document could help?"

"Jesus was a Jew," Dov said. "His first followers were Jews. If this document is authentic, it was written by the Jewish brother of Jesus who was the first leader of the Christians after Jesus was crucified. Surely, James would throw some light on the true history of how the first followers of Jesus became uniquely separated from the rest of the Jewish people."

"You want this ancient manuscript because you think it might bring reconciliation and understanding?" The priest crossed his arms over his chest and looked askance at Dov. "You really want me to believe such an idea?"

Dov looked down at the floor for a moment. "My closest relatives died at Auschwitz where they were consumed in the flames of a crematorium. Only by an unexpected stroke of Providence did my parents come to Israel, but it cost great pain. Yes, my interests arise from the ashes of enormous personal sacrifice."

The priest stared as if captured by what had just been said.

"You must remember that the Viennese Jew Theodor Herzl began writing about the creation of a new state of Israel because he watched the humiliation poured on Alfred Dreyfus by the French. The innocent man was hustled off to Devil's Island for no other reason than that he was a Jew." Dov's voice quivered slightly. "The word *pogroms*—a Russian idiom for violent mass attacks—came from their assaults on our people. Even the head of the Russian Orthodox Church in the late 1800s clarified the policy of the Russian state toward all Jews living in their country. He suggested that maybe one-third would convert, one-third would die, and one-third would flee the country. Don't you find it interesting that these worshipers of the Jewish Jesus hated Jews?"

The old priest shook his head. "Such treatment has certainly been a plague on the church. I can only say that no religion can be judged by the example of its worst practitioners. You must remember that one-third of all the priests in Poland died in the Nazi concentration camp at Dachau for opposing Hitler's murdering hordes. Even under Hitler, there were Christians who hid the Jews."

"Absolutely and we are grateful for the righteous gentiles as well as the sacrifices of Poland's priests. But we must remember that many Christians looked the other way. Isn't reversing this history of hate worth the cost?"

"Yes, it is." The priest set his coffee mug down. "And I find great pleasure in being able to do a deed that would have burned my old bishop's hide. I'm going to tell you the secret that only a handful of people know. I do so in the name of tolerance and magnanimity with a poke in the ribs for my long-dead old rotten bishop. Regardless of how leaders of the church have functioned in the past, we still exist and serve in the name of truth and goodness. Sitting down here in this forlorn dungeon has taught me how important it is to stay consistent with the highest and best."

Dov took a deep breath. "You are a good man, Father Donnello."

"No, I'm only an old sinner living out his final days in relative seclusion, but I choose to live them with honor. Come here, my son, for no one else must hear what I'm about to tell you."

Dov stood up and turned his head toward the priest. The old man cupped his hand over Dov's ear and whispered.

Dov stiffened and gasped. "*The Prologue of James* is hidden *there*!

"Yes. You would never have expected it."

21

MICHELLE TOWNSEND WALKED UP THE PATH TO THEIR OFFICES WITH HER arms filled with books while her husband sauntered along behind her. An October morning in Rome always felt exhilarating, and she walked at a brisk clip.

"You trying to set a new record for the sprint," Jack asked.

"How can I answer a tortoise with the energy of a snail?" Michelle quipped.

Jack reached over and pinched her on the bottom. "That'll teach you to be smart with your husband."

Michelle giggled. "Maybe I should upgrade you a tad from a turtle status, but only a tad."

"Definitely." He shut the door behind them.

"Well, my, my," Dov Sharon said. "Here they are. The love birds from Texas, the Bobbsey Twins, Mr. He and She. At it again."

Jack set his briefcase down on the desk. "You have a way of getting here before the sun comes up, Dov. Seems to put you into gear."

"It's a little hard to dance all night when you walk up and down the stone stairs in the Vatican's hidden basement," Dov answered sarcastically. "Forces one to go to bed early. That will definitely get you up with the dawn."

"Let's sit in the conference room and discuss where we are this morning," Jack suggested.

"I think everyone needs an update."

Michelle watched Dov shuffle some papers together. Obviously, Jack didn't agree with her doubts about him. She'd have to admit he'd done an amazing job at the Vatican Library, but her skepticism lingered. If she was totally wrong, then nothing was harmed. On the other hand, if she were right and Dov was mixed up in the dark side, her concern would be significant. She simply couldn't dismiss her hesitation.

She carried her books into the conference room and set them on the old table. Jack opened his briefcase and pulled out a file. Last of all, Dov shuffled in and slowly slid into the chair at the end of the table.

"Let's review what we've found to date," Jack started the session. "What about the project to find the ending to Mark's Gospel. That's the main objective we're pursuing. Any progress on that front?"

Dov shook his head. "Not to date. I've wandered around down there in that dungeon of a library on the bottom floor, but all I've picked up is insignificant. The most important clue I've stumbled across is that a trail points toward a Laterani family. Apparently they were important in the first century and had a great deal to do with building the first church facility in Rome. Actually, the Vatican wasn't the site of the first edifice. San Giovanni in Laterano, or St. John of Lateran, is the most ancient church in Rome. I don't know where this path is going, but it's a good lead for us right now."

"I haven't found anything in the research that I've done on the writings of Clement of Rome at the end of the first century and Ignatius of Antioch at the start of the second century," Jack said. I've also studied Hermas of Rome in the same period. I don't find evidence that any of them dealt with the problem of the ending of Mark's Gospel. I'm still looking though." He turned to Michelle. "What's on your plate, kid?"

"The most important matter that I have to report is that I'm extremely happy with the work Guido Valentino has done. The man is amazing. I've never met anyone with a grasp of Roman history like he has. We have indeed found an important friend."

"You're right about that," Dov said. "Guido's a good scholar. He's going to be important for the future."

"Dov, what have you come up with in your quest for *The Prologue of James*?"

The telephone rang.

"I'll get it." Michelle jumped up and went back to the other room to answer the phone on her desk.

Dov rubbed his chin thoughtfully. "It hasn't been easy," he began more seriously than usual. "I've talked with Father Donnello at great length and only our friendship has helped me get information. He gets edgy when we start talking about *The Prologue*, but I've made a breakthrough. I've waited to tell you the extraordinary news I have because it must be kept in the highest confidence. My discovery is for your ears only."

"Really?" Jack smiled. "Good job, Dov. I'm all ears. Do you have any clues about why they are hiding the parchment so tenaciously?"

Dov leaned closer and cupped his hand over his mouth, speaking more in a whisper than in his usual voice. "The document's existence destroys the idea that James and the other children were cousins of Jesus. If the document is true, it verifies they were all siblings. Right off the bat that's a blow to Roman Catholic doctrine. However, I'm getting the suggestion that some of what James wrote reconstructs the picture of Jesus that the Roman Church currently holds. I'm not sure what the document asserts, but it seems to raise entirely new issues."

"What do you think they might be?" Jack asked.

"Hard to say," Dov answered. "But put yourself in the position that James must have been in. No matter how you stack up the debate over cousins or brothers, James grew up with Jesus and must have watched his brother become an entirely different person than they would have expected. Consider the options. Did he consider Jesus a fanatic? a genius? deluded? maybe, just plain nuts? the long-expected messiah? What did he think?"

"We don't want to buy an idea that is blasphemy," Jack said. "We've got a great deal at stake here, too. Being a Jew, you're in a slightly different position, Dov."

"True, but it doesn't change the fact that there's something in that document that profoundly troubles the Roman Catholic Church. That's why they've kept it concealed under lock and key. I now know where it is hidden."

Jack's mouth dropped. "You're kidding me!"

"Nope. Father Donnello leveled with me."

Michelle came briskly back into the room. "No big deal on the phone. I was going to tell you that I've been trying to see what's behind *Teaching of the Twelve Apostles* that dates from A.D. 130 to 160. and trying to find any clues hidden there," Michelle said. "No luck so far, but I have one thing I want to show you." She turned to her pile of books. "Oh, gosh! I left it in my briefcase in the car. I'll run out and get it." She stood up. "I'll be right back."

Hurrying through the kitchen and out the back door, Michelle rushed to their car parked in the reserved space. Her briefcase should be in the back seat. Picking up the armload of books had distracted her, but then again, she couldn't have carried everything at once. Halfway down the path, she wondered if she put the briefcase in the car or might have left it at home. Could be either.

Her body suddenly left the ground followed by a roar engulfing her with a terrifying boom that shook every bone in her body. When she hit the grass, Michelle bounced, catching a glimpse of a piece of wooden siding flying passed followed by a shower of broken glass. She came up on her hands and knees but a hunk of something dark careened toward her face. Michelle tried to block it, but felt it catching the top of her head and sending her flying backward. Everything blanked out.

Voices seemed to be drifting in from somewhere. She tried to open her eyes but found it difficult to focus. Noise increased, and she heard men running somewhere out there in front of her. No matter how hard she pushed, it seemed impossible to get off the ground.

"There's a person over here!" A man yelled in Italian. "Over here in the grass."

Michelle kept blinking, and shapes became more defined. Wherever she looked, splintered pieces of boards were scattered on the yard. Only then did she look at their offices. She looked again. Pieces of the roof were gone and the walls at the kitchen entrance had cratered inward. Entire sections of the wall were ripped away. It looked like a volcano had erupted through the floor. Michelle kept blinking, unable to grasp what she was seeing.

"Here she is!" a familiar voice yelled. "My God! Get a stretcher over here!"

Father Donald Blake leaped over the broken pieces of wood on the ground, rushing toward her. The heavyset priest appeared to be flying through the air. She still couldn't grasp what he was about.

Father Blake dropped on his knees beside her. "Oh, you poor dear. How badly are you hurt?"

"I-I don't know," Michelle mumbled. "W-what's happened?"

"You're bleeding from the top of your head," Blake said. "We've got to get you in an ambulance."

Michelle got a tight grip on his coat sleeve. "Tell me what's happened."

"An explosion went off under your offices," Father Blake said. "Apparently, you weren't inside."

"Inside?" Michelle mumbled slowly. "Heaven help us! Jack was in there."

"You're sure?" Father Blake pressed.

"Yes, and our assistant Dov Sharon. Both men were . . ."

Father Blake stood up. "There are two more inside," he shouted at the top of his voice. "Somebody get in there and see where they are! Get me a stretcher over here."

"J-Jack was in there," Michelle mumbled, finding it difficult to talk. "You've got to find him." She pulled frantically on the priest's arm. "Understand? We've got to get him out."

"We will. Don't worry. We will."

Oh, my poor husband," Michelle groaned. "Lord help him."

Everything around her began to shift and swirl. Michelle felt nauseated and her stomach wrenched. A white glaze began descending over the pile of debris and the men running around the smashed house. The whiteness increased, and she couldn't sit up any longer. Grass pressed against her face and suddenly everything disappeared.

22

When a bright ray of sunlight fell across Michelle's face, she awoke but nothing made any sense. She pulled her arm over her eyes to shield them from the brightness and only then realized she was in a strange bed. Rising slightly, she stared at the face that didn't seem to fit.

"It's me," the man said. "Donald Blake."

The man's features slowly took a familiar shape. "F-Father Blake," she stammered. "Where am I?"

"Your in the hospital, my dear. You've been unconscious for several hours."

Michelle lay back down. "The hospital? What am I doing in a hospital?"

"You got hit in the head and received a concussion when the house exploded. They stitched your head, but you've been unconscious for some time."

"Concussion?" The idea didn't make any sense. "What house?"

"Your offices," Father Blake said. "Don't you remember any of what occurred?"

"I remember leaving to go to my car, but nothing more."

"A bomb went off underneath your building," Father Blake said. "Did you have any idea or warning the explosion was coming?"

"A bomb?" Michelle struggled to grasp what the priest was saying. "A bomb?"

"Caught you by complete surprise?"

Michelle pushed herself up and stared at the man. Nothing was making any sense. She didn't know what to say.

"OK," Blake said. "I think I have your answer."

"You're here?" Michelle said. "Where is Jack?"

"Jack was in the house," Blake's voice sounded grave. "I came here with you in the ambulance."

Michelle lay back down and tried to think. Jack should be here with her. Why hadn't he come in the ambulance. Maybe he and Dov were still talking. Busy. Yes. Preoccupied.

"They were having a conference," she said. "He and Dov. We were talking . . ."

"Yes," Father Blake leaned forward.

Everything felt too heavy. She could feel her eyelids fluttering as if they were independent of her control. Michelle couldn't finish the sentence. That was the last thing she remembered.

23

THE FIREMEN WORKED BACK AND FORTH IN THE WRECKAGE TRYING TO MAKE sure the ruins of the old house didn't erupt into flames. While there had been some charred wood, only smoke still curled up out of the wreckage. A crowd of people from the neighboring office buildings and houses had gathered and stood next to the church staring at the pile of smoldering rubble.

Tony Mattei pushed his way through the crowd to the front. For a moment the diamond merchant watched the workers throwing broken lumber into piles. The police were guarding the perimeters and holding the crowd back. The situation looked grave.

"Officer! Mattei called out and beckoned with his hand.

A policeman looked at him and strolled over. "*Ciao.*"

"I am a close friend of the Townsends who have an office in that building. Can you tell me what happened?"

"You knew the residents?" The policeman said.

"Quite well. I am their personal friend."

"Come with me." The policeman led him out of the crowd over to a small command station that had been set up near the back of the church. "I want you to speak with my supervisor and give him any information you have."

"Certainly," Tony Mattei said.

"This man knows the Townsends," the officer said to a skinny inspector in a worn sport coat making notes on a small pad. "He might be able to report something. Please meet Alfredo Pino."

"How many people were in there?" the detective immediately barked.

"I don't know," Mattei said. "Usually three people worked in those offices."

"Three? Hmm. We've found three so far."

"Probably got 'em all," Tony said. "Did anybody survive?"

"Don't know yet," Pino said. "Took two away in ambulances, but I didn't see them. Can't tell if everyone survived."

Mattei held his arms in the air in a helpless gesture of consternation. "What happened?"

"We believe a plastic explosive device was placed under the house," the inspector said. "At least that's my hunch at the moment. We'll know more later."

Tony Mattei nodded. "Doesn't look like anybody could have survived."

"Best we can tell a table fell over on one person and shielded him from the direct blast. Another guy apparently was standing over the spot in the kitchen where the bomb was planted. I'm sure he's gone."

"Terrible, terrible," Tony muttered.

Another man came out of the crowd and walked straight toward the detective without speaking to the policeman. When the cop reached for him, the man glared furiously and the policeman let go. The intruder kept walking.

"I am Dr. Albert Stein," he said forcefully. "I'm an associate of the Townsends. We work on the same projects and do research together. I am sure they will be concerned that their investigations not be destroyed in the blast. Since I am an anthropologist, I would be delighted to help recover any material scattered in the ruins."

Tony studied the professor with the arrogant look on his face. His appearance looked foreboding.

"At the moment, we're attempting to make sure a fire doesn't break out," the detective said. "We'll need to make certain there are no other explosives planted in or around the building. Once we're certain, we'll be ready for a salvage operation. Perhaps, you can help with that. Of course, it will be tomorrow before we know for certain."

Stein nodded perfunctorily. "I see. Yes. It's best to return tomorrow?"

"That would be my suggestion," Pino said.

"I'll be back," Stein said and turned away.

Tony Mattei watched the man walk back toward the crowd. Stein remained unintimidated by the police.

24

By the time Michelle awoke, night had returned with the darkness feeling far more soothing than the early morning bright sunlight. For several minutes, she stared at the ceiling and tried to make sense out of what had happened but only drew a blank. She stirred and felt a sharp pain race through the top of her head.

Carefully touching the top of her scalp, Michelle felt bandages running over the crown of her head covering a throbbing ache. For the first time, she realized that with each beat of her heart, another sensation of pain surged through her body. Glancing around the room, she appeared to be in a hospital. A strange place indeed.

Scooting up in the bed, she found a button and pushed it. A soft, gentle light appeared from behind her head. Yes, she was definitely in a hospital room. She glanced at a digital clock fastened to the wall. It said 8:00 p.m. How could it be night? It had just been morning when she left for the office?

Michelle felt up and down her side, which felt like it was covered by a huge bruise running the length of her body. Could she have been in a car wreck? Maybe she had been coming to work and got blindsided. But why would she have been driving

154

by herself? That didn't make any sense. Jack was always with her. Where was Jack?

Michelle laid back on the pillow. Where had Jack gone? Jack should be there with her, but she couldn't remember when she had seen him last. Her memory seemed to have turned to mush.

But something had happened. Something she couldn't quite remember. Something that lay just beyond the tips of her fingers. Something . . . something . . .

She took a deep breath. Somewhere along the way she had heard the word "concussion" and obviously had been hit on the head. A blow of some kind had knocked everything out of her, leaving her feeling numb, disconnected, emotionally flat. Nothing made any sense, but she had no idea what was missing.

Missing? Yes, that was the word that described her condition. *Missing!* Some important piece of the day had disappeared, vanished like fog in the morning. *Still missing . . .*

The door to the room cracked slightly, and she caught sight of an eye peering in.

"Yes?" Michelle said.

"Are you awake?" a man's voice ask.

"Yes. Come in."

To her surprise Guido Valentino walked in holding a small vase with flowers. "I wanted to make sure you were awake before I disturbed you. Please tell me if you need quiet and I can leave immediately."

"Guido!" Michelle felt relieved that she recognized him. "Thank you for coming to see me."

"I thought maybe the flowers would cheer you." Guido set the vase on the bed stand. "They tell me you've been unconscious all day."

"I guess I have. You're the first person I've seen. Thank you for the flowers. They help. I can't remember anything except going to work early this morning."

Guido nodded and rubbed his chin. "I see. So, you know nothing of what has happened today?"

"I-I guess not. I can't remember anything."

Guido pulled a chair over by the bed. "They found you outside, lying in the grass. Does that bring anything back to mind?"

Michelle dropped back on the pillow. "In the grass? What was I doing on the ground?"

"There was an explosion. An extremely loud noise. Remember?"

"Explosions frighten me. Actually, they leave me terrified, but I don't remember hearing one."

"A bomb went off under your offices."

"Oh, no! No!"

"Yes, no one is sure why you weren't in the house, but it appeared you were going to your car. Maybe you were leaving."

"Wait! Jack . . . Jack . . . and Dov were in the building?"

"I am afraid so."

"God help us!" Michelle shrieked. "What happened to Jack?"

"The firemen believe the conference table collapsed in front of him and shielded him from the blast. The table probably saved his life."

"He's hurt!" Michelle pushed herself up fully in the bed. "Tell me now, Guido! How badly?"

"Jack is down the hall in Intensive Care, but he is alive."

Michelle felt her heart skip a beat and then beat intensely. A light-headedness settled in and she gasped for air. "H-how b-bad is he?"

"I don't know, but for now they are not letting anybody in to see him."

"Heaven help us!" Michelle could only barely moan. "I-I must see him."

"I'm sorry, but they won't let you in until tomorrow. Moreover, you haven't been out of bed all day. It would take a nurse to help you with a wheelchair."

Michelle clutched the sheets tightly in her fist. "My husband is my life. Do you understand? We are inseparable. I have to be with him."

"I can only tell you what the doctors have told me. It won't be until tomorrow at the earliest."

Michelle wiped her eyes. "Oh, my poor husband." She stopped. "And Dov? Is Dov . . ."

Guido took a deep breath and looked away.

"Tell me!" Michelle demanded.

"Apparently, Dov was standing right over the area where the bomb went off. He never felt a thing."

"H-he's g-gone?" The words barely came out of Michelle's mouth. "Gone?"

Guido nodded his head.

For a moment she couldn't speak. Then she felt emotion arising from within and coming on like an unstoppable freight train. The very depths of her affection and concern erupted in hysterical sobs. Her body shook and her hands trembled. Only after several minutes could she stop crying and lay quietly on the bed.

"Dov is gone," Michelle finally said. "I just can't believe it."

"There is no way that I can express the depth of my condolences," Guido said. "Please know that I am here to walk beside you. You and your husband are not alone."

Michelle nodded her head. "Thank you, friend." She reached out and squeezed his hand. "Please watch over our offices. Possibly you can check to see if anything remains from our research. We had papers and books around the office with important notes in them."

"I will do so in the morning," Guido said. "Is there anything more that I can do for you tonight."

"Thank you. I needed to know what happened and you told me. Thank you for that information as well."

Guido stood up. "I will return in the morning. You remain in our prayers."

"I appreciate the remembrance so much. Pray for Jack. Thank you again for coming."

Guido bowed at the waist, turned and walked out.

Michelle laid back on the pillow. Their offices blown away? How could such a thing happen? And Dov killed? The thought overwhelmed her once again and she cried bitter tears.

She had been wrong about Dov Sharon, terribly wrong. And, now she knew how seriously she had misjudged him. Jack had been right all the time. Realizing how seriously she had misjudged him only added to the weight of his death. Michelle wept into her pillow. How could so much have gone so wrong?

25

Michelle slept later than she expected, but as soon as the nurses came in and helped her to the shower, she was ready to see her husband. The nurse left a terry cloth robe behind for her to put on. No amount of hesitation on the hospital's part would keep her from entering the intensive care unit today.

Someone knocked on the door.

"Just a moment." Michelle finished tying the robe around her and sat down slowly on the bed. "Come in."

The door opened slowly. "Excuse me," a skinny man in a worn sport coat said. "I'm Alfredo Pino, a detective with the police. Might I come in."

"Certainly."

"Mrs. Townsend?"

"Yes."

"We are trying to understand what happened when your offices were blown apart," Pino began and handed her his card. "I guess you know a bomb exploded?"

"That's what I've been told," Michelle studied the card for a moment. "I'm sorry, but I received a concussion. It's hard for me to remember much of anything today.

Pino pulled out a small notebook. "Yes." He scribbled on the page. "I understand that you are Bible scholars. Can you tell me why anyone would want to bomb the offices of such studious people as yourselves?"

Michelle shook her head. "It doesn't make any sense. No. We're about as straight as it's possible to be. No. I don't have any idea why this would have occurred."

"Yes, it is strange," Alfredo Pino said. "You've never been involved in any form of illegal trafficking?"

"Heavens no! What are you suggesting?"

"My job is simply to ask questions," the detective said. "I'm sure I have bothered you long enough. I will be going. The best to you Mrs. Townsend." The skinny detective left the room.

Moments later the door opened again and a nurse wheeled in a chair. "I imagine you are more than ready to see your husband. I believe we can go now."

"I feel like I can walk down the hall by myself," she told the nurse.

"That's good," the older woman said, "but we can't risk falling."

"A wheelchair is a must?"

"We will definitely use one," the nurse said. "I will go with you. Once we're inside intensive care, you can stand alone, but you must remember in your condition you can become dizzy. Take it easy."

"Sure. How's my husband this morning?"

"I don't know because I don't work on that unit." The hesitation in her voice suggested that she did know and the problem was serious.

"You know he's in bad condition?" Michelle pressed.

"Your husband was in a horrific explosion. The fact that he is alive is significant. I must leave it there."

"But you know what injuries he received?"

"I know his arm is broken, and he has facial contusions." The nurse stopped. "You really need to talk with the doctor attending him. I can't say anymore."

"Certainly." Michelle lowered herself carefully into the wheelchair and adjusted her feet on the rests at the bottom. "I'm ready."

The trip down the long hall turned into a much longer trek than she had expected. After turning several corners and going a significant distance, she found the swinging doors beneath the Intensive Care sign.

"Let's go in," Michelle urged.

"It's not visiting hours, but the staff felt your visit might be important for your husband," the nurse said. "We'll enter now."

"Thank you," Michelle said. "I'm anxious to see Jack."

The nurse pressed the button on the wall and the doors swung open. Cubicles lined the walls around the large room. An antiseptic smell drifted down the corridor and made the area smell sterile. Very little noise drifted in, and the staff seemed to be functioning in an effective, expeditious manner. The nurse pushed her toward a nook with the number six above the cloth drapery.

"You can go in by yourself," the nurse said. "I'll be here waiting."

Michelle hesitantly pulled the curtain back and stopped. A plaster cast ran from Jack's wrist to his shoulder. Bandages covered most of his face with red seepage along the side of his chin. She only saw one eye still closed, the other was covered by bandages. A thick bandage covered the top of his chest with plastic tubes running down the side to bags on the rail. A bag of glucose hung from a rack, dripping into a needle in his good arm now tied to the bed. Michelle felt her knees buckle and thought she might faint.

"I'm here," the nurse said. "Don't worry. I'll catch you. Maybe, you should sit down."

"Definitely."

After a couple of minutes, Michelle felt her stamina returning and stood up slowly. Tenuously, she leaned over the bed. A closer look at Jack didn't encourage her. He remained in a coma, and she could tell his breathing was labored. Nothing looked good.

"Jack?"

He didn't move.

"Jack, it's Michelle." She squeezed his hand.

No movement.

"Jack, I'm here with you."

His breathing continued in an interrupted steady pumping of his chest up and down. Slowly. Struggling. Suffering.

"Jack?"

No sound.

Michelle withdrew from his bedside and looked at the machines around his body monitoring his heart, breathing, and vital signs. A quick glance said the pattern was regular on the low side. She gestured for the nurse to follow her outside the drapery.

"Jack's in serious condition," Michelle said.

The nurse nodded.

"Will he live?" Michelle asked with a firmness in her voice that conveyed she wanted a straight answer.

"No one can say for sure right now," the nurse said soberly. "Obviously, the blast was substantial. The next twenty-four hours is crucial." The woman looked Michelle in the eye. "Jack won't be conscious for a period of time."

Michelle sat down in the wheelchair. "Please take me back to my room," she said. "I need to rest." She closed her eyes and held her face in her hands.

Michelle could feel the tension building as the nurse wheeled her down the hall. Never in a million years would she have imagined her husband dying. Even the hint of such an idea overwhelmed her and started pumping wild emotions through her mind. The longer it took to get to the room, the more anxious she became. An avalanche of hysteria seemed ready to roll down on her, compounded by the absolute terror that Jack might die.

Once inside her room, she insisted she be allowed to sit alone in a chair. The nurse rolled the wheelchair out the door and left. Her knees turned wobbly once more. Flashing visions of the city of Cerignola blipped through her mind. Michelle could feel her emotions shifting and becoming like a child's descending into the darkness of a stormy night. A speeding gasoline truck surged toward her and the room began to shake. The side of the chair started to lift. For an instant, her father's face came out of the darkness and then receded. Her mouth turned dry and her hands became sweaty. A roaring noise erupted in her ears and drops of sweat slowly ran down her cheeks. Her entire body felt clammy and the muscles in her arms became rigid. She was about to be swallowed.

With the deepest breath she could take, Michelle grabbed the chair and clung fiercely. Another thought arose beyond the landslide of fear. She, and she alone, was all they had left at this moment. Jack couldn't do anything for who knows how long, if ever. No matter how difficult it might be, she couldn't allow her childhood experience to control her life. Even if the memory of the car collision had worked its way into the fiber of her very being, she couldn't let it take over her life. The hallucinations had to stop, and that wouldn't be easy. When the trauma surged, it always began in her body before she even grasped it was coming. Michelle had no idea how to control what occurred physically within her, but she couldn't let anxiety win. It might take everything in her, but she would no longer be ruled by the fears from the past. Loud noises, banging, gunshots couldn't be allowed to dominate. Whether she liked it or not, she would have to take control of their eruptions and keep their project moving while Jack recovered . . . if Jack recovered.

26

A cold wind blew down from the top of Santa Maria Church sweeping rubbish across the back yard of the church. Workmen had already been separating debris from the foundation of the bomb-scattered house. A few people hung around watching the workers sift through the devastation. Guido Valentino stood on the sidelines talking to a detective and observing several men stacking the ruins of the bombed house in a pile to one side. Windows had been completely blown out and the roof cratered with shingles blasted away. The front porch had sunken and the door completely disintegrated.

"Strange about bombings," detective Alfredo Pino made casual conversation. "They don't explode in a consistent direction. Some of the house was blown away while other parts remained surprisingly intact. I guess the one guy was standing right over the bomb when it went off. Got hit straight on. Horrible." The detective shook his head. "Worst I've ever seen."

"Why would someone bomb these people?" Guido pressed.

"Doesn't make any sense," Pino said. "They're not political. I guess the fact they were Americans with a Jew working for them might be part of it. Just don't know what to think.

Confounds me. Everyone is speculating that this group called The Scorpion set it off. Seems they don't like Americans." The detective shook his head. "Bizarre. Don't see any connections between those two explosions, but they might be related."

"I work with the Townsends and, of course, wasn't in the office," Guido said. "I can't see any reason for any of this destruction either. The Townsends have been the best people I've ever been around. Yet, I can't believe this was a random act."

"Like that subway explosion. No good explanation."

Guido noticed a well-dressed figure walking around from the side of the church. The man stayed bent over as if desperately searching for something. Wearing elegant clothes, the man looked completely misplaced wandering through the rubble. Swaggering into the rubble, he started kicking boards around as if he owned the place.

"Who is that guy?" Guido pointed at the figure. "Strange-looking fellow."

"I don't know," Pino said.

"Looks like he's trying to ransack the wreckage." Guido watched him more closely. "I've been around here working with the Townsends for several weeks, and I've never seen the likes of him. He's not somebody you'd forget."

"He's picking up pieces of paper and books," the detective said. "Might be some sort of hack trying to find materials he can sell to a secondhand bookstore. We can't have any of that monkey business." Alfredo Pino started stepping over pieces of board to get to the man.

Guido followed from behind, watching closely.

"What's going on here?" the detective demanded. "Do you have any identification?"

Pushing a few strands of his blond hair aside, the man looked at Guido and the officer suspiciously.

"Why are you asking?" He sat the books down and looked harshly at them.

"I ask the questions," Pino fired back. "If you don't have identification, you will be charged with trespassing as well as stealing and taken into custody."

"I work with the Townsends," the man said indignantly. "I am a PhD from Tübingen, Germany."

"Let's see your paper," Pino said impatiently. "I won't ask again."

"My name is Dr. Albert Stein." He reached for his billfold. "When I heard of the explosion, I volunteered to be of assistance. Opening the billfold, he pulled out a driver's license. "I don't carry my passport when I am doing physical labor."

Guido looked over the policeman's shoulder. "I work with the Townsends," he said dogmatically. "I have never heard your name mentioned once. Not once! Can you explain that?"

Stein leaned forward, studying the face before him. "How long you been there?" he asked skeptically. "A matter of weeks?"

Guido flinched. "Not long," he said. "But I would have expected them to have mentioned you."

"Well, your expectations were wrong," Stein barked.

"Officer, I cannot vouch for this man. I'd suggest you take his information and send him on his way."

"You running the project now?" Stein sneered. "I also have a *Permesso di Soggiorno* for study purposes, but don't carry the papers on archaeological digs."

Guido said nothing, but the detective was already copying the information down on his notepad.

"We don't allow anyone in at a crime scene," the officer said. "This certainly is not an archaeological site. You obviously didn't check in with us when you arrived. I'm not going to arrest you, but your information will be examined and better add up. I'd suggest you leave now."

Stein looked back and forth at the two men for a moment with a fierceness that left the impression he might bite one of them. Guido felt his fist tightening and had to force his fingers to relax.

Without saying a word, Stein stomped out of the wreckage and marched away down the path between the church and building next door. In a matter of moments, he was gone.

"Strange-looking individual," the officer said.

"More than strange," Guido said. "I have no idea who that character is, but he obviously was more than a little interested in whatever he could pick up.

Guido Valentino stayed throughout the day, observing the workmen, the detective, making sure nothing was carried away that might have value. Slowly, the wreckage of the broken walls and the dilapidated roof were pulled back. The house looked like it had been over a hundred years old with pieces of molding from around the ceilings that might have antique value. Beyond a few old remains, nothing else had any value. Computers and bookcases had been destroyed. By noon, a truck rolled in with a backhoe and started tearing down the rear of the house. The work went much faster, and the pile of splintered boards continued to grow higher.

The new priest who had been appointed to Santa Maria Church came and went several times, standing quietly watching, saying little. Guido introduced himself to Father Alberto Kajetan and told the priest the name of the hospital where he could find the Townsends. The priest assured him that he would visit this afternoon.

By mid-afternoon, a few shadows had started to fall across the ruins. The roof had been completely torn away, exposing the floor and a few remaining walls. An ugly jagged hole in the middle of the front office exposed the deadly spot where the bomb had gone off and Dov Sharon had been standing. No one said much when they walked around the hole that exposed the dirt beneath the house.

"Hey!" one of the workmen suddenly shouted. "I need help deciphering what we've found.

Guido joined the officers huddling around the man standing with one leg on the broken flooring and the other on the ground. A board had been turned over with wiring running along its length.

"What is this?" the workman ask. "It's got an apparatus of some kind attached to this board. "Looks like the piece was in this conference room somewhere and got torn loose."

The policemen gathered around and stared. "Don't know, but it looks like a transmitter of some kind," one of the men said.

"This house was bugged!" another policeman said. "Don't touch it. We should check it for fingerprints."

Guido stood up. "Whoever planted this device could have set off the explosives."

"Yeah. We've found something important," the workman said.

27

THE 11:00 A.M. FLIGHT OF THE LUFTHANSA FOKKER 100 LANDED SMOOTHLY on Rome's Leonardo da Vinci Airport runway, turned around, and headed back to the terminal. A cold wind blew rain across the window and left dampness in the air.

"Now that we are back in Rome," the detective said, "Klaus Baer can once again become Klaus Burchel. You can forget about that frightening grandfather of yours and go back to being just an everyday crook." The man laughed.

Klaus bit his tongue. He'd had enough of Stein's envoy to last six lifetimes. Big and strong, the man was inescapable and was the only one who enjoyed his asinine jokes.

"Actually, you are an extremely lucky fellow," the detective said. "Most employers would have written you off. Some would've had me just put a bullet in your head. Not Dr. Stein! I'm amazed that he wants you to come back to work for him after you knocked off a priest and ran. Actually, bumping off that man wasn't too cool."

Klaus kept looking straight ahead.

"Don't worry about getting through passport control. Nobody's connected you to the killing but Dr. Stein."

Klaus took a deep breath.

"I don't think you'll be in the mood to run once we get in the terminal, but remember all I have to do is pick up a phone and report a killer on the loose, give them a description, and you won't make it to the front door."

"I have no intention of running."

"Good. My car is in the parking lot. I'll take you to Stein's apartment. I think the good doctor even has a task ready for you to do immediately."

The pilot signaling the release of the seat belt sent both men to their feet. The detective stepped behind Klaus. "After you, young man," he said. "I'll be behind you all the way."

After a long hour of driving through congested streets, the Mercedes stopped in front of the familiar apartment on Via del Gracchi. Pulling over to the curb, the detective pointed at the building. "Think you can get up there by yourself or do I need to follow you?"

Klaus shook his head. "Don't worry. If I was going to try and make a break for it, I would have done so before now."

The man patted him condescendingly on the hand. "Good boy. Now you go up there and make your ol' Uncle Albert happy. Don't be a wise guy and make me run you down again. Next time it might prove to be truly painful."

Klaus nodded, opened the door, and stepped out.

"Be a nice boy just for me."

Klaus started to tell him where to go but thought better of it. He was already in enough trouble. Walking straight ahead, he entered the apartment building and took the elevator up to the second floor. Klaus had been there so many times that there was no mystery to finding the way. With a hesitant step, he walked to the door and knocked.

"Enter!" Stein shouted.

With intimidation, Klaus turned the knob, walked in, and shut the door behind him. Wearing a maroon robe, Stein was bent over his desk working on something. He glanced at Klaus and went back to whatever he was doing without saying a word. Klaus stood awkwardly waiting for Stein to unleash the fury of hell on him, but Stein said nothing. After a long minute, Stein closed a notebook, stuck his hand in his pocket, and looked at him. Reaching across the table, he picked up a small Walther P5 pistol.

"You're a grotesque little frog," Stein said.

Klaus caught his breath, but stood at attention, saying nothing. He felt his hand start to tremble.

"Why didn't you come back here after you killed that priest at the Santa Maria Church?"

"I panicked," Klaus mumbled. No point in lying. "I didn't mean to kill him. The man crept up on me, and I stabbed him more by reflex than anything else."

Dr. Stein studied him for a moment. "You know, I think you are telling me the truth, Burchel."

"Why would I lie? You've caught me."

Stein nodded. "Fortunately for you, I still need your services, but I don't want you ever to run again. Do you understand me?"

"Yes, sir."

"Next time I won't be so generous." Stein put the gun down on the table and pulled his hand out of the pocket of his robe. "I will be keeping this cassette recorder in a safe place." He held a small tape recorder before him. "The confession you just made is recorded here. You'll want to do your best to keep me alive so no one finds it."

Klaus stiffened. It was not what he had expected.

"Now change into those old clothes hanging behind the door in the bathroom. We have work to do today and tonight."

28

THE HEAVYSET MAN SPED DOWN VIA APPIA NUOVA IN HIS FIAT UNTIL HE reached Grande Raccordo Anulare road where he slowed. The *Anulare* formed a ring around Rome, and beyond lay the suburb of Ciampino where a small airport made travel in and out of the area easy. Two men had flown in from America just for this meeting, and he eagerly awaited their report. Parallel to the highway ran Via Appia Antica, the Appian way, the ancient highway entry into Rome proper that all first-century travelers walked down to reach the heart of the city.

Before stopping, he drove past The Catacombs of St. Sebastiene twice. The other four men should already be there. Even though it was 2:00 in the morning, he could not risk anyone seeing him enter or leave. Once satisfied that the area was safe, he slowed and parked across the street where no one would connect his car with the ancient burial site that the first Christians had used two thousand years ago.

Each of the five men had a key to the side door of the church that allowed them to enter and descend into the dark catacombs where tourists visited. Stopping in the black of night, he slipped a stocking-cap face mask over his head before letting himself in. Black gloves not only offered protection against leaving fingerprints but added prevention of his hands being recognized. With cautious steps, he descended to the lowest level where the ancient Romans had once carried their dead. Only then did he switch on his flashlight.

At the bottom of the steps, the leader caught sight of a faint glow down the earthen tunnel to his left. A larger area had once been a little chapel. Inside stood a stone slab altar standing on the dirt wall. All around were the indentations in the walls where bodies had been placed for their eternal sleep. The candles on the altar and around the small room had been lit by the men who arrived first. Dressed in black with hoods over their entire heads, each man sat on a rock stool, waiting anonymously for him to arrive.

The leader walked in and nodded to the group. In turn, they responded.

"Gentlemen," the leader began quietly. "I welcome our two guests from outside the country to this important planning meeting. To date, we have done well. We have exploded two bombs in the city with significant results. A subway tunnel was closed and a train derailed. Most recently, we bombed American scholars and blew their offices to pieces, killing one associate. No one has yet picked up one clue as to who we are."

The group mumbled their appreciation.

"With such success, I believe that the title *general* would be appropriate. From henceforth, you will address me in that manner." He paused and looked across the faces of the four men. "I'm not sure we have yet made our point with the government that American control must stop in Italy and around the world. Perhaps, we must be more specific the next time," the leader said.

No one answered.

"Only two of us know the identify of the rest of this group," the leader continued. "Anonymity provides security. I want you to feel completely free to speak your minds. We must be candid. Understood?"

The group murmured their compliance.

"One of the reasons that we are meeting tonight is to plan our next attack," the general said. "We are now called The Scorpion by the media." He chuckled. "Conveys the message that we leave a powerful sting. I believe an attack in the United States would make an additional important statement. Perhaps, blowing up a school in Los Angeles, or striking an airport in Chicago would get big media attention."

No one spoke.

"Come now, gentlemen. You must have some response."

One of the foreigners held up his hand. "We have studied the situation across America," he began. "Since the 9-11 bombing, our country has become armed to the teeth. While we are not an identified terrorist group and have no connections with radical Muslims, we have those factors in our favor, but that is all. We believe a terrorist strike would be a disaster."

It definitely was not what the general had expected to hear.

"It is the unanimous opinion of both of us that it is not a wise idea," the American said.

"This was not what we agreed upon earlier," the general growled.

"Correct," the other American said. "But at that time we had not fully surveyed all of the possibilities. We have now. It is our conclusion that you are dealing primarily with an Italian problem and it should be kept in Italy."

The compatriot sitting beside him nodded his head solemnly.

The leader rubbed his chin thoughtfully. "What would you suggest?"

"You must be more specific when you attack," the American said. "You have not left the police with enough information to understand why these assaults are happening. The attacks require you to be clearer about your objectives. You are leaving the impression that you are amateurs. Your work must become sharper."

"How dare you criticize us!" the hooded man nearest the altar exploded. "No one even has a hint about who we are. Two successful bombings right under the nose of the police is not a small matter. Do you realize that?"

The American cursed. "Of course, we understand! You are too thin-skinned. We're telling you the way it is. Take it or leave it."

"You are Americans," the general said slowly. "I suppose it was not clear in the beginning that you were also part of the problem. We will leave it at that."

Jerking a gun from his belt, he fired quickly. The first American lunged forward and then tumbled sideways. The second turned to run, but the leader hit him in the back twice, and the man sprawled on the floor.

"We should never have trusted them," the hooded assistant said. "They were a drag from the beginning."

The third man stood immobile and speechless.

The leader stuck the gun back in his belt. "We can't leave them down here. We'll have to carry their bodies out."

"My God!" the third man choked. "You just killed them like they were rats crawling out of a hole."

"They were rats," the general growled. "You don't fiddle around with vermin. You get my meaning?"

The general watched the man's eyes widening. He said nothing, but finally nodded his head obediently.

"Remember that we don't leave one behind who might rat on us," the general said and laughed. "Get it? *Rat* on us."

"Yeah," the second assistant said. "But what are we going to do next? Their resistance has messed up our plans."

"I hate those worthless Americans," the general said. "Can't trust any of them. Now we have to find another follow-up target. These Uncle Sams screwed everything up. We'll have to give more thought to this next attack. I guess we must strike in Rome. You know, we could bomb the American embassy."

"If that Townsend guy doesn't die, we could shoot him," the assistant said. "That's a real option."

"Hmm," the leader mused. "We'll see how he comes out of the coma. Of course, he might die in the hospital." He kicked at the American lying on the floor nearest him. "Let's get these bodies upstairs and haul these guys off. We'll meet again in ten days."

The third man still said nothing.

29

Michelle Townsend had dressed early and packed her bags to leave the hospital. After visiting her comatose husband, she came back to the room before checking out. Seeing Jack lying comatose left her drained and feeling woozy. Michelle didn't want to leave him behind, but she knew she had been dismissed and had no choice but to go home. After three days in the hospital, the doctors had released her with a warning that her concussion remained an issue. Michelle had promised she would pay attention. The heavy bandage across the top of her head remained, leaving her looking like a war refugee.

Guido walked in with a nurse pushing a wheelchair. "They tell me that they have to wheel you out of here regardless of how good you feel."

"Afraid so," Michelle said and sat down in the wheelchair.

"How was Jack this morning?" Guido ask

"I'm afraid there's been no change. He's still in a coma and doesn't look good. I keep praying for progress. That's about all I can say."

The nurse started pushing her out of the room and toward the elevator. When the elevator reached the ground floor,

Guido pointed toward the entrance. "My car is already parked out front. We'll be out of here in a flash."

The nurse helped Michelle into the front seat, wished her the best, and waved good-bye. Guido pulled away, and they were back on the streets of Rome. The insanity of Roman traffic ran full tilt, and she had little choice but to hang on.

"I want to go back to what was once our offices," Michelle said. "I was unconscious when the ambulance took me away. I must see the wreckage. I just have to see the disaster with my own eyes."

"It's not a pretty sight."

"I'm sure that's true. Anything happen lately?"

"A guy named Dr. Albert Stein showed up and said you were associates. True?"

Michelle bolted forward. "The man has been a source of constant severe problems. Our book *An Answer to the Cynics* violently upset him. Jack always said Stein would remain our enemy until the clocks quit running."

"I caught him rummaging through the debris and had the police check him out," Guido said. "I thought something was wrong with the guy."

"In the rubble?" Michelle shrieked. "That scoundrel was trying to steal from us! In the past, he has been obsessed with whatever we were doing."

"Exactly what I expected. He hasn't been back."

"This report is alarming," Michelle said. "There's no telling what he's up to."

Guido wound his way skillfully through the traffic and slowed for a stoplight. "We found one other clue," he said softly. "Your offices had been wired. Someone had been eavesdropping on your conversations."

"Stein is capable of such a thing," Michelle said. "I'd put him at the top of the list."

"The police are checking it out. We'll see."

"I trust so." Michelle looked out the window. "Jack's condition has kept my attention focused on him, but Dov Sharon keeps coming back to my mind. The Jewish community has already buried him?"

"Yes," Guido said. "They have."

"He loved working on the *Sarajevo Haggadah*. I was never sure what he was after, but Dov will always remain in our hearts as a precious person. I know he was thrilled when he came up with this search for *The Prologue of James*, or the Brown Book, as the backroom boys at the Vatican call it. I must write his parents today and tell them how much we cared about Dov." Michelle's voice trailed away. "Who would ever have thought such a thing could . . ."

They drove in silence for a considerable distance. Finally, Guido said, "Earlier, Jack said that loud noises affect you negatively."

Michelle took a deep breath. "You might as well know that I have a psychological hangover from a childhood accident, but I can't allow it to control me, Guido. I'm forging ahead regardless of what I feel."

"You are a brave woman."

"I'm not brave," Michelle protested. "I'm simply faced with an inescapable alternative. Jack would want me to make sure that our work continues. While he is hanging on to his life by a thread, I can't let old fears stop the work. I must carry on. I believe that is what God would want me to do as well. So, I must grit my teeth and keep trying to jump through the hoops regardless."

Guido turned slowly and studied her face for a moment before looking back to the road. "I find you and your husband to be two of the most Christian people I've ever met. I am highly impressed. I want to say it again. I will stick with you regardless of how long it takes Jack to recover."

"Thank you," Michelle said softly. "I can't tell you how much I appreciate your steadfastness. We've got an uphill road ahead."

"But together we can climb it."

"Yes," she said. "We can with God's help."

Guido turned into the alley and pulled into the reserved parking space left for the Townsends. Michelle stared out the window at the ruins. All the walls were now gone. Only a pile of broken slats and split 2x4's stood in a heap to one side.

"It's all vanished," she lamented. "Disappeared."

"I went through the wreckage with the workmen and saved many of your books and papers. They have been stored in the church. Of course, much was lost, but your books did surprisingly well all things considered."

Michelle got out of the car and walked toward the ruins. "It's hard for me to imagine who could have done this to us. In five lifetimes, we couldn't have offended anyone this bad, or so I thought. The whole disaster is nothing but craziness."

Guido stood beside her, but said nothing.

"We are not going to stop," Michelle said. "No matter why this happened we won't allow a bombing to terminate our work."

"Why would they do this?" Guido ask.

Michelle shook her head. "We have apparently stumbled on to a serious matter with our pursuits of hidden manuscripts like *The Prologue of James* codex that Jack and Dov were chasing before the explosion. It's hard to believe anyone in the Vatican would destroy our offices because we had such an interest. On the other hand, Albert Stein has been sinister and draconian in the past. This bombing would be extreme, but he is an extreme character. Then, there's a conversation that Father Don Blake had with Jack. I overheard him warning that anti-American sentiment had been behind the bombing of the subway and he was worried that we were vulnerable."

"You've named enough enemies to start World War III," Guido said. "You'd better rethink what you just said. Sounds to me like you've got everything from religious nutcases to sinister terrorists on your trail. Obviously, Father Blake knew what he was talking about.

"Blake?" Michelle said. "It's vaguely coming back to me that he was with me at the hospital. Have you seen Father Blake recently?"

"No," Guido said. "I have no idea where he's gone."

30

THE FALL AIR FELT BRISK AND SNAPPY, LEAVING MORE THAN A HINT OF autumn in the air. Leaves had already fallen from the trees along the Virginia highway. A black Ford SUV sailed down the highway with the windows so heavily tinted that no one could see in. A man in the backseat watched the scenery drift by while the almost barren tree branches shook in the wind.

"I trust you are comfortable," the driver said. "When I pick up our agents at the airport coming in from abroad, I always want them to have the amenities of home."

"Thank you. I am quite fine."

The large vehicle slowed at the edge of Langley. Once again beyond the city limits, the driver picked up speed until he came to the Central Intelligence Agency entry gates. The driver flashed his credentials, and the SUV continued through. Only then did the man in the backseat pull the clerical collar from around his neck and unfasten the shirt at the top. Setting aside the image of a priest, Donald Blake reached in his coat pocket for his personal credentials. At the next checkpoint, the driver leaned out the window. "I have Agent Donald Blake returning from Rome. We have an appointment on the third floor."

The guard flipped through the pages on his clipboard and signaled for them to go on through. The SUV drove away.

"We've gotten even more strict," the driver said over his shoulder. "Since the 9-11 attack, we dot every 'i' and cross every 't' with no exceptions. You know how it is."

"Sure," Donald Blake said. "That's the new reality."

The vehicle pulled into a parking zone and stopped. The two men entered the large gray building and took the elevator to the third floor. Once they had exited, Blake walked toward a door marked PRIVATE, and the driver sat down on a bench along the hallway. "I'll be here when you come out," he said and pointed at the door. "Have a good time in there with the big boys."

Donald Blake nodded, and went in. Immediately, a man at the head of the table stood up. "Don! Great to see you. I believe you know our special assignment people."

"Thanks, James." Two men on each side of the table stood up. Blake nodded. "Sure. Sam. Brad." They shook hands. "We've worked together before." The men sat down.

James started the interview. "Please update us on what is unfolding in Rome."

Blake leaned back in his chair. "By masquerading as a priest, I've established contacts all over Rome and made inroads at important points. I can cover those areas if you wish."

No one nodded. James shook his head.

"Good. I'll leave the descriptive data out for the moment. Following the bombing of the terminal at the Piazza del Cinquecento stop, I began working to discover the source of the attack. As we all know, the Italian police aren't the sharpest in the world and let many details slip. However, my contacts led me to an informant that I have been paying for information. Through him, I was able to penetrate the cell that set off that blast. I now have inside information on what is going on in the terrorist attacks."

"Excellent!" James added. "Exceptional work."

"A single man stands behind the blasts and is now supported by two other assistants he acquired for this operation. The media calls these punks The Scorpion and thinks they're a multitude of terrorists lurking behind every street corner. Fortunately, there isn't. One of the lead man's assistants is my informant. The mouthpiece told me that they are not connected with any other groups. The lead man simply hates Americans. Believe it or not, that's the whole point of what these hatchet men are in to, killing Americans and their influence."

Sam smiled. "Nice work, Don."

"After I got the big picture of what these hair bags were doing, I noticed that an American scholar got his big story published in *Ill Messaggero*. His name's Townsend, Dr. Jack Townsend. I warned him that this wasn't a good time for Americans to be getting publicity. Unfortunately, Townsend didn't take me seriously. To make some kind of bizarre point, The Scorpion boys blew up his offices, killed one of his associates, and put Townsend and his wife in the hospital. Bad news."

"These terrorists are Italians?" James said.

"Yes," Blake replied. "They can't be extradited to America."

"Hmm," James said. "That could create a problem."

"What brought me back today was the most recent information I picked up on these guerrillas. One of the options they are now pondering involves bombing the American Embassy. They apparently want to raise the ante."

James leaned over the table. "I thought the three of you needed to hear this report as it changes the game we've been playing in Italy. They may be local Boy Scouts playing with dynamite, but when one of our embassies is mentioned, it's no longer little boys picking up merit badges. We have to be highly concerned."

Brad held up his hand. "When could this occur?"

"I have no working target date yet," Blake said. "At this point, I felt it was necessary that I be debriefed and you have time to consider options."

"Good planning," James said. "Obviously, we are deeply concerned when one of our citizens is hit. However, we must immediately start preparations to make sure that our embassy remains secure. Don, I'll have Sam start the debriefing. As soon as we're through, you can return to Rome."

Blake smiled. "Gentlemen, let's start the show."

31

Klaus Burchel carried the last box of electronic equipment in and set it on the floor of the new apartment. Albert Stein stood by the window, mumbling to himself. On the street below the humdrum of honking cars and speeding traffic echoed down the block. Via Glustiniani ran behind the Pantheon, an ancient place of worship with a vast domed ceiling, but the neighborhood wasn't shabby. Still, the apartment was a step down from where Stein had been.

"I don't like this location near as well as the flat on Via del Gracchi," Stein said. "Much closer to Vatican City over there." He shook his head. "But this is an address the police don't have, and I must protect my residence at all cost."

Klaus nodded. "We got your furniture moved in through the night quickly enough that no one will know you are missing for days. If they don't catch you for something else, you'll be safe."

Stein glared at him. "They didn't *catch me* doing anything! I was at Townsend's demolished office and they wanted information. Understand? Information!"

"Yes, sir."

"I'm waiting to see if Townsend survives," Stein said. "I'm sure that stupid wife of his will hang in limbo doing nothing until the man's fate is settled. It slows us down as well."

"I could go up to the hospital and sneak in," Burchel thought out loud.

"Stupid idea," Stein growled. "The nurses would be all over you in an instant. Give it some time and then we'll consider sending you in."

Burchel shrugged sheepishly. "Just a suggestion."

Stein started pacing back and forth. "From our hidden surveillance system, I picked up that they are on to a new chase for a document hidden somewhere in the Vatican. I could start looking for that little gem, but I must be careful not to raise any suspicion." He kept walking back and forth. "We've still got to hunt for that ending to Mark's Gospel."

"Now that the worthless Jew is dead," Burchel said. "It makes matters easier. Doesn't it?"

"Not necessarily," Stein said. "He was the one leading the search in the Vatican Secret Library for this new interest. If he was still around, he'd be the one whose head should be put in the vice."

"I'd love to do that," Burchel grumbled. "I hate Jews."

"You're not exactly in love with the Americans either," Stein sneered.

"I had time to think about it while I was in Munich," Klaus said. "The Americans ruined everything with their victory in World War II. They destroyed the way of life that my family had developed and reduced them to poverty." He pounded his fist into his palm. "These Yanks can't be allowed to do it again. I think we ought to kill the Townsends." His voice raised. "Kill 'em if nothing else just for the sport of it!"

"My, my, Klaus. You do have a nasty disposition, don't you? Admirable trait."

Mad Jack's on Via Arenula was an Irish pub with a festive atmosphere, and at night the music was loud while the drinks floated away like the Tiber River. In the afternoon, Mad Jack's usually stayed relatively quiet. Michelle didn't stop there often and always came with her husband. They'd often laughed about Jack's and the pub's names being the same. Sitting and talking on this late fall afternoon seemed somewhat nostalgic and made her feel closer to her husband. She and Guido Valentino talked over coffee.

"Have you heard anything from the hospital today," Guido asked.

"Just the usual. Jack's still in a coma, but they hope he will come out soon. Maybe his vital signs have improved some, but there's not much good news."

Guido nodded his head. "Very difficult. Yes, the situation is not good."

"I've thought a great deal about what Jack would want me to do," Michelle said. "It wasn't in his nature to slow down or put things on hold. I believe he would want me to continue our work. We still have important projects floating out there. I can't sit still and let them dangle in the air."

Guido took a sip of his coffee. "You are a courageous woman, Michelle." He held up his hand to keep her from protesting his compliment. "Even with your post-traumatic stress problem you are ready to struggle on with the work. I have some suggestions. Please hear me out."

Michelle raised her eyebrows. "OK."

"I told you that I was here to be of help and I meant it. I am willing to assist you in anyway that I can. I am more than serious. You and I can continue the work. We can do it together."

"Thank you, Guido. I know Jack would profoundly appreciate your availability. I certainly do. I'm just not quite sure where to turn."

"Let's consider what's before you," Guido said. "Tell me what the next step might be."

Michelle thought for a moment. "Now that Dov Sharon is gone, his interest in the *Sarajevo Haggadah* has ended. The book was in Hebrew and that was his expertise."

"OK," Guido said. "We can take that project off the list."

Michelle nodded. "It's a shame, but you're right. Did Jack share much with you about the Brown Book, as the Vatican calls it? *The Prologue of James*?

"Enough that I am highly intrigued. Finding that material could be revolutionary. I'd be profoundly interested in locating and reading such a manuscript. However, only Jack and Dov really understood where the search was going. I'd be at a loss to know where to turn next."

"The problem is that I'm a woman and the Vatican isn't hot on women wandering around in their library. They're not known for dishing out good treatment to nuns, feminists, ordained women of other denominations, and scholars like me. I'm afraid I'd almost have to dress like a man and trim my hair down to a crew cut to go researching around in their archives."

"Afraid so. It's almost like that project awaits Jack's return." He stopped and rubbed his forehead thoughtfully. "Of course, we don't know when that will be and if he'll be able to remember what they did a few weeks ago."

Michelle looked away, but tears welled up in her eyes. "I'm afraid to think about it."

"At least, the situation at hand suggests we must wait for Jack's return before we do anything on *The Prologue* project.

Michelle nodded, but didn't say anything.

They sat silently and watched the cars and tourists walk passed. Finally, Michelle spoke.

"Our pressing work is finding the original ending to *Mark's Gospel*. That's where this trek began and is Jack's passion. The original interview with *Ill Messaggero* had been about our search. A reporter named Mario Corsini was intrigued over the possibility of what we might turn up. I think that's the logical project to continue working on."

"And that is why I first came to you after I read the article in the newspaper. What I didn't tell you was that I did an extraordinary amount of research on both of your backgrounds. I wanted to know everything I could about you before I told you why I volunteered to help."

"Really?" Michelle squinted. "You're kidding."

"After the explosion in your offices, I continued to observe you carefully. I had to know that you were genuine Christians and completely trustworthy."

Michelle grinned. "Come on! Why would you do such a thing?"

Guido pushed back from the table and looked her straight in the eyes. "There is much that I have not told either of you about myself," he said. "Only after I have shared with you the entire story will you be able to understand."

"Understand? What don't we know about you?"

"I can only tell you one piece of the story at a time. I must watch how everything plays out before I'll be able to convey all that I know, but I can assure you that what I have is vital to your work."

Michelle blinked several times. "Guido, I don't have any idea where you're going with all of this. We checked your resume with Musei Capitolini, and their report back to us was excellent.

"Of course. I worked at the museum under the name Guido Valentino, but you must understand that is not my true name."

Michelle gasped. "Not your *true* name?"

Guido shook his head. "No. My actual name will blow your mind."

Part Three
Midnight Approaches

32

THE FALL AFTERNOON HAD SLOWLY BEGUN TO SLIP AWAY AND THE TRAFFIC on the street had picked up. After 4:00, all the stores opened again from their two-to-four nap break that many took every day. A few more customers had come in, and Mad Jack's had started the usual upward climb toward its nighttime peak, but Michelle remained unconcerned with the crowd strolling by. She leaned over the table to talk more privately and cupped her hand over her mouth. Other patrons in Mad Jack's Irish Pub walked by without paying much attention to her intense conversation with Guido Valentino.

"OK, Guido. What's this name you have hidden away that's suppose to scramble my mind? Some magic incantation you dug up from beneath the Roman streets?"

Her cell phone rang.

"Just a minute," Michelle said and picked up the phone. "*Ciao.*"

"This is the hospital," a female voice said. "We need you to come here at once. It is urgent."

"I'll be there as quickly as I can grab a taxi," Michelle said. "I'm on my way."

"What's happened?" Guido said.

"I don't know, but I've got to get to the hospital. I'll catch you later."

Michelle ran into the street and started hailing a taxi. Within moments she was on her way across the city. "There's an extra ten euros in this trip if you hurry."

"Presto!" The driver started swerving erratically in and out of the crowded lane. Like a teenage stock-car driver, he maneuvered wildly down the streets.

Michelle settled back in the seat and worried over what she had not heard. Whatever it was that Guido had to tell her, it couldn't compare with the urgency of making sure Jack hadn't taken a turn for the worse. Within record time, the cab swung in front of the hospital and Michelle jumped out.

Running down the long halls toward Jack's room, she realized that blood was pounding in her head and remembered the doctors had warned her to take it easy. She slowed to a quick gait. As she reached the room, a nurse was coming out.

"Is Jack OK?" Michelle grabbed the woman's arm.

"Look and see." The nurse pushed the door open.

To Michelle's astonishment, Jack was sitting up in bed with his eyes closed, leaning against a pillow propped up behind his head. It was the first time in weeks he had been out of bed.

"Jack!"

Jack slowly opened his eyes and looked at her.

"Jack?"

He blinked several times as if he was trying to bring her into focus.

"It's me. Michelle!"

"Michelle?"

"I'm your wife."

"Wife? I'm not sure that . . ."

The nurse stepped in behind her. "He's having trouble putting things into perspective. After all, he's been unconscious for a long time."

Michelle pushed the chair up next to the bed. "Jack, I'm your wife. Remember we work together, do research together, do everything together. You've been through a terrible experience. Remember?"

Jack kept looking at her as if he should know her. "Y-yes," he said slowly. "I do remember you. Remember . . . from . . . somewhere." He leaned back on the pillow and closed his eyes.

Her heart was pounding. This wasn't what she had expected at all.

"Jack? Jack, are you with me?"

"We've had a definite breakthrough today," the nurse said. "The doctor will be excited when he comes tonight. The fact that your husband has regained consciousness is a major step forward."

"But he doesn't know me," Michelle protested in a pleading voice.

"Sometimes it takes a while for memory to kick in. Don't worry. He'll be more alert tomorrow. It was important for him to see you today."

Michelle searched the woman's face. She wanted much more of an answer than she'd heard so far, but the professional distance she saw in the woman's eyes made it clear that the nurse wouldn't tell her more.

"It would be best for us to let him rest now," the nurse said. "You'll be able to come back later." She gently tugged on Michelle's arm and kept the trained smile in place.

Michelle walked out of the room and down the hall at a slow, unsteady pace. Many times, she had heard Jack explain to groups that through redemptive suffering, healing could come to the brokenness of the world. He had passionately believed that undeserved pain resulting from the pursuit of good released the power to change the destructive potential of evil situations. Certainly, they had been in just such a violent predicament. Michelle could only hope Jack's ideas were true and good would come out of this horrid mess they were in. Without question, Jack had been plunged into dire straits for no reason other than he was trying to make something positive happen.

But whatever she had hoped for today hadn't happened yet. Jack had come out of the coma and that was important, but if he didn't remember her, he certainly wouldn't remember anything about their work. If his memory did return fully, it would take considerable time before he was fully functional. As the realization sunk in, it seemed as if the autumn had suddenly turned to winter. She had to make him remember her.

Klaus Burchel stood in the shadows across the street from the hospital, watching the front door. During the days that had passed since he first watched the Townsend's office on Via Vittoria Veneto, enough of his hair had grown back that he no longer had a bald-headed appearance, but the scar on his cheek remained. If Michelle Townsend had caught a glimpse of him earlier, he might look somewhat different now.

The Townsend woman came out of the hospital and walked to the street curb where she hailed a cab. Burchel watched her and wondered if anything had improved with her old man. She sped away in a battered clunker with *taxi* painted on the door. Burchel hurried across the street and into the hospital. By this time, he knew exactly where Jack Townsend's room would be found. Stein would want an update, and the best way to get it was to look in the room. He slowed as he came closer to the door. A nurse stood outside making a notation on a metal covered chart.

"Excuse me," Burchel said. "I'm a friend of Dr. Townsend. How's he doing?"

"Oh, much better," the nurse said. "He's awake for the first time. We're making progress."

"Wonderful!" Burchel said. "Glad to hear it."

Klaus kept walking. Not good news at all. Stein would want to know about this turn of events immediately.

33

Michelle had awakened often throughout the night, worrying about Jack and praying that Dov had left this world in good stead for his heavenly journey. Dozing off again, the remembrance of a street in the town of Cerignola flooded her mind. Once more, she could see a gasoline truck coming straight toward her. The terror of an imminent collision shook her body. She awoke with perspiration dotting her forehead. Hours passed before she could make herself go back to sleep. Each time old images of destruction returned, and she had to fight them off.

When morning came, Michelle felt like a wrung-out dishrag. She had to shake off fatigue and push herself to get dressed. The trip back to the hospital took forever in the raging morning traffic, but no matter what the obstacles, she needed to be there as quickly as possible. She had to make sure Jack had progressed as the nurse had predicted.

Most of the hospital's regular floor staff knew her and nodded pleasantly as she passed. Michelle appreciated their warmth and reminded herself that no matter what happened, she mustn't allow her churning inner emotional fears to conquer. She had to stop these flashes from the past and keep them from destroying her concentration. Michelle picked up the pace and pushed Jack's door open.

To her surprise, a man was already sitting in the chair, trying to talk to Jack. The diamond merchant Tony Mattei had beaten her to the hospital

"Ah, Signor Mattei!" Michelle said. "How unexpected."

Mattei was on his feet instantly. "I have been dilatory in visiting my injured friend. I see that your husband is awake this morning. Most positive."

"Yes. He's talking to you?"

"Doesn't seem to recognize me, but I am offering him good cheer." Mattei immediately backed toward the door. "Now that you are here, I leave him in your care." He bowed at the waist. "Good to see you, my dear. Yes, good indeed." Tony Mattei disappeared through the door.

Perplexed by his rapid departure, Michelle turned to her husband. "Jack? Jack? Are you awake?"

Jack blinked several times. "Where . . . where am I?"

"You're in the hospital."

"Yes . . . yes . . . the hospital."

"Do you know me?"

Jack stared at her for a moment. "You're my wife. Michelle."

She wanted to shout for joy. If nothing else, he remembered her. Thank God for that discovery. Michelle grabbed his hand.

"My arm . . . I can't move it."

"Yes," she said. "You received a severe injury in the explosion. Your arm is in a plaster cast."

"I don't remember any explosion," Jack said. "When did that happen?"

"Several weeks ago."

"I don't recall anything about an explosion. No, nothing."

201

"You and Dov were in our offices when it occurred."

"Dov? Who is Dov?"

"You don't remember our associate Dov Sharon?"

"The name is familiar. Was he a friend?"

"A good friend," Michelle said.

"Oh . . . oh."

"You and Dov were working on finding a lost book from the first century, *The Prologue of James.* Remember that quest?"

Jack shook his head. "No. I do recall that we were searching for the original ending to Mark's Gospel. Right?"

"Definitely."

Jack laid his head back on the pillow. "So much seems vague, miles away. I can't seem to get my hands around it." He sat up again. "Yes, you are my Michelle. My wife. I love you very much."

"Oh, Jack, those are the sweetest words that I've heard in ten years." Michelle kissed him. "Oh, yes. I love you passionately."

Jack laid back on the pillow and closed his eyes. "So hard to remember." He fell asleep again.

Michelle sat next to the bed holding his good hand firmly for what seemed like an hour. Finally the door opened behind her and Guido Valentino tiptoed in.

"Any improvement?" Guido whispered.

"Much," Michelle said in her normal voice. "Yes, some of Jack's memory has returned. I am highly encouraged."

"Good," Guido said. "Excellent."

Jack stirred and opened his eyes. "You are the doctor?"

"No, no. Remember me? I am Guido Valentino. I work with you on the project on Mark's Gospel."

Jack stared blankly and shook his head. "No, I'm afraid I don't, but there is so much I can't seem to recall. All I remember is working on finding the ending to Mark's Gospel," his voice trailed away. "Trying to find an ending . . ."

"You are much better," Guido said. "Yes, we are going forward."

"I am sorry that I left so abruptly yesterday," Michelle said. "When news came that there had been a change, I had to get up here at once. That's just the way I'm put together."

"No problem," Guido said, "but you did leave at the most inopportune moment. I was almost about to tell you something important."

"Please forgive me," Michelle said. "I'm afraid any change in Jack's condition takes precedence over everything else."

Jack raised up in bed and looked at Guido again. "Yes. I do vaguely remember your helping me with some translation. Yes, you were demonstrating some characteristics of first-century Koine Greek. Something of that order."

Guido smiled. "My friend, you are making excellent progress. Your sentences are coming together much better. Your mind's starting to work."

"I can't tell you how relieved I am," Michelle said.

"I believe I have come at a fortuitous moment," Guido said. "I actually wanted to talk to both of you. I believe now is the right time."

"You might have to repeat this information to make sure we all get the meaning. I hope Jack is up to it."

Guido took a deep breath and began. "My family and I haven't shared this information with anyone for fear of how local citizens might react. My family name could create problems with the Roman Catholic Church, and we don't want any of those issues to erupt. My actual name is Jonas De Lateran."

"Lateran?" Michelle said. "That name came up in our studies." Michelle said.

"Until the 'i' was dropped, our name was Laterani. We are direct descendants of the Plautius Laterani family that extends back to the first century."

"Yes! The Laterani name kept appearing here and there in our search," Michelle said.

"My ancient ancestors owned property that was on the edge of Rome. Eventually this land was sold to Fausta, the wife of Constantine. On that piece of land in A.D. 311 Constantine built the first church in Rome that became the center of Christian life. Not the Vatican, but San Giovanni in Laterano was primary. San Giovanni was Rome's first actual church building. San Giovanni was the original seat of the Pope and remained so until the papacy moved to Avignon in the fourteenth century. Encased in the center of the high altar is a table that is reputed to have been used by St. Peter himself. Needless to say, San Giovanni remains one of the greatest relics of the Christian faith."

"Your family donated that property to the church?" Jack mumbled slowly. "Amazing."

"It was in this edifice that Innocent III met St. Francis in the twelfth century. Yes, obviously my family's history remains consequently."

"And what does this have to do with the ending to Mark's Gospel?" Michelle ask.

Jonas smiled. "That document has been in the hands of my family since the first century."

34

With the coming of November, the nights stretched longer and fewer tourists walked the streets. Sensing that too much time was passing, the leader of The Scorpions had called a meeting in the catacombs beneath the Church of Domine Quo Vadis. Located on the Appia Antica, the ancient Appian Way, the church supposedly stood at the spot where St. Peter was challenged to return to Rome and face crucifixion from Nero. The catacombs beneath the sanctuary remained so extensive, a novice could quickly get lost and disappear. Each of the three men had agreed to arrive thirty minutes apart to avoid notice.

As always, the general showed up last and found his two comrades waiting not far from the entrance to the ancient burial grounds. Each man had on the required black mask.

"I changed our location for tonight's meeting in case anyone picked up any aspect of our trail," the general said in a low gruff voice. "Nothing showed up in the papers about our killing the two Americans. Dropping them in the Mediterranean took care of that, but we can't be too careful."

The other two men nodded.

"Been giving considerable thought to our next attack. How about you? Anything come up?"

"Still thinking about hitting the American Embassy?" the first man asked. "Seeing that thing come down in flames pushes all my buttons."

"Not me," the second answered. "We'd be too exposed at that location. Even though we killed the upstarts from America last time, they had a point. We can't appear to be local amateurs on the prowl or we're dead. An attack on the embassy could make us look bad and wreck everything."

Silence settled over the discussion. The general sat quietly absorbing what he had heard. "I don't like to admit it," he finally said. "But unfortunately, you have a correct view of bombing the American Embassy. They've been hit in other countries and aren't about to let up military coverage here in Rome. With soldiers stationed around with M16s ready to fire, the bombing could well end up being out last attack."

"OK," the first man said. "Then, there's the possibilities with this American egghead Jack Townsend. How about cracking that shell with a few bullets to the brain?"

"Yeah," the general said. "He's out of the coma now. I thought Townsend would die in the explosion, and then I was sure he'd kick it lying up there in that hospital bed, but the guy came out of the bed all alive. Amazing, but the man is still highly vulnerable."

"This reporter Corisini at the *Il Messaggero* newspaper ran several stories on how Townsend's medical condition is progressing," the second man said. "That keeps the man's name out there where everyone knows he is an American."

"This time we've got to make sure that the public understands we're making these hits to bring down American influence," the general said. "That's the whole point."

"Yeah, we've got to do a more complete job of forcing the government to pay attention to the fact that Americans got their sticky fingers too deep in our economy. Maybe, we should write a manifesto of some sort and stick it on his body."

"I'd go for a letter to the newspaper after it's all over," the other terrorist said. "That Corsini guy would be the perfect recipient. Send him an explanation with the suggestion that they read it at Townsend's funeral."

The two men laughed.

"That's not such a bad idea," the general said. "Apart from the funeral nonsense, we could mail a letter to *Il Messaggero* laying out all details of our discontent. Townsend's body would demonstrate we mean business. His wife's turned into a real homebody type on the computer, flying around trying to get their show back on the road. We need to hit her as well."

Leaning forward, the general spoke in hushed tones. "Our next target will be the Townsends. The man's got a broken arm in a plaster cast so he's limited in his ability to resist. We'll have to identify the best time and place to hit them. I'll take care of that angle, then one of you will be the shooter or bomber, depending on what works best. Are we agreed?"

The two men nodded.

"Got it then. We're going to kill Jack and Michelle Townsend."

35

THE EARLY MORNING NOVEMBER SUN ROSE WITH A WARM, PLEASANT GLOW. By the time Guido Valentino had arrived at the Townsend's apartment, the magazine and newspaper vendors were hard at work on the streets. Children filed by on their way to school and a few privileged women walked their well-groomed dogs down the sidewalk. A gentle wind whistled down the streets, sending scraps of paper swirling along the curbs. As has been the daily fare for three thousand years, another day had begun in Rome.

The threesome sat around the small coffee table in the Townsend's apartment. Michelle handed Guido a cup of coffee and set another cup in front of Jack.

"After your jarring revelation, I don't know what to call you," Michelle said. "Is it Guido or should we call you Jonas De Lateran?"

"Let me first establish an important fact. Do you know that your apartment isn't bugged?"

"The police told us that they did a thorough electronic search of everything around here and assured us that nothing is wired," Jack said. "They are maintaining surveillance of this apartment. I hope we can trust their judgment."

"Good. Please keep calling me Guido Valentino. It is important that I keep my identity a secret. Since we do not know who is behind these attempts on your lives, we must assume something sinister is afoot and some scoundrel could slip by us. I have to protect my own family."

"Of course," Jack said. "We will honor your wishes."

"You have a pack of crazies out there with an intense interest in what you are doing," Guido said. "We can't discount any of them."

Jack nodded his head solemnly.

"The Vatican has a most checkered history of intrigue," Guido said. "Lately we have the sexual abuse scandals in the United States coupled with financial malfeasance from massive bank deals. Of course, we always have the Inquisition lurking in the background with Pope Sixtus IV sending King Ferdinand and Queen Isabella on a rampage chasing the Jews out of Spain. We still have scholars claiming Pope Pius XII did nothing to stop the World War II persecution of the Jews. The latest hot stories connect the mafia with the Vatican and include the claims of murder in the death of Pope Paul VI in 1978. There's a Vatican that you see; there's a Vatican that you don't see."

"I am highly aware of these contradictions," Jack said. "You're suggesting that someone in a robe is coming after us?"

"I'm only laying out the facts. It's not impossible that the Vatican has someone who's highly upset about your man Dov Sharon searching for *The Prologue of James* as I've heard you call it. It's enough to send someone after you."

"I still can't remember what Dov told me about where documents are hidden, but I think he did. I get your point, Guido."

"We still got that sweetheart of a gorilla named Albert Stein whom I caught walking through the ruins of your wrecked offices," Guido said. "Think he's incapable of chasing you?"

"Got your point," Michelle said nervously. "I don't like running through the catalog of creeps. Your point is that we keep your name under wraps."

"Yes," Guido said. "I'll go on being no more than your assistant Guido Valentino."

"The issue is settled," Jack said lowering his voice. "Let's start discussing what it means that your family had the original ending to Mark's Gospel. You didn't finish the story."

Guido took a sip of coffee and leaned back in his chair. "Saint John in Lateran is the oldest and ranks first among the four great patriarchal basilicas of Rome. The Laterani family occupied the site in ancient times. Sextius Laterani was the first plebian to attain the rank of consul. However, during the reign of Nero, Plautius Laterani was accused of conspiracy against the emperor and his goods were confiscated. We believe it had to do with Plautius hiding the lost portion of the Gospel of Mark, but we can't be for sure. We do know the Laterani family never gave up the document."

"Fascinating," Michelle said. "That fits with why the Laterani name kept popping up in our research to find the original ending to Mark."

"The original church that Constantine built carried the name Basilica Salvatorius, which was later changed to St. John because of a Benedictine monastery of St. John the Baptist and St. John the Evangelist which adjoined the basilica," Guido explained. "Through the centuries donations by popes and benefactors turned the church into a place of splendor, and it was called for a time Basilica Aurea or the Golden Church. Consequently, when the Vandals attacked Rome, they stripped the church of its splendor. The church had to be rebuilt several times through subsequent centuries. The current edifice has a somewhat tasteless appearance. It was rebuilt by Innocent X after the Avignon captivity of the papacy in France. When the pope returned, the city was nearly deserted and the church left in ruins. Nevertheless, the ancient apse with fourth-century mosaics survived all those assaults until late 1878 when the apse was destroyed to enlarge the area around it. However, the mosaics remained and are still in the church."

"That's amazing," Michelle said. "You've carried this extraordinary history with you for all these years."

"It's part of my family's story. We have a unique relationship to that church."

"Indeed you do." Jack carefully shifted the weight of his heavy arm cast around. "How does this mesh with what happened to the ending of Mark's Gospel?"

"When the story started in the first century, my family were not Christians. Apparently, with time, this changed. They came to treasure the fragment in their possession without realizing how priceless it was. Only after several centuries did they fully recognize what they had. By then, political intrigue had entered the church and touched its leadership. Revealing what they had kept hidden might have had dangerous repercussions for my ancestors. Consequently, they concealed the parchment in an unusual place and told no one except family members."

"Only your family knew?" Michelle asked.

"Only the *inner circle* of our family. It became our guarded secret carefully handed down from generation to generation through the centuries."

"And now you have brought this information to us," Jack said.

"I have come to the conclusion that it is time to release this treasure to the world. From all that I have learned about the two of you, I believe you will deal with this revelation in a manner that honors our family and its diligence through the many centuries."

"We are profoundly honored," Jack said. "Can you tell us now where this fragment can be found?"

Guido shook his head. "If for some reason we are wire tapped or someone overheard what we have just said, all chaos would break loose. We must take this journey a step at a time. Only as I know each piece in the puzzle is safe will I reveal where the next piece can be found. This will protect you as well. No one can come after you because you won't know."

"My, my," Michelle said. "We're in on a mystery scavenger hunt."

"I'm afraid so," Guido said. "I don't see any other way to keep us safe."

"I guess that puts you in the driver's seat," Jack said. "I'm still on the lame side, but Michelle is already back at work."

"They've moved our offices inside Santa Maria Church in a back room," Michelle said. "The new priest was gracious enough to allow us to work inside. We had a significant amount of material destroyed in the blast, but the books and papers that remained have been stacked in the new offices. I am still trying to get everything back in order, and it'll take a while to do so."

"OK," Guido said. "I will start work in those offices."

Michelle smiled. "You bet. We're ready for that next big step."

36

THE TOWNSENDS' APARTMENT HAD STAIRS LEADING UP FROM THE STREET, making it a challenge for Jack to come and go easily. Small, the flat had one bedroom with a kitchen, living room, and dinning room almost comprising the entire area. On a side wall, books sat on a large brown shelf piled up nearly to the ceiling. Most of the flat looked pedestrian and only functional. The bedroom barely accommodated a bed and a chest of drawers. Jack's heavy cast still required some assistance to get him out of bed and this morning wasn't any different. Holding him tightly, Michelle eased Jack through the bedroom door and onto the couch in the living room.

"You don't need to hold me like a china cup," Jack said. "I'm doing much better, and my memory is improving.

"Remember anything more about Dov Sharon?"

"What a funny, brilliant guy he was, but none of the other details are there. I just know he worked for us and you said he had been killed."

"You don't remember any aspects of the search for *The Prologue of James*?

"Sorry dear. It's just not come back yet."

Michelle sat down across from him. "We could certainly use any hints about where it's hidden. *The Prologue* would be an extraordinary find."

"Right now I'm walking again and that's big time for me. I'm not to worry about our projects yet. Lying in that bed on my back for days didn't help my stamina, but a little physical therapy put the punch back in me. I just hate having to lug this cast around day and night."

"Won't be long until you get those lovely biceps out of the box again."

"Lovely nothing. I'll be shriveled into diminished flab. Don't kid me. It must have been a bad break."

"Jack, the conference table saved your life. If it hadn't hit your arm so hard, the blast would undoubtedly have killed you. We're talking serious stuff here."

"I know." Jack shrugged. "Nothing of that day remains in my head, and my memories of Dov are only fleeting. Let's pray the rest of the story filters back in."

"Absolutely." Michelle stood up. "Let me fix you a cup of coffee. A little java might offer some encouragement."

"Good idea."

A knock sounded from the door.

"Who in the world could that be?" Michelle said. "Only a few people know our address."

"Beats me. Take a look."

Michelle opened the door. "Buongiorno."

"Buongiorno, indeed!" Father Donald Blake said.

"Why, it's our American compatriot and foremost male chauvinist," Michelle said.

"Ah, you women are all alike. Never let a poor man off the hook. Are you going to let me in or make me shout at your husband from out here in the hall?"

"You old fraud," Michelle jabbed back. "Come in before we call the police on you for disturbing the peace."

Father Blake walked briskly into the small living room with his overcoat hanging heavily from his shoulders. "Jack, my boy! How are you?"

"I'm still struggling to get my memory back. Forgive me, but I don't recognize you."

Blake sat down slowly. "I'm an American priest in Rome. I went to the hospital with your wife the day of the bombing and stayed with her most of the day when she was unconscious. We've been friends for some time."

Jack smiled. "Please forgive me. Pieces of my memory were simply blown away, but much has come back. I hope the Father Blake portion returns quickly."

"We've missed you," Michelle said. "You've been gone awhile."

"I had to go back to the United States. It was a personal matter, but I'm back again and making my rounds of my parishioners on the street. Always fascinating to have my many friends share with me."

"Interesting," Jack said. "We appreciate your dropping by."

"I didn't know you had our address," Michelle said.

"Oh, I have my ways of coming up with whatever I need. I'm simply pleased to see both of you doing so well. I see that you're out of that ball of bandages they had around your head, Michelle."

"They've even taken the staples out of my skull. A little on the ouch side, but I'm glad to be nearly healed. It was quite a blow that hit me when some part of the house flew by and knocked me to the ground."

"Indeed! I was there not long after it occurred. The bomb proved to be a highly nasty event. Jack, you probably don't remember me warning you that Americans could be the target of such explosions."

"He doesn't, but I do. I overheard your confidential conversation. Unfortunately, we didn't take you seriously enough."

"Exactly," Father Blake said. "I hope you'll take what I'm about to tell you far more earnestly this time."

Michelle stiffened. "Don't tell me you have more bad news."

"Afraid so." Father Blake stood up and reached into the pockets of his overcoat. "I know good Christians don't believe in violence and that you practice peaceful responses. I'm hoping you'll listen to me and also practice a little self-protection." He pulled two pistols from each pocket and lay them on the coffee table.

"Guns!" Michelle gasped.

"Hear me out," Blake insisted. "Jack has a broken arm and is still recovering. No condescension intended, but you are a woman, Michelle. Brilliant, beautiful, a scholar, but a frail creation if you had to fight off an attacker. The two of you are completely vulnerable to another attack. Whoever set off that bomb isn't through. Finishing you off could well be their next line of attack. You need a gun."

Michelle felt the inner throbbing that usually preceded an emotional attack. Light-headedness settled in, and for a moment she felt as if a tsunami was about to land on her. Gripping the chair tightly, she swallowed hard and fought to stop the assault.

"Believe me, you need to be armed," Blake said.

Jack stirred nervously in his seat. "I've never kept a gun. We've always believed that Providence provided our security. "I-I don't know what we'd do with a weapon."

"You're talking to a priest. I'm surely not casting any aspersions on divine guidance, but that didn't stop the bomb from nearly killing both of you, and you're sitting there with a broken arm. When Father Raffello was stabbed, the heavenly hand didn't shelter him from the knife. I'm concerned that neither of you end up lying on the lawn with another blade in you. Remember that God helps those who help themselves. It's not in the Bible, but it should be. Understand me?"

"You're walking on the edge of heresy," Jack said.

Michelle's heart kept beating faster, but the attack had stopped before her memories went wild. Breathing more heavily, she kept trying to push the surging wave of emotion back.

"Exactly what are you suggesting?" Jack asked.

"I've brought two pistols with me and the papers that allow you to carry them legally. Jack, I thought a Browning double action 9mm would fit you well. It's a heavy enough pistol to stop an attacker dead in his tracks. For Michelle, I came up with a Walther PPK that's lighter. It only carries seven rounds but is more easily concealed. I want both of you to start carrying these weapons."

Michelle took another deep breath. "I-I don't know if I could."

"You *most certainly can*," Blake demanded. "Your life may well depend on it. Put these weapons in your briefcases or a purse. If the bad boys come sneaking around again, at least you're armed. Surely, you get the significance of what I'm saying."

"Yes," Jack said slowly. "It's a little hard for a couple of biblical scholars to imagine running around with guns like we're James Bond. That's not even close to our world. I don't know. We'll have to think about it."

"Think hard," Blake pushed. "This problem is far from over, and I can assure you more trouble is coming."

"Jack," Michelle said slowly with a reserved tone in her voice. "I didn't tell you this earlier because I didn't know if you'd remember the name, but there is an important piece of this puzzle you should know about. Remember Dr. Albert Stein?"

"Stein! Good heavens, I couldn't forget him. Yes, of course. I remember Stein."

The morning after the explosion Guido caught Stein walking through the ruins. I didn't know the significance of this fact, but the man could be dangerous."

Jack stared at her for several moments. "I trust God has strongly as I ever have, but I recognize the peril Father Blake is talking about. Yes, we could be in jeopardy. That's a fact we can't ignore. Leave the guns."

Albert Stein leaned next to the curtains and looked out the window. From the corner of his eye, he kept observing Klaus Burchel, sitting like a statue across the room and staring straight ahead with a frown across his face.

Stein turned around. "Something eating at you, Burchel?"

Klaus blinked several times and ran his tongue over his teeth. "I've been in on a few police chases and I've had my share of run-ins with authorities. You know I've been high on coke and smoked pot. Yeah, I was even forced to listen to the denazification indoctrination at school." He shrugged and turned nervously in his chair. "Sure. I was running from the police on this last trip to Munich. I've already told you that I panicked. But when I realized how much the Americans ruined my family's way of life, which led to my grandfather's death, it really flipped me out. Torched me." He looked up at Stein with a hard, stern stare. "Yeah, it bothered me a lot."

Stein nodded. "The Americans put the sharp blade in all Germans." He uncharacteristically softened his usual arrogant voice. "My family came out of the war better than yours," he said in an unusual thoughtful reflection. "We were lucky that the Americans needed what we could produce. Didn't stop me from hating them though." He cursed violently.

"Twice they brought Germany down," Klaus continued. "Those dog-faced Yanks pushed our heads underwater. Makes me want to put a gun in Townsend's face and blow his head off."

37

Pushing with her elbow, Michelle pried open the front door of Santa Maria Church and struggled through the entrance with her arms filled with books. The reverent sound of an organ playing signaled that worship was unfolding in the sanctuary and people would still be on their kneelers. Down the marble floor to her left, the door was already open to the offices the new priest had given them. Her steps echoed down the hall as she hurried toward their nook in the large church. She found Guido already hunched over a desk, studying some document.

"Buongiorno," Guido said politely and returned to the material in front of him.

She set the books down on the edge of the desk. Two desks had been pushed together to make room for a third now sitting against the wall. One empty file cabinet stood near the door. Paint had started to peel from the wall, and the color had faded long ago. An old statue of some saint stood in one corner as if watching over everything that might happen in the room and keeping an eye on a dilapidated fireplace in the center of the room. Someone had hauled in a small table placed in another corner with a coffeepot and cups ready for use. Recovered books from the wreckage had been stacked on the floor next to the wall and Michelle's desk was piled high with papers that Guido and the workmen had gathered up after the explosion. One look told her it would be days before the mess was completely straightened out. Not an encouraging thought.

"Looks like we've got our work cut out for us today," Michelle said.

Guido took off a pair of reading glasses and settled back in his chair. "I had no idea where to put what we picked up so I left the loose papers in a stack on your desk. I hope that is acceptable."

"More than acceptable. Jack and I appreciate all of your efforts while we were out of commission. Acquiring this room from the church officials helped infinitely more than I can say. Our apartment is simply too small to accommodate the research we are doing."

Guido held up the manuscript he had been reading. "This morning I took a long look at the *Sarajevo Haggadah* Dov had been working on. He must have found something fascinating in there that he never told any of us about."

"He probably did. Jack first met Dov while researching in the Armenian Library in Jerusalem. We quickly realized that Dov had an unusual ability to work with languages. From there, one thing led to another until he was part of our work here."

"Yes," Guido said. "I found him to be a thorough scholar. "We cannot make up for his absence."

Michelle whispered to Guido. "I think he stumbled on to where *The Prologue of James* might have been hidden if only Jack could remember what he said. We can only hope we will eventually recover that information.

Guido nodded. "Are we sure this room is electronically clear?"

Michelle shook her head and mouthed a no.

"As I suspected, we must be cautious."

"Unfortunately," Michelle said.

Guido got up and came around to sit on the edge of her desk. "We must not discuss any sensitive matters in this room. It is one of the reasons that I haven't told you and Jack about the next step in our search. If you knew where we are going, you'd be subject to attack and search. Not knowing allows you to stand above the chase. When the right moment comes, I'll tell you what comes next."

"I understand. You are a thoughtful man, Guido. I know you will reveal this crucial and strategic portion of our pursuit at the right time. Jack and I are both comfortable with this arrangement."

"For the moment, we must allow matters to settle and make sure the police really are on top of the pursuit of the criminals. As soon as we get some sense of where it's all going, we'll be ready to move."

"Super."

Guido pointed at the old fireplace with one hand and cupped the other over his mouth. "When you push the top of the irons in the fireplace, it opens a secret door that allows you to walk down to the crypts below. Apparently it was a little escape mechanism that Cardinal Antonio Barberini built in here back in the 1600s. The Capuchin monks apparently were surrounded with considerable danger back in those days."

"Back in those days?" Michelle laughed. "I bet no one ever put a bomb under their bed."

"Good point. Today's world isn't a hair safer than theirs."

"I suppose I should get this office straightened up first thing," she said. "We want to be able to move the moment you're ready to tell us where we're going."

Guido smiled and went back to the *Haggadah.*

Late afternoon shadows had already fallen by the time Michelle got the last of the papers off her desk and in order. The file cabinet no longer stood empty and many of their reference books had been placed in order. The complete collection of the works of *The Ante-Nicene Fathers* and *The Post-Nicene Fathers* had been stacked together for a quick grab. She knew well they contained all the writing of the earliest Christians during the first couple of centuries. Next to them, she had arranged other books that they used frequently.

"I can give you a ride home although I'm not sure it will be any faster than the subway," Guido said.

Michelle laughed. "This time of day it's a madhouse out there on the streets."

"I think that tomorrow we will be able to accomplish more," Guido said. "You have done a great deal today."

"We're getting there." Michelle slipped her topcoat on. "I guess we can go out the front door."

"I'd suggest the back," Guido said. "It's closer to my car."

"Whatever you say." Michelle picked up her briefcase. "Let's go."

Without saying anything more, they walked down the corridors Jack had always followed in his many excursions through the church ambling around like a fascinated tourist. Candlelight had now illuminated most of the building with the high altar bathed in a soft glow. Stepping outside, Michelle could see the moon had not yet come up, but the ruins of the house looked like a jumbled mess of splintered boards still sticking up at strange angles, looking like an abstract painting in black and white.

A figure emerged out of the alleyway, and Guido grabbed her arm, jerking it toward him.

"Watch out!" he whispered.

The man leaped forward and raised his arm.

"He's wearing a black hood over his face!" Guido pushed her toward the door they had just existed. "Run!"

The pinging sound from a pistol with a silencer sliced through the quiet, and a bullet ricocheted off of the back of the church. Michelle ran like she never had before in her life.

Guido swung the door open and they rushed in. He grabbed for the latch, but the defective lock didn't catch.

"Keep running!" he shouted again.

Dashing through the halls they'd just come down, they headed for their office. Michelle grabbed her keys and unlocked the door. The sound of racing footsteps wasn't far behind them. Once inside, they locked the door and darted behind the desks. Fumbling with the briefcase, she pulled out the Walther PPK Father Blake had given her. Barely able to hold it steady in her shaking hand, she made sure a bullet was in the chamber. The running noise increased.

"Do you think he knows we're in here?" Michelle whispered.

Guido groaned pessimistically.

Footsteps increased, and it was obvious that the assailant had come out in the narthex.

"What's going on out there?" Some man's voice echoed down the hall. "This is a church. What . . . what are you wearing . . . on your face?"

The gun cracked again and the man's voice stopped.

Guido crawled across the floor and grabbed the irons on the fireplace. A creaking noise sounded and the panel behind the grating slid open. "Let's get out of here."

Michelle could hear the assailant coming closer to their door. She started creeping backward toward the fireplace.

"Get in there," she said. "I've got the gun and will be the last one in."

Guido darted inside as Michelle kept inching toward the opening.

Suddenly the man in the hall threw his weight at their door. The old portal made a cracking sound, but didn't come open. Michelle fired two shots at the door before dashing into the fireplace and hurrying down the ancient stone steps behind Guido.

"I've got five bullets left," she said.

"Hang on to them. We've got to get down into the crypt to escape."

The noise of the door breaking open and slamming into the wall above them echoed down the hidden stairway. Two more shots rang out.

Michelle and Guido ran down the dark passageway filled with the bones of dead monks. When they came to the first corner, she stopped. "I've got to see if he comes down those hidden steps," she said. "That's everything!"

Guido cowered against the wall and held his breath.

At the other end where they'd come out, Michelle saw movement and fired three shots. The assailant fired back.

"Get out of here!" she gasped. "I've only got two bullets left."

Michelle ran down the corridor until it ended, and they turned to the right. Fifty feet away they realized they had come to a dead-end wall. Standing in total darkness, Michelle knew they were trapped.

"Get down," she whispered. "Flatten out on the floor and don't make a sound."

The smell of dirt filled her nose, and she remembered that soil from the Holy Land had been sprinkled on the floors and was never swept up. Sticking the pistol straight in front of her and resting the butt of the gun on the floor, she tried to stop shaking and aimed into the darkness.

Only then did the fierce thumping of her heart signal that an emotional rumble was beginning. Like a runaway gasoline truck careening down the road straight at her, she felt the tearing pain of raw emotion exploding within her. Her eyes started to blur, and a roaring noise filled her ears. Her mouth turned dry and her hands shook fiercely. She couldn't close her eyes, fearing the attacker would come running straight at them. All she could do was gulp in the sour, soiled air arising from the dirt on the floor.

No sounds echoed down the corridors. For five minutes, she and Guido lay side by side staring into the darkness. No other noise filled the tombs of the dead.

"Police!" a man yelled from somewhere far away. "We're the police. Put your weapons down."

"It could be him," Guido whispered. "Don't be deceived."

Michelle nodded.

"We're the police," the man shouted.

"We're with them," a different voice yelled. "We're the *carabinieri*, the military police. We're behind them."

"Thank God," Michelle said. "I think we're rescued."

"Oh, I hope so." Guido stood up slowly. "Let me get some light. I've got a cigarette lighter in my pocket."

"Back here!" Michelle shouted. "We're being chased by a gunman." Her voice echoed down the long tunnel with a hallow sound.

Guido flipped on the light. Crunched up in a small space carved in the wall, a skeleton sat wrapped in a deteriorating brown robe. Six inches from his face, a skull stared at him through empty eye sockets. Breathless, Guido sputtered, trying to catch his breath.

"You down there?" Detective Alfredo Pino's voice echoed through the crypt.

"Barely," Michelle answered.

Long after the detective and the police had gone, Michelle sat in the small office alone, looking at the pistol laying on her desk. Her father had kept a gun hidden in the large chest in their bedroom, but she always feared the weapon. When Father Blake brought the guns to their apartment, she would never in her wildest dreams have imagined firing the Walther PPK at someone. In truth, she would have completely rejected the idea of keeping the weapons if Jack hadn't accepted them. Michelle had always hated violence in any form. And yet she had fired at the person pursuing them.

It was a hard thought to accept, but she could see that the saying was absolutely true. Violence begets violence until the world is filled with the uproar of a volcano of fury. Right here inside this church with its gospel of peace, lives had been taken. Father Raffello had fallen as well as the man killed just outside their door. Jack had nearly been destroyed and Dov Sharon murdered. And all they had been interested in was completing their work on Holy Scripture. With only the best intentions in mind, they had marched into a battle with evil that had nearly taken her life that very afternoon.

What a strange world, Michelle thought. *The absolute best can bring the total worst. Never would I have expected such a possibility. I suppose I have no choice, but to keep this weapon close at hand. Even holding this loaded pistol violates my deepest and most heartfelt intentions. Then again, I have no other choice. The battle is joined to the final blow and I cannot acquiesce lest the other side win.*

Michelle put the gun back in her briefcase, locked the door behind her, and headed home.

38

Father Donald Blake strolled up Via di San Cosimato at a leisurely pace, keeping his eyes fixed on the Da Vittorio café across the street. At a table on the sidewalk, Tony Mattei sat hunched over a plate of food he appeared to be devouring in record time. Periodically, he stopped and took a big gulp of wine from the large glass sitting on the table in front of him. Thick, black hair hung down over his eyes as his heavy cheeks rolled with each inordinately large bite. Even from across the street, Blake could see that Mattei wore his usual three massive diamond rings, flashing in the bright sunlight with the sparkle of elegance.

Breaking through the traffic, Blake continued his casual stroll across the street and walked up behind Mattei. "Buonasera."

Mattei jumped. "What?"

"It's your old friend." Father Blake sat down across from him.

For a moment Mattei glared and then burst into his usual jubilant expression. "Ah! God has blessed me with a visit from heaven! I am being graced by his Excellency, Father Blake."

Blake smiled pleasantly. "Tony, you are an old-fashioned sack of . . . sayings."

"Of course. Of course. What else can I be when I stand before the radiance of the sun shining down on me with the light of eternity."

"You ever think of running for political office?"

"Yes, as a matter of fact I have. The time has come for someone to straighten out the economic mess this country is in. I think I could be just such a man."

"Indeed." Blake kept smiling.

"Someone must shoulder the responsibility that the import situation has placed on small merchants like myself. We need relief."

Blake looked at Mattei's diamond rings. "I wasn't aware that you were having a hard time. You look prosperous to me."

"I must maintain appearances." Mattei raised his shoulders as a sign of resignation. "It is only appropriate for business."

The waiter stepped to the table. "You wish?"

"A cup of coffee will be fine," Blake said.

The waiter hurried away.

"I suppose you've already heard about the shooting at the church last night," Blake said.

"Terrible! Who could imagine such a thing?" Mattei kept eating.

"Did you know that one of the parishioners got shot out in the narthex trying to stop the attacker?" Blake folded his arms over his chest and leaned back in the chair.

"That is what they told me. Sad situation."

"Apparently, the gunman ran Michelle Townsend and her assistant around the church before the police appeared."

"That is the rumor," Mattei said.

"Why do you think anyone would want to hurt such lovely people as my friends the Townsends?"

Mattei's eyes narrowed and he looked pointedly at Blake. "Now, you've become the questioner?"

"Just asking," Blake said.

"I didn't know we were in an examination," Mattei answered.

Blake laughed. "How quickly matters can change in Rome."

"You should try the Neapolitan pizzas they have here. The oil-drenched crust is called pizza bianca. *Magnifico!*" Tony shook his fingers in the air. "Excellent! Da Vittorio restaurant not only sprinkles mozzarella cheese across the top, but they create a sauce with a festive bouquet of arugula and cherry tomatoes on the top. This is a wonderful café."

The waiter set a cup of coffee in front of Blake. "For you, padre. On the house." The man moved on to the next table.

"Thank you," Blake said.

"My father brought me here when I was a boy," Mattei continued. "So many good memories associated with this little nook."

"Let's get back to the shooting in the church last night." Blake stirred his coffee slowly.

"Yes," Mattei said. "Why do you think anyone is attacking Americans?"

"Americans?" Blake rubbed his chin. "You are among the first to use the term *Americans* in speaking of these attacks."

"What else would you call the Townsends? Are they not your countrymen?"

"Yes," Blake said. "I didn't think of their nationality as being distinctive in these attacks."

Mattei shrugged. "Seems evident to me. Someone doesn't like Americans."

"Hmm. Appears their old offices were wired for surveillance before the bombing. I wonder if their new office inside the church has the same problem."

"Anybody find evidence of it?" Mattei asked.

"Wouldn't know," Blake said.

"I can only hope for the best for my friends," Mattei said and took another large bite of the pizza. "If you find any inside information, please let me know."

"And what would you do with such information?" Blake asked.

"Why, I'd go straight to the police!" Tony clapped his hands. "Yes, I'd want to report the same immediately."

"Interesting. Well, I'm sure you'd be among the first to know."

Tony Mattei smiled. "What more can a humble jewelry salesman do but keep his ear to the ground?"

Blake finished his coffee. "We shall see what the day brings." He nodded and started back down the street.

39

Rome still buzzed with disquieting rumblings in the streets. Bombings and shootings hadn't ever been the order of the day and the locals worried about what might happen next. In his day, Benito Mussolini had once strutted around town, but no one fired at him. Pickpockets and petty adolescents pulling off heists on tourists were run-of-the-mill, but that was about it except for an occasional crime of passion. These expectations changed with the explosion and persistent assaults on the Townsends that had given them a near celebrity status with the tabloids. Newspapers picked up from somewhere photos of Jack in bed in the hospital with Michelle at his bedside and splashed the scene across the front pages. Paparazzi hovered around their apartment, making it increasingly difficult to complete their work in private. The attacks had turned into a circus with onlookers hovering nearby for a peek at whatever went by when the parade came marching through.

Guido had started entering the Townsends' apartment through the alley, which kept him out of the line of view of the gawkers and allowed him to enter their flat unobserved. A freshly grown beard had changed his appearance enough that he wasn't immediately recognizable.

On this morning, Michelle opened the back door to the apartment and let Guido in. "I see you've escaped the procession rolling down the street this morning."

"How could something so conventional as scholarly research in a library have turned into such a freak show?"

"Bizarre," Michelle said. "Come in and take a look at what's waiting in the living room."

Guido flinched. "I'm almost afraid to ask what's in there."

"I think you'll like this one," she said.

Jack Townsend sat on the couch with his feet propped on a small stool. The plaster cast had vanished, and his arm hung leisurely in a cloth sling. "Well, our ol' exploration buddy is here."

"Good heavens!" Guido said. "You've escaped the jail."

"Getting out of immobilization in plaster was a gift from heaven. I can get around like a normal human being again."

"You have to keep the arm in a sling?"

"For probably another week," Jack said. "But I'm back on my feet and ready to work. Still got a few blind spots, but most of my memory is working again. Unfortunately, I don't remember a thing about what happened the day of the explosion and much of what Dov and I discussed. Outside of those important areas, I think that I'm back in the saddle. We'll have to see."

"Excellent," Guido said. "Do you feel safe talking this morning?"

"I thought we might push the small kitchen table onto the balcony and let the sunlight shine on us," Michelle said. "Traffic noise in the street ought to cover us even if some eavesdropping device is around here, but the police checked every room. We're covered."

"I'll help pull the table over to the open area," Guido said. "Then we can get down to business."

Michelle and Guido carried the table toward the small balcony. She placed steaming coffee mugs before them and the threesome let the morning sun settle over them.

"Feels so good to sit in the sun," Jack said. "I had a hard time getting adjusted to the hospital. Not an easy place to like. For the last month, I've been inside for such long hours that this morning feels like a stroll down the beach."

"The police almost drove me crazy questioning me over and over about the shooting in the crypt," Michelle said. "They hinted that we might be in some nefarious activity we weren't admitting. It was hard for them to believe we were only scholars trying to go about our business without bothering anyone. Then, these maniacs with cameras started popping up." She pointed to two men standing next to a light pole in front of the apartment building. "Those guys are part of the shutterbug club that now meets on our doorstep."

"Rome has an inordinate taste for the sensational," Guido said. "I'm afraid they won't go away until this struggle subsides."

"What does that mean for our search?" Jack said.

"I've given that considerable thought," Guido said. "On one hand, we could stop everything that we are doing and let the ruckus fade away. The option of retreating into solitude sounds highly inviting. On the other hand, I don't believe your enemies will stop trying to assault you. Whether it's the Vatican or terrorists with dynamite, I think they'll be after you until this project is finished. Moreover, this Scorpion group doesn't seem to be in a mood to retrieve their stinger either. So, who are the bad boys?"

Jack rubbed his chin and stared down into the street. "It's simply beyond me to figure out who these scumbags actually are. I don't know how to answer your question."

"Me either," Michelle said.

Guido took a long sip of coffee. "Therefore, I must answer my own query. We don't know who the culprits are. Therefore, I believe we must act at once to protect you as well as the fragment ending to the Gospel of Mark."

"Excellent! If nothing else, I'm in better shape to be of some value in a hunt than I was a week ago." Jack shook the sling. "Let's go get 'em."

"Before we start down the trail, let me tell you more about the Laterani family history," Guido said. "The period of the Crusades that began in 1067 came in the midst of a time of economic peril. Between 970 and 1040, there were forty-eight years of famine. From 1085 to 1095, the problem became even worse. These troubled times produced a deepening of religious feeling. It was a combination of economic struggle with the adventurous call to purify the Holy Land that started the Crusades."

"Agreed," Michelle said. "We've studied the popes from Hildebrand through the Latin Patriarch of Constantinople. We know a considerable amount about the battle with the Muslims during those times of struggle. Jack and I studied this period in history."

"What few people know was that the Laterani family was a major force during the Crusades. Much like the Templars, they were entrusted as depositors of treasure captured during these holy wars. We kept the treasures here in Rome, and much of it was stored around the Church of San Giovanni in Laterano. Because these treasures amounted to a vast amount of wealth, it was important that their security be ensured. During this period, my family changed their name to De Lateran as a protection against attack."

"Fascinating," Jack said. "So your ancestors accumulated a highly significant amount of wealth during this period."

"To put it mildly! We became one of the wealthiest families in Italy. Of course, the Laterani family already had accrued considerable affluence before this period. However, it was during this time of concealing the treasures taken in the Crusades, that they hid the ending of Mark's Gospel in its present location and it became our family's most precious secret."

"It's been there all these years?" Michelle asked.

"Never touched."

"Do you think the document has deteriorated?" Jack ask.

"I honestly don't know. When we take it out of hiding, we'll be the first to find out in a thousand years."

"I'm ready!" Jack shook his good fist in the air. "Let's go get it!"

"Easy there, Superman," Michelle said. "We don't want to have to put you back in a cast again."

"And that is exactly why we must deal with this matter in complete secrecy," Guido said. "I don't want anyone getting killed. Even with possible danger, I believe this is the hour for us to strike. I think tomorrow morning would be a good time to start out."

"Oh, man!" Jack exclaimed. "This adventure is beyond my wildest dreams!"

"In the morning, I will show up with an old Jeep to make us look obscure, and we will drive to the location I mentioned. Only then will I tell you where we are going."

"I am overwhelmed." Michelle slumped back in her chair. "We are standing on the threshold of one of those great historical moments that could change everything."

"Everything." Guido looked pensively out over the street. "Absolutely everything."

Klaus Burchel slid back from the top of the building directly across the thoroughfare from the Townsends' apartment. The International MicroPower WM-1 had been modified to pick up what was discussed across the street with great precision. Klaus wore a small earphone to monitor the transmission going straight to Stein's van.

When the windows were closed, Burchel picked up nothing, but on a bright day when the Townsends opened the shutters, he picked up enough bits and pieces to get the drift of a conversation. Today's exchange on the balcony had been extraordinary. Every piece of their chatting with Valentino came through like going to the movies.

"Did you get all that?" Burchel said into a cell phone.

"Absolutely," Albert Stein said.

"I think tomorrow we'll be waiting out front for the Jeep to show up," Burchel said.

"Without question," Stein answered.

40

MICHELLE WATCHED HER HUSBAND SLEEPING SOUNDLY. WITH THE SUN beginning to shine in the old window facing the street, he held his arm defensively to shield his eyes from the increasing brightness. His usual early morning cherubic countenance always carried a solemn smile. No question that atrophy had diminished the size of his arms where the break occurred, but he was alive and back to his old self again. The realization of what might have happened swept over her, and Michelle recognized that she could have ended up in bed by herself forever but for the grace of God. She watched him for a moment as tears welled up in her eyes. Jack had become more precious than life itself. She rolled over in bed and kissed him softly on the cheek. Jack stirred. Michelle kissed him again, but this time more forcefully.

"W-what?" Jack blinked.

"I just thought you'd like a little personal wake-up call this morning."

Jack pushed himself up and looked around. "I was dreaming about being in the hospital . . . seemed like . . . I was there . . . forever. More of a nightmare I guess. Am I ever glad to be home and out of the plaster cast." He pumped his arm back and forth several times. "Flexibility is coming back. A little more exercise and I'll be ready to lift weights again."

Michelle kissed him again. "By the way did I tell you lately that I love you? Love you more than you love those *alla giudia* artichokes at the Dar Poeta café?"

Jack laughed. "Hey, this relationship could develop into a full-blown hanky-panky thing. You up for such a kooky possibility?"

"On your life." Michelle kissed him fervently.

Jack's cell phone rang. "Hang on," he said and picked it up. "*Hallo.*"

"Jack," Guido Valentino said. "You awake?"

"Yeah. I had to get up to answer the phone."

"Ha. Ha," Guido said. "Don't be a comedian. I'm concerned about our trip today. We've got the problem of the paparazzi and the sidewalk observers to consider. Do you think it might be safer for me to pick you up in the alley behind your apartment?"

"Sure. Let me know the exact time you'll be here and Michelle and I will come dashing out the back door."

"I'll be there at 9:00 and we'll be on our way," Guido said.

"You're on!" Jack said and hung up.

"Our man is ready to roll," Jack told Michelle. "Looks like our dreams are about to come true." He stared out the window. "Amazing, isn't it? We've been chasing this prize for a long time and then it abruptly falls at our feet because Jonas De Lateran walked into our lives. I would have never expected this turn of events."

Michelle leaned against the headboard. "Do you have any idea where we are going?"

"There are so many nooks and crannies in Rome that have sprouted endless options that it could be anywhere. To make matters worse, the fabulists run around creating new myths all the time. Anywhere is a possibility. The Palazzo Massimo alle Terme is a museum with collections that span the centuries. A fragment of a document could be tucked away in there and no one would find it. San Clemente is out there in the valley between Esquiline and Oppio Hills. Down there in the basement are the remains of an ancient Temple of Mithra. Now there's an ancient site covering two thousand years of history. Wouldn't that be an unsuspected zone for hiding a document?"

"You're right. Rome is packed with the unsuspected, and we haven't picked up any significant clues from our research so far. I guess we're completely in Jonas's or, as he wants us to call him, Guido's hands."

"I think we'd better hit the shower and get ready for a big day," Jack said. "The clock is ticking."

Michelle put her hands on his shoulders and pulled him closer. "We must never let the clock shape our relationship. When it's all said and done, we've only got each other."

Jack kissed her gently. "Even *before* it's all said and done, we're all we've got."

41

THE ALLEY HAD THE USUAL SHABBY LOOK OF GARBAGE CANS, LITTER, JUNK, and the muck that had collected for a thousand years. A slight scent of decay drifted through the air. Empty cars parked here and there only added to the disorderly appearance. Jack and Michelle stood in the apartment's back door waiting for Guido to drive up in the Jeep.

"You've got that gun that Father Blake left us?" Jack asked.

Michelle patted the large handbag at her side. "I've started paying careful attention since we were chased through Santa Maria. I don't like it, but it's here."

"Got my Browning and a small power-pack flashlight," Jack said. "The gun's a little awkward under this coat."

At a few minutes after 9:00, Guido pulled into a space directly behind the back door. The black Wrangler with a canvas top looked more like a trailblazer in the Swiss mountains than a vehicle on the streets of an ancient cosmopolitan city. The couple hurried out and jumped into the Jeep.

"Hit the road." Jack bounded into the front seat. "I've been waiting a long time for this trip. Today is our Christmas."

Guido glanced in the rearview mirror. "Can't ever be sure whether this is Christmas or Halloween. You people seem to live more on the trick-or-treat side of town."

Michelle glanced up and down the alley. "Don't see anyone. That's got to be a good sign."

Guido pulled away without answering.

"Getting through Rome's traffic won't prove easy," Jack said. "Got any shortcuts in mind?"

"We're going to drive around for a while," Guido said. "The paparazzi have their own unique ways of turning up, and we don't want that tribe on our trail. We'll see how things unfold."

Jack leaned back in the seat and relaxed. "I'm only glad you're behind the wheel and not me. I'll enjoy the sights."

For ten minutes Guido glided around the narrow streets and broad thoroughfares. Alternating between a slow drag and sudden bursts of speed, Guido kept maneuvering down the boulevards. Finally, he turned to Michelle. "I want you to watch directly behind me. It seems like a black Audi's been following us for several blocks."

"You're kidding," Jack said.

"Pay attention. I'm going to cut a sharp right, and we'll see what they do."

Jack watched over the seat while Guido veered to the right and then hit the gas pedal.

At the next corner, he jerked to the left.

"They did exactly the same thing," Jack said. "It's not by chance."

"I don't know where I picked them up, but I noticed the Audi back there on Piazza Santi Giovanni. They're after us."

Michelle clutched the safety belt tightly. "We're in trouble again, aren't we?"

"I don't know," Guido said. "We've got to think about this carefully. Obviously, we can't go to the location I intended. Got to be cautious since we have no idea what they're about."

"Won't be good," Michelle said. "We've been down this rocky road before."

"OK," Guido tried to sound calm. "We're not that far from the ruins of the first-century city of Rome. Tourists flock to that sight. I don't think they can chance an attack on you while you're mingling with sightseers. Too much risk of getting caught. I'll swing into the sight and drop you off at the back. Run into the excavations like you're part of an archaeological team. On second thought, you'll find a monumental drain that's been turned into a tunnel. It will take you under the ruins to the Temple of Minerva, the goddess of household tasks. Run down that drain tunnel and keep going no matter where the path leads. You should be safe hiding down there."

"What'll you do?" Jack said.

"I'm going to circle back on these tailgaters and see if I can get some idea of who they are."

"Listen to me!" Michelle barked. "We've already been down this road with a bombing, murder, and a chase through the crypts under the church. You need to stay out of their way. Keep going south."

"Thanks for the suggestion," Guido said. "I'm pulling into the parking lot of the ruins of ancient Rome. Get out and move it!"

Jack grabbed Michelle's arm with his good hand. "Start moving when the Jeep pulls to a halt. We've got to walk fast."

Michelle took a deep breath. "Something tells me that I won't like this."

Guido hit the brakes. "Go through that entrance over there by special parking. The authorities are likely to think you're archaeologists. You know how to speak the dirt digger's language. Get going."

The Jeep swung away, heading back toward the street. For a moment, Jack and Michelle watched Guido angling back into the traffic. Hardly a minute had passed when the black Audi emerged from the boulevard, aiming for the same parking lot.

"Let's go!" Jack said. "Get in that drainage tunnel!"

With one last look over her shoulder, Michelle watched the black car speed into the parking lot and stop. A man was getting out.

"They're on to us," Michelle gasped. "We've got to hurry!"

Jack led the way, dashing down the drain's wooden steps descending into the darkness. A single lightbulb dangled from a bare socket, only throwing dim light on the steps. Clutching the railing, the couple stumbled down the stairs, hoping that whoever was behind them hadn't seen their descent.

"I've been down here before," Jack whispered. "I remember that the tunnel runs into the ruins of the Temple of Minerva. In the seventeenth century, one of the pope's tore a load of stone out of the ruins, but I also know that they called it the Passageway Forum, because it once provided a road from the old Roman Forum to another part of the city. Keep your eyes open."

Distant footsteps scrambling down the top steps behind them echoed down the tunnel.

"Sounds like an irritated Tasmanian devil's after us," Michelle whispered. "He's bounding down those steps like a maniac on speed. Pick up the pace!"

At the bottom of the steps, the tunnel straightened, allowing them to run down the dirt floor toward the Temple. Footsteps behind them stopped, and Michelle paused to listen. The explosive roar of a gun vibrated through the dark and a bullet whistled by frighteningly close.

"God almighty!" Jack grabbed her hand. "I've got to fire back to hold him off." He dropped to one knee and fired straight into the tunnel.

Another wild shot careened into the tunnel wall above them, but all running had stopped. Grabbing Michelle's hand again, Jack dashed into the dilapidated Temple. Dropping behind the remnant of a waist-high wall, Jack pulled out the small flashlight and made a quick survey of the area.

"There's the entrance!" he whispered and pointed to his left. "That's a continuation of the street that once ran into the city. We've got to get over there and stay as low as possible. Start crawling."

On hands and knees, they shuffled along in the dark. Behind them they heard only a slight noise, which meant their pursuer had only slowed down.

Jack dropped beneath the bricked entryway opening into the black tunnel that once emptied into Rome's housing district for the general population. "I'll delay the shooter. Run down the tunnel, and no matter what you hear, don't stop."

"No, Jack. I can't leave you here alone."

"You can and you will! This is no game of 'got ya last.' Take my flashlight and get going."

Michelle backed away slowly. "I d-don't want—"

"Run!"

Michelle plunged into the darkness with her heart pounding and fear surging through her limbs. Her arms stiffened and her breathing became more difficult. Stumbling onto the hard floor, she scrambled to get back on her feet. Once again old scenes began swirling through her head. Flashes of fires exploded and debris blurred her vision. Pounding her chest, she knew another emotional attack mustn't stop her in the midst of the danger descending on them with the ferocity of a pack of starving wolves. She had to stop the post-traumatic stress surge from overwhelming her.

Switching on Jack's flashlight, Michelle edged forward. It looked like archaeologists had been digging in the sides of the walls and leaving hunks of rock strewn over the floor.

Two sudden exchanges of gunfire behind her caused her to run again. The path seemed to wind like a meandering trail through a long-gone forest. Piled together through the centuries, mounds of dirt around her stood as remnants of a bygone age. Michelle kept running.

The shallowness of her breathing made it hard to maintain a pace. Finally, she dropped down behind a pile of rocks. Another blast echoed down the tunnel with a fearsome roar. She had to get her mind organized and push the increasing trepidation away.

Michelle began crawling on her hands and knees into a side tunnel. Keeping the Walther pistol in her right hand, she inched her way through the blackness. The air felt damp, and a hint of moisture filled her nose. When she turned on the flashlight again, Michelle found a still pool spreading in front of her. Like a small pond, the surface of the quiet water stretched to a distant rock wall. She must have stumbled on to drainage from who knows how many centuries.

The black surface reflected like a giant mirror. With Jack's flashlight gleaming across the water, she recognized the black hair and dark eyes of a striking Italian woman and knew men found her attractive. The image wasn't a little girl crouching in the backseat of a car flying out of control. She had become someone different and always would be. What happened to that child was in the distant past and had to be kept there. The danger they were struggling with at this moment wasn't the same frightening experience from childhood. She could push the past away.

Squinting her eyes as tightly as possible, Michelle pressed with all her might to force the old images to float away. Slowly, the tide drifted out and calm returned. Even with a terrorist shooting at them, she could face the assault without allowing it to become confused with long ago. Michelle got back on her feet and steadied the gun she held in front of her. It was time to help her husband whether he wanted her assistance or not. They were a team, and running away down some dark tunnel didn't help either of them.

With cautious, slow steps, Michelle retraced her path back through the musty tunnel. All shooting had stopped and no other sounds echoed down the way. If she yelled, it might disclose her location and endanger both she and Jack. Michelle kept walking.

After a turn in the tunnel, she recognized a dim glow of the entrance straight ahead. Unless he'd been hurt, Jack had to be close. She crouched down on the floor, watching for a shape to emerge in front of her. She saw nothing. Could he have been hit? Could their attacker be waiting just on the other side? Absolutely. The only option was to wait in the dark and see.

Time hung heavy. Finally, she decided to try a ploy. With her gun held straight in front of her aimed at anyone that might come around the corner, she called out in a near whisper, "Jack?"

"I'm around the corner," a quiet voice said.

"You all right?"

"Yes," Jack said. "I think our adversary retreated. He probably didn't expect us to be carrying weapons."

"Can I come around the corner?"

"I think so. We've got to be cautious. The man could be lurking ahead of us in the tunnel."

Michelle crawled around the corner. "Jack, we must be doing something awfully right or big-time wrong to stir up this much of a struggle. Who'd think that the pursuit of the ending to a Gospel could set off World War III under the remnants of a three-thousand-year-old city?"

"Hand me my flashlight," Jack said. "Let's see if we can spot anyone in the tunnel who was shooting at me. Maybe an exchange of gunfire sent him sprinting back out of the tunnel. It's possible that the noise never got above the ground and no one knew we were down here slugging it out."

"Yeah, and we've got to make sure that nothing happened to Guido during the struggle."

42

Tourists walking around the ruins of ancient Rome watched from a distance while police combed the area around the drain hole. Detective Alfredo Pino walked back and forth in front of Jack and Michelle sitting on a broken marble column, seeming genuinely upset. The Townsends sat quietly, saying little.

"If I hadn't worked on my English for years, I wouldn't even know how to talk to you people," Pino said. "I have more trouble keeping up with you than any five criminals in Rome." He kept scribbling in a small notebook.

Jack looked at the ground and said nothing.

"You've gotten yourselves involved in a murder, an explosion, a personal attack in a church with a man killed, and now a gunfight in an archaeological ruins. Don't you think that's amazing for two people who say they're nothing but scholars?"

"Remember that the explosion put Jack in the hospital and killed our associate," Michelle protested. "We certainly wouldn't have been responsible for such a tragedy."

"That's the only thing that keeps me from thinking you're running drugs or pushing stolen automobiles," Pino said. "I swear! How can you get into so much difficulty when you say you're only trying to figure out Bible problems."

"Look, Alfredo," Jack said. "We are as baffled by these attacks as you are. We simply don't have any better explanation than what we've discussed so far. Some people think it's all connected to that explosion in the metro system back in September. Others feel the Vatican has been offended by our explorations."

"The Vatican!" Alfredo Pino exploded. "Lord, help us out on that one. Please, don't mention that idea again around me."

"I'm only trying to help."

"That thought isn't helpful for certain," Pino said.

"I honestly don't know what else to tell you except the shooter was definitely trying to kill us," Jack said. "Getting shot under an archaeological dig isn't exactly my idea of an indoor sport."

Alfredo Pino shook his head. "We have our staff working on your problems night and day. It hasn't been easy. I'd suggest you limit what you do on the streets until we get this mess cleared up."

"Believe me, we'll do our best," Michelle said. "We're not interested in being used for target practice. Please believe me. We're not out looking for trouble."

"Everything OK?" Father Blake came walking up. "I heard you were being chased again."

"Ah!" Jack exclaimed. "Father Blake, please tell this detective that we're not causing all the trouble we have experienced. I'm afraid the police think that we're the source of all the turmoil. Can you help us?"

"I can vouch for them," Father Blake said. "These are good people being chased by bad men."

Alfredo Pino scratched his head and flipped his notebook shut. "I'll take your word for it, Father, but this is getting old. Tell them to keep their heads down next time." The detective walked away.

"I think I once mentioned something about a hate group chasing Americans like they were wild turkeys in hunting season," Blake said. "As I recall, no one listened to me."

"We're listening," Jack said. "Carrying those guns you gave us saved us down there in the Minerva Temple or we'd have bullet holes in our heads."

"If nothing else, guns are a step forward in keeping you alive. I'm telling you these terrorist are mean guys. By the way, have you seen that Dr. Albert Stein guy lately? Seems like he's disappeared."

"No one's heard of him since the first day after the offices got blasted," Michelle said. "Maybe he went away."

"I don't think so," Blake said. "Just wondering."

"I guess we're free to go," Jack said. "Want a ride anywhere, Father? Guido will be waiting to pick us up. We can take you."

"No, no," Blake said. "I'll be off on my rounds, but you people need to pay careful attention to who's following behind you."

"We were," Michelle said. "That's how the whole chase scene started. The thugs were following us in a black Audi. We ran down the underground tunnel to keep them from blasting us."

"Black Audi? Hmm. Well, you got away this time," Blake started walking away. "Keep watching your back."

"Sure thing." Jack took Michelle's hand. "Believe me. We're trying harder to stay out of trouble than either of you two guys believe."

Wearing a black overcoat, leather gloves, and a wide-brimmed hat to protect against the cool wind as well as to conceal his identity, the man hurried across the piazza and crossed the street. Staying close to the walls of San Pietro in Vincoli Church, he looked up and down the street before entering a side door. Staying in the shadows, he looked carefully to make sure no one was nearby. An inside contact had already told him that this one door would not be locked even though the front doors were secured. Certainly, none of the staff would be around at 2:00 in the morning.

For a moment, he paused to stare at the magnificent ceiling decorated with a fresco commemorating the supposed miracle of the chains. San Pietro's claim to fame was their possession of the relic of the chains that held St. Peter. Supposedly one set was used in Jerusalem and another set fashioned when Peter was held in the Mamertine Prison in Rome. The legend proclaimed that when placed side by side, the two sets of chain merged into the one chain and cuffs that the church now exhibited. Overlook the fact that there's no record Peter was chained in Jerusalem before he was captured in Rome.

Forget the medieval nonsense, he thought. *The ceiling is impressive and let it go at that. I've got business elsewhere.* He hurried toward a side chapel waiting behind closed doors.

Pulling a black face mask from his pocket, he positioned it over his face. His connection with the church had garnered a promise that the chapel door would be unlocked, and he could expect his two comrades to be waiting inside. Inside the chapel only light from the street cast shadows over the chairs. Two men sat in the rear with face masks concealing their heads. He hurried to the back and sat down in from of the men.

"Any problems getting in the church?" the general asked.

Both men shook their heads.

"Unlocked just as you said it would be," the first man said. "Walked in like I owned the works."

The second man only grunted.

"OK," the general said. "Where are we tonight?"

"Nobody's getting our message," the first man said. "They're not finding what we left behind telling what we're about."

"At least, they haven't caught us," his associate replied.

"Not much consolation in that twist of fate," the first man said. "The whole point of these strikes was to warn about American intervention. This last go-round didn't even touch that issue. Lucky I didn't get shot. We fell on our faces again."

"We've got to do better," the general said. "Be more decisive. The newspapers like to call us The Scorpion. We've got to strike like one. Really stick the stinger in deep."

"Forget the American Embassy," the second man said. "I've been casing that bull pen and noticed they've beefed up the police. The only reason to mess with them is if we wanted to commit suicide."

"Here's what I think," the general declared. "Tonight we hit an American airplane parked at Ciampino Airport. There's one out that was flown in this morning. A nice small American Super ATR sitting out there waiting for us to smash it. It shouldn't be any hassle to get in because security at Ciampino is nothing like Leonardo da Vinci airport. We can hit 'em fast, hard, and get out. May have to shoot a couple of guards, but that should be about it."

"Now wait," the second man said. "We haven't even cased the field, and killing our own countrymen is another matter"

"I checked out the scene," the general said defiantly. "And I've got wire cutters in my car to get through the back fence. The fact we do the job tonight will catch everyone off guard. And if we hit an Italian or two, it's regrettable but necessary."

"Yeah, but—"

"This time we're going to spray a big painted message on the tarmac showing them that The Scorpion has struck and the target is American intervention in the world economy," the general said. "No question about our purposes after they read that script. Everything is in my car, and we can leave now."

"Excellent," the first man said. "This will make up for our botched attempt on the Townsends."

"Oh man!" the second man mumbled and cursed. "We could lose our necks on this one."

"What are you grumbling about?" the general hissed. "When we started these strikes you were with us from top to bottom. You turning jelly-belly on us? Getting gutless?"

The man glanced back and forth between the two men and squirmed. "No, no. Nothing like that."

"Then cut the whining and let's get moving."

"Can't we at least give this a day to think about?"

Reaching into his heavy topcoat, the leader pulled out a Beretta 81 handgun. "Do I hear resistance? Maybe I'm hearing wrong."

"OK, OK." the man's voice rose an octave. "I withdraw my question."

The leader kept the Beretta leveled straight in front of him. "I've got night-vision goggles and a personal-size 20-watt fuel cell should we need power for some reason. Explosives are in my trunk. I'm ready to hit the airport."

The first man nodded. "This ought to prove interesting."

The second man said nothing.

43

KLAUS BURCHEL PICKED UP THE *IL MESSAGGERO* NEWSPAPER AND GLANCED at the headlines. After a second look, he hurried to Dr. Albert Stein's apartment behind the Pantheon. Clamoring up the stairs, he knocked on the door and waited to be summoned.

"Enter," Stein's growl echoed from a distance. "Make it snappy."

Burchel entered quickly, made a slight bow, and extended the paper to his boss.

"So?" Stein glanced at the *Il Messaggero* but didn't take it. "What?"

"Another bombing last night," Burchel said. "The story says that this Scorpion group struck at the Ciampino airport and damaged an American airplane as well as leaving a message sprayed on the concrete. Shot a couple of guards. Those guys really hate Americans."

"Good for them," Stein grumbled.

"Yes, and the police don't have any clues about their identity yet."

"The police are morons," Stein said. "Absolute pack of fools."

"I thought you'd want to know what's happened."

"Let's see." Stein snatched the newspaper. For several moments, he glanced at the article. Finally, he said, "If they hate Americans so much, maybe they'll go after the Townsends."

"I wonder if they have not already struck," Klaus answered. "The explosion at the house might have blown away some message they left behind. Who else would have hit the Townsends' office after I went to the trouble of wiring the whole building for communication?"

"It fits," Stein said. "The police certainly ran me off before I got to take a good look through the wreckage. Yes, it makes good sense even if these Scorpion boys are rank amateurs." He pointed his finger at Klaus. "And that's what they are! Real pros would have blown that American airplane into a million pieces, not just damaged it."

"Agreed."

"You've done better since you returned." Stein leaned back in his chair and eyed his lackey cynically. "Any explanations? Have you learned anything?"

"I was surprised you sent a man to bring me back. Even though the guy frightened me, your allowing my restoration has inspired me to work harder."

Stein snorted. "You've had your problems, Burchel, but you also have promise and that grabs my attention. Of course, I never knew your grandfather, but Richard Baer was a great man who performed an expeditious job in running Auschwitz. I am sure he passed on significant heredity that still resides in you somewhere. You've got to release it! Let it grow! Even though you have wallowed in decadence, I am depending on that hereditary dimension from your past to arise to the occasion. Is that possible?"

"I am doing my best."

"About time." Stein crossed his arms over his large chest. "We will anticipate results."

Klaus shrugged. "I'm trying."

Stein turned back to his desk. "We have learned two important matters from the Townsends so far. They are still searching for the lost ending of Mark's Gospel, which is hidden somewhere in Rome. Along the way, they stumbled on to a second gem. This so-called Brown Book, *The Prologue of James*, could be the jackpot. Since we are the only ones who know the full truth about their two objectives, we are positioned to steal either or both documents before the Townsends make another smash publishing hit with a breakthrough discovery."

"You've heard of this *Prologue of James*?" Klaus asked.

"Never! And I've studied everything in the library. It's either a total fraud or the breakthrough of the century." Stein pulled at his shagging chin. "The Nag Hammadi Library unearthed in Egypt by some local numskull peasant was a collection of twelve leather-bound papyrus books and an individual tractate. At first, everyone thought it was nonsense or a fraud. Quickly, they concluded it was three cherries on a million-dollar slot machine. Takes a while but once the truth is out, the archaeologist discovering the find goes right up to the top of the ladder."

"So, this *Prologue* might be nothing?"

"Wouldn't say nothing, but it might be a dead-end street."

Klaus scratched his head. "What would you bet on, Dr. Stein?"

"With the Roman Catholic Church trying to hide it? I'd bet it's bigger than Piazza San Pietro. We could be talking blowing the lid off the church."

"That would be some accomplishment," Klaus said.

"Absolutely."

"Unfortunately, the Townsends' windows have been shut since it turned cold, and I haven't been able to pick up much of anything with my eavesdropping device. It's hard to say where they are in their search at this point."

"This only means we must keep on their trail with constancy," Stein said. "Townsend's wife has been working more than I expected. So far, we've been able to stay on top of where they're going. Following them through Rome's heavy traffic wasn't easy, but they didn't lose us. That's an important sign that we can keep up with them."

Klaus scowled. "We know for sure they're carrying weapons now. I wouldn't have expected either of them to be shooting back. Of course, this raises the ante. It's going to be much more difficult to stop them when they're running around armed to the teeth."

"And what does that mean to you, Burchel?" Stein asked with more than a touch of cynicism in his voice. "Makes you run for the cellar?"

Burchel shook his head. "I swear I'm going to kill that worthless dog yet."

"OK. Next time *do it*."

44

WITH POLICE STATIONED OUTSIDE THE TOWNSENDS' APARTMENT, THEIR abode felt much safer. Over Michelle's protest, Jack still took his morning subway ride to the Dar Poeta café for the newspaper, a survey of the people walking by, and his favorite artichokes cooked *alla giudia*. With the continuing upheaval in their lives, starting a day with style put tranquility back in the turmoil and seemed to press order into disorder. He needed to think and did that best alone.

Jack massaged his arm where the plaster cast had been and felt muscle returning. Before long, he'd be exercising with heavy weights and then the right proportions would return. How could he languish in despair when they'd been able to slip by the catastrophes? With police watching the street and the alleys, they could sleep at night without fretting over an assailant dropping in from some unguarded entry. Normality might be on the horizon. As soon as he got back on his exercise routine, even his body would be completely in shape to take on the chaotic world.

Guido would be returning, and they'd go after unearthing the ending to Mark's Gospel. He had disappeared after the attack under the Roman ruins to give the excitement and confusion time to settle, but time was running out, and he'd be back soon to continue the search. Unfortunately, he didn't get a look at who was in the black Audi pursuing them.

"Your artichokes *alla guidia*." The waiter set the dish in front of him. "You are the first person to order our specialty this morning." Luichi smiled. "A little early for most folks."

"Of course. Then again, I live on the unusual side. Thank you, Luichi."

The waiter smiled and sauntered away.

Jack took a bite and closed his eyes in a moment of delight. "Excellent," he murmured to himself and took another fork full.

A rotund woman wearing a solid green dress came strolling by. Over the top of her attire, she had a white baker's apron with a bright pink scarf tied over her black hair and hanging loose down her neck. Her ponderous body bounced down the street like a half-inflated basketball as she made her way to what was probably a meager paying job in one of the many piazzas. The clash of pink and green seemed strange and out of place, but a collision of colors reflected so much that was Rome. The Santa Maria Church made for worship was actually a bone collection. Detective Alfredo Pino worked on finding their attackers but seemed to think them guilty of something or the other because of the continuing assaults. An ancient city filled with thousands of years of priceless buried treasures hid the hoard of the past so completely it was nearly impossible to find anything. Contradictions hid in every alley and lurked behind the endless monuments on every street corner. He and Michelle had taken on a formidable task when they waded into the sea of paradoxes in trying to find the ending to Mark's Gospel.

Jack bit into another artichoke and held it in his mouth, savoring the flavor. Artichokes had a smooth, gliding sensation, sliding across his tongue. The aroma of the Roman-Jewish style of cooking lingered. The problem was that Rome had a billion hiding pockets. Everywhere one turned, new excavations turned up. Jack knew that the document could be anywhere and that was what made their chase so frustrating.

He thought of Dov Sharon. Even though much younger than either he or Michelle, Dov had been like a teasing brother who could turn anything into a chuckle. His dry sense of humor had kept them going and giggling through the hardest of times. The tragedies his family endured decade after decade had taught him it was better to laugh one's way through difficulty than to succumb to moroseness. And now he was gone.

Tears edged their way forward. Since coming out of the hospital, Jack had not allowed himself to think about what had occurred the day of the bombing. Getting his head back together had been difficult enough that he had avoided mentioning Dov to Michelle. Going on without his friend seemed almost impossible. For the first time, he let himself feel what had been lurking beneath the surface. Tears broke loose and ran down his cheeks. For several minutes, he kept his head ducked while his body shook gently beneath the weight of the loss of Dov's life. Finally, the heaviness settled some and he felt he could breath easier. Jack sighed and tried to let the pain slide. He quietly allowed a sense of resolution to set in and kept nibbling at the artichokes.

Abruptly, his mind opened as clearly as turning a page in a book. He could hear Dov speaking to him almost as surely as if he were sitting across the table from him.

"James grew up with Jesus and must have watched his brother become an entirely different person . . ." The remembrance of the voice drifted away and then returned. "Did he consider Jesus a fanatic? a genius? deluded?" Once again the voice slipped away.

Jack sat entranced, staring at the empty chair. He could almost smell the ancient stale scent of their old office. It carried the odor of carpets left on the floor through decades and seldom cleaned. The walls imparted a tasteless hint of peeling paint. The memory of the day of the bomb rushed back to him.

"Something in that document profoundly troubles the Roman Catholic Church," Dov had said. "That's why they've kept it concealed under lock and key. I now know where it is hidden."

The scene disappeared like a soap bubble popping. Jack lurched forward. One second it was there; the next it was gone. Whatever Dov started to tell him about the location of the document vanished into blackness. But one fact remained. Jack was certain that Dov had told him where *The Prologue of James* was hidden. Unfortunately, the revelation had disappeared with the blast.

Two old cronies walked by. Like typical Italians, the first man wore an old fedora hat with a sport coat that he must have slipped on his back every day for the past thirty years. A gray sweater covered a maroon shirt buttoned at the neck. The white-haired man talking next to him wore a light blue sweater under his dark blue sport coat with gray worn-slick pants. Both men were shaking their hands fervently as they talked. The Italian language was as much about gesture as about words. Like the multitude of old men all over Rome dressed exactly like them, they went on down the street indifferent to the explosive circumstances erupting across the city.

Jack couldn't be like them, not allowing tragic events to roll on down the street like the Tiber River on an endless journey. He couldn't let his sudden insight be just another blip in his memory. He had to recover what Dov had told him. The trouble was the mirage had disappeared, and he couldn't open it by exerting sheer willpower.

Finishing his artichokes, he opened the newspaper. *Il Messaggero's* headline story described the bombing of an American airplane at Ciampino airport. Terrorists with The Scorpion organization had broken through a back fence and shot a couple of guards before damaging the American Super ATR parked on the tarmac. A message had been sprayed on the cement warning American capitalism to stay out of Italy. Anarchist were still on the loose. Jack immediately folded the paper and stuck it under his arm. Laying the money on the table with a tip for Luichi, he trotted back to the subway. He had to get home before Michelle picked up this story so he could attempt to soften the blown.

The subway lurched back and forth in predictable unpredictable jerks. Hanging on to a pole, Jack tried to read the article again. Some guard had seen three men leave through a hole cut in a wire fence, but wasn't sure if that was the number of the assault team. Maybe more than three men had been involved. The police thought so. The story said national security was at stake, and the police would be beefing up their watch. Nice thoughts, but it didn't mean much. Jack had seen the police at work up close and wasn't reassured. Michelle certainly wouldn't be.

For a moment he thought again about the sudden encounter that had returned only minutes earlier. Had that experience of Dov talking to him been real or did it pop out of the disorder that had ruled his mind during the past weeks? Could he have just made it up? Maybe the bombing had made him unstable. Then again, the recollection could be extremely important. Everything about the recall had seemed real, but what if it wasn't? The idea felt unnerving. It wasn't only a memory, but the entire episode might be an exposure of his crumbling stability.

The subway car slid to a stop and Jack bounded through the door. Without slowing, he rushed for the gate. Within the usual time, he was back at the apartment where Michelle sat at the kitchen table reading. Attempting to create a look of casualness, Jack walked into the living room at a much slower pace.

"How's things going?" he ask.

Michelle looked at him for a moment. "Why do you ask?"

"Oh, just wanted to make sure you were OK."

"Because if I heard that the Ciampino Airport got bombed last night, I might freak out?" She held up the *Il Messaggero* newspaper.

Jack caught his breath.

"Yes, the story is all over Rome this morning and I haven't gone crazy yet," Michelle said. "Who knows? I may slide over the edge at any moment. Actually, I'm doing quite well. Living through a bombing and two attempts to kill me seems to have helped suppress my problem. You can breathe easier, Jack. I'm as cool as a candy bar."

"What a relief," Jack said. "I thought that maybe—"

"Yes, I know what you thought and you can stop being my father. All right?"

Jack walked in and sat across the table from her. "I'm not trying to play parent. I simply worry about you."

Michelle leaned across the table and kissed him. "You're the kindest man in the world and I appreciate your constant concern, but I'm truly fine."

"Michelle, I've been down the street," Jack paused.

"At Dar Poeta," Michelle's voice took on a condescending air. "I can smell the artichokes on your breath. Let's be a little more exact."

"OK. OK. I was sitting down there reading the page when I had a flashback. At least, I thought I did. It seems that Dov did tell me where *The Prologue* document was hidden, but I simply can't bring it back to mind. The entire experience might be a figment of my imagination, but I can't lay it down. Before we go any further in our search with Guido, I think I ought to go see that priest who leveled with him. I believe his name was Father Donnello. Maybe he would be equally straightforward with me."

"You had some kind of remembrance about what happened just before the bomb went off?"

"Yes, it sort of popped up when I remembered how much I mourned Dov's death." Jack stopped and couldn't say anymore. His eyes filled with tears. "I guess I've been avoiding allowing myself to think about him." It became harder for him to speak. "Sorry." He choked up.

"Dear, it's OK. Don't fight it. You need to let your emotions out."

Jack wiped his eyes. "Sure." He sniffed. "I have to give remembering a big try," Jack said. "I must talk to that old man. If for no other reason than my own sanity."

45

BECAUSE VATICAN SECURITY AGENTS KNEW DR. JACK TOWNSEND, PASSING through their check points proved to be only a momentary pause. Even though he was a Protestant, Vatican officials liked his and Michelle's *An Answer to the Cynics* and had on occasion recommended the book. Controversy over the book from the theological Left had only propelled his reputation up the ladder with the Roman overseers. Being considered a friend provided freedom in wandering through the Vatican Library and Secret Archives.

Once beyond surveillance, Jack walked quickly down the elaborate corridor. The ceilings towering above him had been covered with gold designs increasing a sense of their height. Artists had massaged frescos of saints and theologians into the exquisite designs giving the hall an overpowering sensation. Once inside the second room in the Secret Archives, Jack paused to study the dramatically colorful ceilings covered with angels flying through a painted sky of elegant proportions. Around the walls, pictures of long-dead heroes like Steven I the Saint, Duke of Hungary, and Demetrius, Duke of Croatia, as well as the coat of arms of Cardinal Scipione Borghese reflected an era when the Pope reigned as king of all kings rather than only a spiritual leader. Jack had studied the details of the lives of the saints and didn't pause for a second look. Unfortunately, the ornamented room reeked of medieval opulence. As he had previously done with Dov at his side, Jack worked his way toward the back of the archives, stopping here and there to study some obscure detail in order to leave an impression that he was working in the archives on an assignment.

Once he reached the rear, he entered the room where Dov had first worked with the collection of fragments unearthed in a street excavation in Rome. The dusty box containing pieces of manuscripts sat just as he and Dov had last left it. Once assured no one was observing him, he slowly disappeared through the obscure door that opened into steps descending to the final basement and the area of an ongoing archaeological dig. Shutting the door carefully so as to not make a sound, he started down the worn granite stairs.

A few lightbulbs attached to the walls kept him from dropping into opaque blackness. Dov had come down this same hidden descent over the slick granite. No one would go bounding down this chasm with any speed.

No record existed of how this hidden area had been developed, which meant the Vatican was still keeping it under wraps. Probably they wanted to plumb the depths of whatever had once been down there in the Circus of Nero and Caligula dig before they let anyone in on the big secrets. The fact that old Father Donnello had been banished to the bottom of the ladder had its own implication. Whatever he had done, Jack figured the old man had probably offended somebody big time.

A musty smell drifted up from the bottom as if someone were digging in soft dirt. Probably archaeologists had already gone to work for the day. Jack turned the corner and observed three men bending over holes in the ground far back in a recessed area, slowly, painfully working to expose what had once been a wall at the side of the racetrack. Chariots must have once raced around the outer perimeter of the track two thousand years ago. For a moment, he allowed his imagination to re-create the horses with their imperial officers trotting around the arena while the crowds cheered wildly. The scene reminded him of the majesty that had once been the Roman Empire.

When Jack reached the bottom of the stairs, the office of the priest stood not far ahead next to racks of books and manuscripts of antiquity. To descend to this pit of ancient history day after day took a special variety of endurance. Perhaps the old priest had a gift of tenacity. Jack walked toward the door and knocked.

"*Che?*" echoed from the office.

"*Un amico,*" Jack answered.

"A friend?" The door opened slightly and a white-bearded head poked around the door.

"It's Jack Townsend. Remember me?"

"Why, yes! You are Dov Sharon's colleague. The author of *An Answer to the Cynics.* A surprise indeed.

"Might I come in for a moment?"

The old man nodded. "Most certainly. I seldom get visitors down here. In fact, Dov was about the only new face I've seen in this hole in years." Father Donnello sneered. "I think they do everything possible to keep me in isolation."

Jack walked in and glanced around. Sitting down on the only footstool in the small room, he noticed that the white-haired old man's scraggly beard hung at odd angles from his face. Bent over with a slight hump on his back, his skinny arms dangled like toothpicks. Probably always small in stature, Donnello left the impression that time and a touch of some disease like osteoporosis had shrunken him. Wearing a clerical collar with a faded black shirt and pants, he gave the appearance of a figure emerging out of antiquity.

"A little tea?" The priest pointed to his beat-up old tin pot. "Maybe a coffee? The water's hot." He rubbed his hands together. "It can get cool down here."

"Thank you," Jack said. "Some hot tea would warm me on this cool November day. Certainly."

"I haven't seen Dov in weeks." Father Donnello scurried around setting out the cups. "I suppose he has been busy."

"No," Jack's voice fell. "I'm afraid not." He took a deep breath and looked at the floor. "You haven't heard?"

"Heard?" Father Donnello stopped. "What do you mean?"

"A bomb was placed under our offices," Jack's words tumbled out with awkwardness. "We've had a hard time making sense out of the explosion. I barely survived, but Dov was killed."

The old priest froze. Color drained from his already pale face. For a moment, he stood speechless with his mouth partially open. "No," he barely whispered. "Please, no."

Jack could only nod his head.

Father Donnello dropped into his desk chair like lead hitting the floor. He pounded his chest as if trying to make his heart start to beat again. "I-I d-don't know w-what to say." He rubbed his mouth and shook his head. "I-I'm speechless."

"Dov's death has been difficult for me to face," Jack said. "I've only been able to think about it quite recently. His demise has been a stunning blow."

The priest looked away, but tears formed in his eyes. "I didn't know Dov long, but our relationship quickly became intense. The young man touched a nerve that ran through everything I have been about. I wanted to help him, befriend him." He kept shaking his head. "I-I just can't believe he's gone."

"We worked together closely and were intensely involved in a couple of current projects. His help always proved invaluable . . . but . . . now . . . it's over."

Father Donnello pushed his coffee mug aside. "Yes, he talked about your work in finding the original ending to the Gospel of Mark. I admired the effort, and we discussed it in some detail."

"And we were working on the project that you call the Brown Book."

The priest flinched. "We don't speak of that document down here."

"I understand, but it has raised several questions that I must ask you today. Will you allow me the time?"

Getting up out of his chair, Father Donnello went to the door and looked out. Seeing no one, he turned to a small window in the back and opened a Venetian blind. The only people in the area were the three archaeologists working far away on their dig. Closing the blind, he pulled his chair closer to Jack's stool.

"Dov understood how confidential these matters must be. His life had been lived under the cover of threat and danger. He knew well that some issues can only be whispered about and never spoken of in public."

Jack nodded. "I didn't live in his Jewish world, but I understand it well. In addition, to surviving the bombing, my wife and I have been under attack and endured gunfire twice since the explosion. We currently must fear for our lives as well."

"You too!" The old man's eyes widened in shock. "Oh my! How terrible!"

"I don't come here casually, Father Donnello. I need your help because we are now boiling in the same cauldron of hot oil that Dov perished in. This is why I ask for your confidence."

"What do you need to know?"

"Did anyone else besides you and Dov know about our search for *The Prologue of James?*"

The old man shook his head. "I don't think so."

"You know that my wife and I work to protect the integrity of the Scripture. Our response to the cynics was just such an attempt."

"Yes, I know and am deeply appreciative."

Jack scooted closer and lowered his voice further. "I can't imagine anyone in the Vatican wanting to attack us over our search for the ending to Mark's Gospel. Apparently *The Prologue* is another matter. Do you know of anyone in the Vatican who would try to kill us because we were looking for this book?"

Father Donnello kept rubbing his chin. "You are a scholar and know our history through medieval times well. We've had everyone from Cesare Borgia and his murderous ways to Popes promoting their own children for high office. The Vatican has been behind monstrous crusades, and some say Pius XII failed to protect the Jews when Hitler came to town. We've had great and powerful spiritual leaders as well as popes who were nothing more than conniving charlatans. Yes, there have been a few scoundrels around capable of killing, but I know of no one who knew about Dov's interest in *The Prologue.* I think I can absolutely tell you that no one in the Vatican has been after you."

Jack ran his hand nervously through his hair. "I appreciate your candor. It's most helpful to be able to eliminate the Vatican from our list of potential attackers."

"I truly believe you can," Donnello said. "If for no other reason than no one knows about what's going on but me."

"Then, I have one more question. Before Dov died, he led me to believe that you had told him where *The Prologue of James* was hidden."

The priest said nothing.

"I think Dov told me where the document is hidden. Moments later the bomb exploded, and for days I didn't know who I was. Slowly, my memory began returning, but this piece of the puzzle hasn't come back. I can't decide if Dov told me or I dreamed the idea. Can you help me by clarifying what happened?"

Once again, the priest pulled at his chin. "I never speak of these matters. Dov was an exception. My love of the Jewish people cracked the veneer that I learned to keep around myself as a priest. I should never have told him what I did."

"Then, you did relate confidential information to him about where this document is hidden?"

"Why do you want to know?" Donnello's voice took on a more disdainful inflection.

"I have two reasons," Jack said. " I am concerned about my own stability. The hospital thought that I wouldn't survive the bombing. Then, it took me some time to regain much of my stability. It's important that I not walk around like some sort of zombie, thinking that I remember what never happened."

"Hmm, I can appreciate that posture. What else is rattling around in your head?"

"I can't understand why you would have told Dov where the document is hidden after all these years of silence."

"I suppose you'd have to be a Jew to understand."

Jack blinked several times. "I don't grasp your answer."

"The Jewish people have suffered such persecution that they have a right to have a break now and then. I believed Dov Sharon to be such a person, and I knew he would handle the information well."

"But he told me," Jack said. " Wouldn't that validate your passing the same information on to me?"

"I can't answer you today," Donnello said. "I will have to give this considerable thought. I suppose I must measure your intentions carefully."

"I understand. Just remember that Dov considered me to be his brother."

46

THE AFTERNOON SUN DRIFTED THROUGH THE LOCKED FRONT WINDOW AND the lacy curtains, throwing light across the Townsends' living room. Detective Alfredo Pino paced nervously back and forth across their living room. Father Don Blake sat passively in a chair across from Michelle. Pino's constant fidgeting and sighing made her nervous, but she tried not to overreact.

"Really, detective," Michelle said. "My husband will be home shortly. He only had to make a trip to the Vatican Library. We don't have any problems to fret over today."

"No problems!" Pino exclaimed. "For people who've been nearly blown to Sicily, you have no problems? If so, I don't know what a problem is!"

"Come now, Alfredo," the priest said. "There's no need to go into orbit."

"But she said he'd be back thirty minutes ago," the detective protested and pointed at Michelle. "I don't see him."

"That was a figure of speech," Michelle said. "If nothing else, the traffic can slow anybody down."

"Our friend detective Pino tends to get a little nervous on occasion," Father Blake said. "Personally, I don't think any of us are in a great hurry."

"Oh, really?" Pino barked. "I have important business elsewhere. Let's be frank. I'm going to have to get on my way if Dr. Townsend doesn't show up quickly."

"He's coming any moment," Michelle protested. "I know he's interested in talking with you."

A knock sounded from the front door.

"Let me see who's here," Michelle said and walked toward the door. She peered through the peephole. "My goodness, it's Guido Valentino." She swung the door open.

"Buonasera," Guido said. "I see you have company."

"Come in. We're waiting for Jack to return. He should be here any moment."

Guido walked in. "Ah, Father Blake. How are you?"

"Fine. Yes, I'm fine. I believe you know Detective Pino?"

Guido bowed politely. "We've met several times while walking around the wreckage of the old offices after the bombing. Yes, good to see you sir."

Pino nodded politely with a hint of being put upon.

The back door of the apartment burst open. "I'm home," Jack called out through the kitchen.

"Here he is," Michelle said. "I knew Jack would be here any second."

Jack walked into the living room. "Well, to what do I owe the honor of a visit from my American chaplain and the Italian champion of justice both at the same moment?"

"We have matters to discuss," Detective Pino responded icily. "Perhaps, we should retire to a more secluded room?"

"Guido is privy to everything we're about," Jack said. "He was driving the car when the chase began that sent us running for cover in the ancient Roman ruins. Signor Pino, you can talk freely in front of Guido."

Pino looked as if he didn't appreciate the situation, but would have to accept it. Looking "put upon" seemed to be his forte.

"Jack, I can leave," Father Blake said.

"Heavens no!" Michelle said. "You were the one who got me to the hospital and have been with us all the way. You're fine, Father. Stay put."

Pino pulled out his small notebook and began writing. "OK, I am noting that we are talking with a larger group in a conversation that has been approved by the Townsends." He made quick flourishes across the page. "Please everyone sit down."

Michelle watched the men take a seat in the crowded small living room. Probably this conversation would only be routine, but she hoped Pino had come up with something new.

"We are still attempting to make sense out of the bombing and the two attempts that have been made on your lives," Pino said. "We have two strong suspects. Dr. Albert Stein is one. Then, we have the terrorist group called The Scorpion." He paused and looked at Jack. "I hate to mention it, but you suggested that the Vatican might have some involvement."

"I'm late because I've been exploring the possibilities in that accusation," Jack said. "I've been checking out the possibilities, and this morning I made inquiries. In my opinion, you can cross the Vatican off of your list.

For the first time, Alfredo Pino looked relieved. "Excellent! You are not a detective, Dr. Townsend, but I am going to accept your word on this matter. Running down that alley could have turned into a riot. Don't worry. I'm dropping the Vatican from my list immediately." He made a quick notation.

"As I was saying," Pino continued. "We've got this strange fellow named Albert Stein. Problem is he's disappeared, and we don't know where he's hiding. I say hiding because he appears to have simply vanished and that isn't natural. I'm sure he's somewhere around Rome slithering around among our 3 million people. We simply haven't been able to nail down where the man is holed up."

"Stein is one troubling entity," Jack said. "He's been on my back for a long time. Of course, he's got the financial resources to cover his tracks because his family owns the Stein Motor Company in the outskirts of Berlin."

"Stein Motors?" Pino stiffened. "You didn't tell me that earlier."

"I guess I overlooked that detail. My mind's been somewhat wobbly since the explosion." Jack massaged his forehead. "Afraid I'm still trying to get everything back in order. Since the concussion I forget things."

Pino kept scribbling. "Stein Motors should make it much easier. We'll check out that angle."

"What's your next issue?" Father Blake ask.

"We still think the terrorist group that hit the subways and the Ciampino Airport could be behind your problems," Pino continued. "As strange as it sounds, they seem to hate Americans enough to blow up your offices. If they're instigators in this chaos, they probably won't quit until they've hit you hard again. Trouble is that we're still running down their identity."

Father Blake gave Jack a telling glance.

"Exactly what does that mean, Signor Pino?" Michelle asked.

"You're far from off the hook," the detective said. "We keep your apartment and the church under surveillance and will continue to do so. However, that doesn't mean these people have retreated one inch. They are a vicious group of hatchet men. We don't how large their group is, but they could be many men."

"I think we've got that picture," Jack said. "We still have the weapons that Father Blake gave us, and the guns offer some assurance."

"They're also fine Christian people," the priest quickly added. "The Townsends depend on the hand of Almighty Providence to hover above them. God is the true source of their strength, but a little help on the side doesn't hurt anything."

Alfredo Pino didn't say anything, but gave them an askance look.

"I can assure you that we've done nothing to attract these attacks," Michelle said. "We're keeping our heads down for sure."

"We've been over this before," Pino said. "My strongest advice remains to continue on that secluded path. You have my card. If anything comes up pertaining to these attacks or attackers, please call me at once."

"We will," Michelle said.

"I'll be going now." The detective closed his notebook. "My best to all. I can let myself out." With a slam of the door, he was gone.

"Alfredo is interesting," Father Blake said. "But I think he watched one too many American detective movies. When he gets nervous, it generally is a sign that he's not sure where the train is going. I think this latest attack at the airport really flipped Pino and his men. Everybody from the army to the prime minister is in a tizzy over that one." He picked up his hat. "I'll be going too. Don't worry, my friends. Everybody's hard at work on this situation."

Michelle opened the front door. "Thanks for coming. Keep us in your prayers."

"Keep those guns close at hand." Don Blake smiled, nodded, and was gone.

Michelle listened to his footsteps disappearing down the stairs and then shut the door.

"Everyone seems to be interested in us this morning," Jack said. "Not exactly the notoriety that I was hoping for. I liked that first article by Mario Corsini in the *Il Messaggero* much better. I think the reason for Pino's visit was to pick up any clues he might have missed earlier. Apparently, my tidbit about Stein Motors pressed one of his button. We'll see."

Michelle sat down. "Guys, what's our next step?"

"I came this morning because I strongly believe we must keep moving," Guido said. "Matters are coming to a head. If anybody has been getting inside information on your work, they already know of my involvement. I believe we must move and act quickly. I would suggest that we finish the job tonight."

"Tonight?" Michelle exclaimed. "You're serious?"

"I am. Jack's clarified where the Vatican is so we can discount men in clerical collars with machine guns. That's important because of where I want to take you. In my opinion, I believe we ought to move immediately."

Jack grinned. "I can't possibly tell you how ready I am to go, but we've got the problem of police surrounding this building. They'll see us coming out."

"That's why I think we need to move at night," Guido said. "Once the cover of darkness falls, we'll be able to travel easier and shake off surveillance. This time I won't pull up in the alley. We're going to take a different route."

47

MICHELLE PUSHED THEIR APARTMENT DOOR OPEN WITH HER FOOT. BACKING in, she laid the large shopping bag on the couch. After removing her coat, she kicked off her shoes.

"Is that you?" Jack called from the bedroom.

"I'm home," Michelle said. "I think I got everything we need."

"Great." Jack strolled in. "You found two black overcoats in our sizes?"

"I did. Found them in a used clothing store over on Via della Navicella. Both look worn and on the dirty side. I think that's what Guido would go for." She dumped the plastic bag on the table. "What do you think?"

Jack held up the shabby overcoat. "Looks straight out of the costume department for *The Grapes of Wrath*. Yeah, they'll work."

"Shadows are beginning to fall," Michelle said. "I think we need to get ready to move as soon as it is dark."

Jack looked at his watch. "The afternoon is gone. Our evening rendezvous with Guido will come up quickly."

"He wanted me to put on pants and pull my hair up so we'd look like two guys walking down the street. I'll get ready."

Jack followed her into the bedroom. "Do you think the police followed you?"

"No question about it. These cops are about as clever as a truckload of snails. I spotted the first cop immediately after I left the front door. The second one hopped on the subway, and I saw him hiding behind a column as well as tailing me in the department store. I know they were trying to offer protection, but any crook chasing me would have seen the surveillance if he had half an eye."

"Those are the people we have to shake tonight," Jack said. "Guido's instructions surprised me, but I see the wisdom in his idea. They won't be looking for two men." Jack shrugged. "I still struggle to believe Guido's real name is Jonas De Lateran. After all this time of research and investigation, our answer was sitting right here waiting to fall in our lap."

Michelle shook her head. "Truly amazing. And the fact is that Jonas is such a good person. I am left with nothing but astonishment. My prayer is that tonight we'll make the big breakthrough." She paused. "Getting a little stuffy in here? I'm feeling warm. Could you open the window and let a little fresh air in?"

"Sure." Jack swung the bedroom window wide open and gentle coolness drifted in. "It's a little brisk. After all, November in the United States would be quite cold today."

"Could be here," Michelle said. "But remember a nice wind from the Mediterranean Sea keeps Rome much warmer."

"Sure can."

She nodded. "Once I get my hair pulled up on top of my head, I'll be ready to start the transformation into looking like a guy. Thankfully it's only wearing a pair of pants under the overcoat."

Jack sat down on the bed. "This entire scenario from the moment Father Raffello was found dead in the grass has been as bad as it gets. We've been running down tunnels and through church crypts ever since. I am tired of the nonsense."

"Exactly," Michelle said. "If we didn't have such a significant project, I'd be packing it up and moving back to the USA." She slipped on a pair of black slacks and put her feet into a pair of Nike walking shoes. "OK. What's our plan of attack tonight?"

"We'll go out the back door of our apartment building wearing these overcoats and men's hats. Guido suggested we walk toward the opposite end of the alley as we never go that way. Often there's not even one cop at the front end of the alley. If we walk in the shadows, we should be able to get out the opposite end without the police noticing."

Michelle pulled her hair up behind her head and began pinning it in place. "I suppose Guido will wait for us if we run into any delays."

"Sure. But if something happens that we get separated, don't stop and wait for me. Keep moving and get on the subway. We're heading for Piazza di San Giovanni station and the church outside. Understand?"

Michelle shrugged. "Certainly, but I'm not worried about separation. We'll both walk into that metro station together."

"I trust so." Jack put on the black topcoat. "Doesn't smell too great, does it?"

"Hey, this is used bargain-basement stuff. It doesn't come with any guarantees." She reached into the sack and took out a narrow-brimmed men's hat. "Do I look like Kid Rock? Same kind of hat, you know."

Jack snickered. "Doesn't exactly propel you into a men's dress review, but it will do."

"Should we put the shoulder hostlers on? I'm not crazy about wearing a gun, but of course, it saved my life when we were attacked in the church. I keep on struggling with ambivalence."

"I think we better," Jack said. "Father Blake's big on weapons. If a man of the cloth keeps encouraging us, I think we should."

"Doesn't make sense that a clergyman would be urging us to be armed," Michelle said. "Usually they oppose all forms of violence."

Jack shrugged. "The Catholic Church encouraged the Crusades, which were about as brutal as you get. Blake might be from that school of thought."

Michelle picked up the shoulder holster. "OK, I'll put it on just in case." She slipped her arms through the straps. "OK, I'm ready."

Jack took her hand. "Out the back door will do just fine." He led her across the living room toward the kitchen. "We're on our way." Jack pulled her closer. " If there was anything I could do to change this situation, I'd do it. I know you're afraid to walk down that dark alley. Fear always remains a highly personal matter for you."

Michelle took a deep breath. "You're right about how personal the journey is. I suppose one of the values of this entire frightening experience has been the growth it has instilled in me. I never thought of myself as being weak, but struggle has made me much stronger. I'm grateful for the progress."

"Score one for our team," Jack said.

"Sometimes I wonder why we're jumping through all these flaming hoops that could devour us when we only want to translate old Bible manuscripts. Got to be a better way to earn a living. Why are we on such a difficult path?"

"It all started back at Tübingen when we were in graduate school. Remember? We dedicated ourselves to help sort out the confusion that permeated the lives of so many students.

We wanted to be part of a work that made a permanent difference in the world. We committed ourselves to pursuing the highest purposes that God had for the world. That's what started us down a path that has ended up with this hunt for the authentic ending to Mark's Gospel."

"I guess so," Michelle said.

Jack squeezed her hand. "But it's always that way, my dear. In this world, we have nothing but turmoil. The mere fact that we are doing something worthwhile makes us a target for evil."

"How is it that working on a project that was nothing but good would have lent itself to so much bad? The harder we work at accomplishing a positive result, the more of a struggle we encounter."

Jack kissed her. "But it's always that way, my dear. In this world, we have nothing but tribulation. Remember that little verse in John 16, promising struggle. The mere fact that we are doing something worthwhile makes us a target for evil. When the job is monumental, like biblical work always is, we're only a larger target to shoot at. I think so many terrible things have happened because we're pursuing a goal of supreme value. The bill has been terribly costly because evil repays the value of the good deed with an equal amount of pain."

"The cost has exceeded anything that I could have ever imagined," Michelle said. "Never would I have anticipated such a price. You're sneaking out for artichokes at Dar Poeta without telling me turns out to be absolutely and totally nothing."

"You know that I love watching people walk by because it reminds me that we are all in the same boat. Occasionally I imagine what the strollers must be confronting because none of us is exempt from strife. Often the struggle is registered on the person's face walking by. You can see conflict in the lines around their eyes, their drooping mouths, or foreheads creased with deep wrinkles. I watch them emotionally limp by and know that there are splinters driven into their feet. They've all been stung and have to keep on trudging, not unlike Dov and his family once did. We're all in the same war together. Some of us are trying to climb the mountain; others attempt to push the climbers off the mountain. The truth is that being righteous doesn't exempt us from battles with detractors. In our case, the adversaries are deadly."

Michelle sighed. "Deadly indeed."

Jack kissed his wife again. "We have each other. That's enough. We'll make it."

"I pray so." Michelle squeezed his hand tightly and glanced at her watch. "The hands on the clock are flying, Jack.

"Time to go."

Across the street, Klaus Burchel rolled over on the roof and quickly wound up the wire on his microphone listening device. The open bedroom window had provided perfect contact. His surveillance device had picked up every word, and Stein would be ecstatic with this information.

It was time to move quickly, and he needed to change clothes. Stein would need to be positioned properly when the Townsends emerged from the subway train at the Piazza de San Giovanni. Both he and Stein now knew what this Guido character looked like, and contact should come easy. The Townsends would be easy to recognize with the information he had just picked up.

Tonight would be the night! Old Stein should be able to cash in his chips and take home the jackpot. Before this evening was over, Klaus could fulfill his own agenda. He would turn Jack Townsend into a corpse, just as his grandfather had done with so many in Auschwitz.

48

Jack Townsend closed the rear apartment door behind Michelle and started down the old, steep staircase creaking with each step. With the lights off, the darkness made it difficult to descend the rickety stairs without slipping.

"There's got to be an easier way to take a stroll than walking down a shaft under the Addams family's house," Michelle said.

"Don't worry," Jack said. "I'm in front of you."

"Yes, and who's in front of you? Get my point? You're the guy who had the broken arm. Another fall wouldn't help you any."

"Listen, I'm totally recovered," Jack said. "Well, nearly."

"Just pay attention to the steps," Michelle said.

"I am. I am."

At the bottom, Jack crouched near the door and peered through the glass pane. "I don't see anybody out there. You ready?"

"This shoulder holster isn't comfortable," Michelle said. "I hate wearing a pistol under my arm. The Walther pistol is small, but it still bothers me."

"Me too," Jack said. "But we've been through so much that we can't take anymore chances."

"Guess so," Michelle said.

Jack turned back to the window. "I can't see anyone out there."

"I guess that's both good and bad. If we can't see them, they can't see us."

Jack cracked the door. "Once we're outside, we'll walk along the wall as far as we can. It'll be black enough to cover us." He turned around and looked into her eyes. "We've got to outfox them at every point. Don't be talking."

"You're the one doing all the jabbering," Michelle said. "I'm just listening."

"Get real, dear. We're about to step into a snake pit."

"Hey, I'm ready to roll. Got my Kid Rock hat on, an overcoat, black pants, and my six-shooter. You'd think I was The Shadow. O-o-o," she cooed.

Jack glared at her. "This is no time for jokes."

"Don't be so hyper. The worst that can happen is that a cop picks up us and writes a ticket for window peeking and carrying concealed weapons."

Jack didn't say anything, but turned back to the door. "Stay close and don't talk. I mean it."

"I won't," Michelle whispered and giggled nervously.

Michelle always gets giddy when she's afraid, Jack thought. She'll pass for a guy walking next to me, but it isn't going to be easy to get out of here and avoid the cops.

Opening the door slowly, Jack slipped around the corner and pulled Michelle after him. The edge of the brick building had been littered with broken bottles and trash. Every few feet trash cans sat against the wall in between old cars parked close to the apartments. By crouching low, they could walk the first twenty feet without anyone seeing them. At the end of the stretch, another building jagged out and forced Jack to walk in the alley.

"Pick up the pace," he whispered. "We need to get out of here."

Michelle nodded.

Jack stepped out, but stayed close to the building, walking with his head bent down. Michelle hustled along at his side.

"Hey!" a man called out behind him. "Just a minute."

Jack froze and looked over his shoulder. Some guy had come out of the shadows behind one of the cars and must have been watching them go by.

"Don't mean no harm," the man called out in Italian. "I noticed you came out of that building that the Townsends live in. Want to get your picture in the paper?"

"Keep walking," Jack whispered to Michelle.

"I'm a reporter and only need a little information," the man insisted. "Could I talk to you for a moment."

Jack shook his head.

"Won't take but a second." The man trotted up behind him.

Jack knew it was a moment of decision he couldn't avoid. The guy might be nothing more than a tabloid jerk, but he was persistent. If the man got in their face, the charade was over. He had to make a decision. All his weight lifting hadn't been only to lift his self-esteem. This was one of those occasions where self-protection was the essence of the situation.

"I just want to ask you some questions about the Townsends." The reporter hurried around Jack and stopped directly in front of them.

Jack knew if the man identified Michelle, they would be in danger and there was no time left to warn her. He couldn't allow such a slipup.

Leaning into his face, the reporter jabbered. "Just got a few personal questions." The man turned to Michelle. "Wait a minute! You're a woman!"

"I'd suggest you get out of our way," Jack's voice took on a menacing tone.

"My gosh, you're the Townsends!" the reporter blurted out. "This really is a story!"

Jack turned sideways before swinging his fist into the man's stomach with all his might. His hat went flying backward.

"A-a-ah!" the reporter gasped and doubled over.

"Run!" Jack told Michelle. "Get out of here, and I'll meet you at our rendezvous point."

With a swift thrust of his knee, Jack caught him square in the forehead, sending the guy sprawling backward against the brick building.

"Jack, I can't leave you here!"

Swinging another hard right, Jack hit the reporter in the center of the chest. The man groaned, but lunged forward bouncing Jack backward.

"Run!" Jack repeated. "Get out of here."

Michelle turned and started running for the metro.

The reporter grabbed Jack by the lapels on his black overcoat and hurled him into the side of the brick building. He felt the strength go out of the arm that had been broken and knew he was spent. The impact knocked the air out of him and for a moment he crumpled. The journalist jumped on top of him, forcing him to the pavement. Pounding on Jack's back, he pummeled him fiercely while Jack tried to cover his head.

For a second, Jack thought the man would knock him unconscious. Only then did he remember the pistol in his shoulder holster. Reaching across his chest, he pulled out the gun and slammed it into the man's head.

The reporter froze with his fist still in the air before silently slumping to the pavement. For a moment, Jack sat prostrate trying to catch his breath. He didn't hear the sound of anyone coming, which meant their scuffle hadn't alerted the police. Possibly, the cop had taken a break. Who knows? They might be down the street drinking coffee. He pushed himself up and leaned against the building. His adversary hadn't been a pushover. That was certain. Without a little encouragement from the butt of his gun, he might be on the alley unconscious.

Jack picked up his hat and peered around the corner. He couldn't hear anyone running. Michelle must have gotten to the metro station by now and probably was on the train. Pulling the overcoat closer up around his neck, he put the hat back on and started walking toward the same station, trying to look as casual as possible.

49

NIGHT HAD FALLEN SUFFICIENTLY TO CAST DARK SHADOWS OVER MICHELLE as she ran to the corner. The first block had allowed her to stay close to the side of the building but she had to wait for the cars to pass. A glance over her shoulder told her nothing. Jack must still be struggling in the alley with the reporter because he wasn't in sight. She wanted to go back, but Jack had told her to run. He must have known he could endure the struggle. Michelle knew how strong Jack was and felt certain that he could hang on. Worst-case scenario would be that the newsman had a wild story to print about chasing the Townsends.

Once across and on the other side of the street, she settled to a slower pace to avoid calling attention to herself. A crowd of people was leaving the metro, and she blended into them. Just ahead was the ticket window. She stepped up.

"Going to Piazza de San Giovanni," Michelle said.

The man looked at her a moment too long and stared at her hat. Then, he pushed a ticket under the window but said nothing.

"Got to get rid of the hat," she mumbled to herself and snatched it from her head. "The thing must look weird."

For several moments, she observed the crowd to see if anyone was watching her. Kids on the streets of Rome dressed in weird outfits, and people might have assumed she was only one of the pack, though she was a bit old for that scene. Stepping toward a large bench, she dropped the hat on the seat and walked away. Hurrying down the stairs to the tracks, she realized again how stale the overcoat smelled. No longer was it necessary to keep up appearances, but the overcoat provided a cover for the night air so she left it on. Once she reached the bottom of the stairs, Michelle watched people lining up to catch the next train that would be coming in shortly.

The metro station always seemed to be filled with people. Rome's subway station had forever been a major part of how commuters traveled through the city. While buses and cars plowed through traffic in the street above, the A and B metro service provided a cross-city service that was fast and effective. With standing room only in the coaches, in the summertime the subway could become terribly hot, but this was a November night and on the chilly side.

Standing nearer the edge of the platform, Michelle noticed a man at the other end watching her. Wearing a stylish brown wool suit with a dark purple shirt and a striped bluish tie, he clearly was dressed better than most of the passengers milling around the tracks in faded blue jeans and sweatshirts. His extremely short haircut reflected he had fairly recently shaved his head and was letting the hair grow from a bald look. A scar ran down his cheek. Michelle turned away and pulled up the collar on her overcoat. For a few moments, she turned away, but glanced out of the corner of her eye. The man in the brown suit kept watching her.

She'd seen that same outfit somewhere before, but where? For a moment the memory blurred and then she remembered the man taking her picture across the street from Santa Maria

Church. Jack and Dov had pooh-poohed the idea, but it had concerned her. This was the man! No coincidences there.

Walking cautiously to the front end where the train would stop, Michelle could hear the coach arriving. A strong gust of wind whistled down the tunnel, and the cars careened into the station, shrieking to a quick halt. She jumped into the first coach and turned to watch the man. Hustling along the side of the cars, he stepped into the coach directly behind her and worked his way toward the adjoining door where he could continue to watch her through the coach windows.

Whoever this jerk was, the man was definitely on her tail. She had to play it cool lest she precipitate a response she didn't want. The subway roared down the tracks into the black tunnel and came out at the next stop where she should depart. Michelle watched him in the back car, standing motionless. Clearly, she would have to make the first move, but if she got off now, it could provide a trail to Guido. She couldn't let that happen. Once again the car pulled away from the station and raced down the tracks. Pushing her arm against the shoulder holster, she made sure the gun was in place.

Having missed her stop, Michelle knew every other station would only take her farther from the Piazza de San Giovanni. She needed to act, but what could she do? Whoever this monkey was, he'd be off as quickly as she departed. He could be part of The Scorpion terrorist ring, or he might be one of Albert Stein's men. Of course, the tail could just be one of those crazy spooks that roamed Rome's back alleys and side streets. Nothing added up right. In any case, she had to shake him and staying on the train wouldn't do it.

The car slowed and the recorded voice on the overhead speakers announced the passengers should be cautious in getting off the train. Michelle scanned the crowd waiting to board. She could wait until most of them entered and then dart out. With people stepping in, the creep might miss an abrupt departure. Even if he saw her leave, she could get a significant head start. The train slowed.

The purple shirt and blue tie weren't moving. The first passengers stepped off the subway and people began boarding. The warning light flashed that the doors were about to shut. Bolting between two men, Michelle leaped to the station platform and ran for the exit without looking back. When she rounded the corner, Michelle saw a restroom sign straight ahead. The ladies room was an option that hadn't occurred to her. Darting through the open door, she walked into the crowd of women. Without hesitating, she marched toward the stall and locked herself in.

Could the brown suit be waiting outside the bathroom door? It was more than possible. On the other hand, he might have missed her coming in and gone on down the hall. If so, by now he had to conclude he'd lost her. If he really was after her, he wouldn't disappear quickly, and she might run into him again. Michelle had no alternative but to wait.

Rumblings started in her stomach, and Michelle instantly knew what was coming. She grabbed the side of the wall to steady herself. An attack had not hit for some time, but she knew she couldn't stop the invasion. The stress of being followed had set it off. Taking a deep breath, Michelle tried to relax, but her hands and arms started to shake. She tightened her eyes to block out the sights, but the vision rolled up anyway.

A huge trailer pulling a gasoline tank came straight at her, hurling down the highway at breakneck speed. Like watching a slow motion rerun of an old movie that she'd seen a hundred times, Michelle saw the truck driver's face grimace in horror as he violently tried to pull his eighteen-wheeler back onto his side of the road. The cab jerked to the left, but the trailer swung wildly toward their car. Her mother screamed just as the rear of the trailer smacked the front end of their vehicle. The sound of the front being torn away rang through the automobile with a shriek of metal ripping apart. Their car started spinning wildly.

"Michelle grabbed the door handle that her father always kept locked, but the car started tipping to the side. She heard glass breaking and saw the windshield shatter into a million pieces. The car went sideways and her grip on the handle broke. Pain erupted when she crashed into the top of the car. For a second, it felt like they were going to spin and then the car bounced sideways and started to roll. Her body began bouncing up and down on the top of the car that was crumpling upward into the auto. A massive rock smashed into the side of the rolled vehicle and everything stopped except pain and glass that kept flying like tiny missiles. Pieces of the broken windows hurled past her neck and arms. A trickle of blood started running down the side of her face.

Michelle lay on the top of the car with the bent roof gouging her. Shock had already partially anesthetized her, but the agony kept pumping and she knew she was hurt worse than she ever had been in her life. Outside a voice kept shrieking.

Her father started crawling through where the windshield had once been. Michelle could smell gasoline, and the scent was growing. His strong arms started easing her into the front seat.

"*Padre!*" she cried. "*Padre!*"

"I've got you, dear," her father said. "Don't worry. I'll get you out."

"My leg!" Michelle screamed. "The throbbing hurts so bad."

"Don't cry," her father said. "You'll be out of here in a second."

Michelle looked down and realized her left leg had turned at a strange angle. Legs weren't suppose to do that. She looked into her father's face and saw blood flowing out of his hairline and running down his nose. Without stopping, he pulled her through the windshield and onto the pavement.

"Don't move," her father said. "Lie very still."

Ahead of their car she could see her mother trying to crawl. Her blouse was torn and blood ran down her arm. The smell of gasoline had become so strong that it hung in the air like a pall.

Suddenly an explosion shook the ground. Her father fell backward onto the pavement, and an orange ball of fire rolled up into the sky followed by clouds of black smoke. All sound stopped and only silence prevailed. There were only movements without resonance. Then Michelle saw her mother.

The explosion had slung her against a slab of rock rising from the side of the road. Her neck hung at an obscene angle as if her head had been internally disconnected. She didn't move, but stared straight away with empty eyes.

For the first time, Michelle remembered exactly what had happened, and the horror froze every fiber of her being. She had never spoken of her mother's death nor discussed it with Jack. The matter was closed, sealed, finished, but now it was clear that conclusion had never happened in her mind. Michelle could no longer escape the dead eyes of her mother staring back at her on the side of that road.

She rubbed her clammy hands against the walls of the bathroom stall as she slid to the floor with knees wobbling like putty. Sinking to the floor, she began crying bitterly. She could not avoid the most intimidating fact of her life. The wreck had killed her mother.

Tears rolled down Michelle's face as the penetrating edges of her memory slowly faded. Sounds returned, and she could hear women walking just outside the stall, but she couldn't move. Her weeping continued unabated.

"Hey, lady!" a woman called out. "You OK in there?"

Michelle couldn't answer.

"Do you need a doctor?"

"No," Michelle finally mumbled. "I'm OK." She could hear the footsteps of other women gathering around the door.

"An ambulance?" Another woman shouted.

"Please, no," Michelle said. "I'll be fine in a moment." She began pushing herself back up off the floor. "I'll be out in a few minutes."

Even though her hands continued to shake, control was returning. The sight of her mother's empty eyes had undone her more completely that anything else that had ever occurred in one of these post-traumatic encounters. Michelle could no longer avoid the fact that she had run from every day since the wreck. Her mother had died in the explosion and her death was more than Michelle could face. The curtain had been ripped open. Reality was on the table before her, and she would have to face it.

Michelle finally opened the stall door and stepped out. A few women stood around waiting, wanting to make sure she was all right.

"Thank you," Michelle said to the women and began washing her face.

The old overcoat no longer had a purpose. Even if she was still being followed, jettisoning it might convey a different appearance. Michelle took it off and hung the coat on a hanger attached to the wall. If she was going to leave, she would need to walk out resolutely no matter how wobbly she felt. If the creep was out there, she'd know soon enough.

Drying her hands, she pulled the bobby pins from her hair and the strands tumbled down to normal shoulder length. Her regular look would also help offset her appearance to women entering into the bathroom. Taking a deep breath, she tried to walk resolutely toward the exit, but her legs still felt wobbly. Michelle gritted her teeth and kept moving forward.

Once outside, she glanced around the long corridors but didn't see the brown suit man. Walking slowly and close to the wall back to the platform, she looked back and forth but recognized no one. Once in the loading area, Michelle blended into the waiting crowd.

With a gust of wind, the metro train came sweeping into the station and slowed. The crowd rushed toward the doors sliding open. Michelle hurried onto the train. The doors closed and the train pulled away.

Standing behind the cement column that supported the roof over the metro, Klaus Burchel had watched her leave the bathroom. Michelle Townsend had seen him on the train and was running. He had to be more cautious. She had stayed in the bathroom nearly thirty minutes, which meant the woman was definitely hiding from him. Klaus had picked up the thin-rimmed hat off the bench where Michelle left it. Waiting for her to come out, Burchel slipped it on, hoping to alter his appearance. No. She'd recognize it. Burchel dropped the hat on the floor.

When she came out of the bathroom, Burchel immediately noticed the long hair and guessed she was on her way back to the train. Staying a considerable distance behind her, he edged through the crowd. She had gone over the top walkway leading to the other side, which meant she was going back to Piazza de San Giovanni just as he had heard through his eavesdropping device. No longer did he need to stay close. Jumping on the last coach, he would get off at San Giovanni station. Things were working out just as Stein had said they would. The old man needed an update.

Burchel emerged at the far end of the platform and got on the last coach just as the doors closed. He pulled out his cell phone and began dialing. After a moment, he heard the other end answer even though Stein said nothing.

"We're returning to the Piazza de San Giovanni right now," he said.

50

When Michelle arrived at the Piazza de San Giovanni station, the press of evening passengers had picked up significantly, but nobody paid attention to her. Staying close to the tunnel walls, she walked up the steps toward the turnstiles. Guido should be around there somewhere standing close to the exit. The rush of the crowd made it difficult to see Guido, but he had to be close.

Fifteen feet on the other side of the steps, Jack stood talking to Guido. Still wearing the old black overcoat, he looked considerably dirtier than when she last saw him. If nothing else, they were together again and their struggles had not kept either of them from arriving at the station.

"You're OK?" Michelle said.

Jack turned around. "I was starting to worry. Took you longer to get here than I expected." His right eye looked puffy and his face drawn.

"You're hurt!" Michelle exclaimed.

"No big deal," Jack said. "Just a few punches here and there. You don't look so great yourself."

"I was followed. Some man in a brown suit stayed on my heels clear through this stop. I recognized him as the photographer taking my picture in front of Santa Maria Church weeks back. He really frightened me, and I had one of my attacks. I'm still a tad shaky."

"Oh, no!" Jack Squeezed her hand.

"You've had a rough trip," Guido said. "I was concerned that something like this might happen."

Jack hugged her. "I'm so sorry. I didn't dream anyone would trail you once we were separated."

"How about the reporter?" Michelle asked. "How did you shake him?"

"Let's just say that he's probably still taking a nap in the alley."

"And your arm?" Michelle rubbed her hand up and down his sleeve.

"OK, but not quite as strong as I thought. I'm still dragging."

"Since Michelle's shed her topcoat, I think you can too," Guido said. "Looks a little on the worn side."

"Worn?" Jack chuckled and began dropping the overcoat. "Gives me the old refined panhandler look. It'll go in the trash right now. If nothing else, we got rid of the cops and reporters following us. You were right about that possibility, Guido."

"Our police aren't the sharpest in the world, but we can't have anyone following us to where I am going to take you. My ancestors would scream from their graves if they thought that location was about to be betrayed. My family protected this secret for centuries. That's why I had to assume someone would probably follow you and attempt to ruin everything."

"I think I shook the guy tailing me on the metro," Michelle said. "The jerk looked unusually well-dressed. You discounted the idea that he was taking my picture in front of the church." She pointed a finger in Jack's face. "Wrong. Obviously, he has a history with us. Haven't seen him since I arrived here, but I can't be too sure."

"I can't assume such," Guido said. "I want us to leave separately. Down the street is the church of San Giovanni. We will reassemble inside at the foot of the *Scala Santa*, the holy staircase. Supposedly the steps came from the house of Pontius Pilate in Jerusalem and had been ascended by Jesus just before his crucifixion. Of course, this story is only legend, but the twenty-eight marble steps draw believers who climb up on their knees to earn an indulgence. I will be there first watching to see if anyone shows who is looking for something more substantial like the two of you. We will stand there watching the stairs until I am convinced we can take the next step. Got it?"

Jack nodded. "You'll leave first, Guido, then Michelle and I follow. We walk straight into the church and head for the holy stairs."

Guido studied the station platform, observing the people passing by, going through the turnstiles, disappearing down the crowded street. After watching for a minute, he headed out through the exit.

Michelle watched Guido cross the boulevard and walk toward the large, white, stone church. In the moonlight she could see statues of the apostles lining the rooftop. Without stopping, Guido walked straight through the large doors and went inside.

"I guess I'm next," Michelle said.

"Tell me about the man following you," Jack insisted.

"Frankly, he scared me, but I didn't want to tell Guido. The man appeared to be unusually well-dressed with a stylish flair. I knew that I'd seen those clothes somewhere before. He certainly didn't look like a terrorist type, but he had a scar on his cheek like from a fight or a struggle. Of course, how would I know what one of these killers looks like? He stayed in the coach behind me and watched through the glass panes. No question that he had his eye on me."

"I don't like it. I wonder if we should go ahead."

"Guido's over there waiting for us. We can't stop now, Jack. Anyway, I am sure that I lost him in the scuffle. What bothers me is that he saw through my masculine disguise and kept coming. If the guy wasn't a pervert of some sort, then the alternative is far from encouraging."

"Yeah, I've got that message. Well, I guess we'd better go."

Jack walked through the station exit toward the church's towers standing above the surrounding buildings. He knew the last restoration had come when Innocent X had stripped away the ancient character of the building, leaving a relatively tasteless plain facade that concealed the romance of the ancient history surrounding the church. Jack hoped that the next step in their journey inside would prove equally mundane.

"I had better split until we get over there," Michelle said. "I'll see you inside, dear. OK?"

Jack took a deep breath. "I guess so. I'll be coming right behind you."

Michelle took one last look around the area to check if the man in the brown suit was back there somewhere, but she didn't see him. Without looking back, she walked up the street just as Guido had done. At the corner, Michelle waited for the stoplight to change and then crossed. In a matter of minutes, she stood before the massive figure of Christ surrounded by nine angels. The statue looked ancient and must have gone way back nearly to the beginning of the building.

"Lord, help us," she muttered to herself and walked forward.

Standing behind a towering pilaster, the man in a brown wool suit, wearing a purple shirt with a bluish tie stepped out and fell in behind her. Michelle Townsend walked determinedly toward the *Scala Santa*, which tourists always gathered around. Once he was sure that was where she was going, he dropped back and watched her carefully so as to avoid calling attention to himself. Moving behind another large pilaster, he observed Guido Valentino gazing over the crowd in front of the steps. Fortunately, Valentino still looked in the opposite direction. Jack Townsend would probably be showing up shortly, and he had to get back to where the boss waited for him before Townsend showed.

Slipping across the church, he entered a gift shop selling San Giovanni bookmarks, statuettes, rosaries, prayer books, and a host of items. Peering through the windows, he could see Valentino and Michelle standing at the foot of the steps waiting.

The man with a decidedly German face stepped beside him. "Excellent work, Klaus." Stein murmured. "We are well positioned for the attack."

51

Jack walked casually as if inspecting the peaceful basilica by studying a tourist guidebook. Stopping next to Michelle, he glanced indifferently at the twenty-eight stone steps.

"Looks like regular old Italian marble to me," he said cynically.

"Only a Protestant could be so disrespectful," Guido replied. "You have to be an Italian to understand these sacred objects."

"But since we're Protestants, we don't fall in behind the party line quite so obediently as you local boys do," Michelle said.

Guido grinned. "As if I didn't already know." He whispered to Jack and Michelle. "I don't see anyone watching us, but I am a rank amateur in this hunt-and-chase game. Hopefully we're still clear. I think we can start walking back toward the entry to the church again. Just stroll leisurely and look around, but don't get too far behind me."

"Don't worry," Michelle said. "We've got our radar tuned up to the maximum capacity tonight."

Guido sauntered away from the *Scala Santa*. Once he reached the distant wall of the sanctuary, he looked at the frescos by Nebbia and d'Arpino. Farther on, he paused beneath the work of Torriti for a moment. When he reached the massive front doors, Guido stopped for a final scrutiny of the crowd milling around the church and then strolled out.

Jack and Michelle maintained a slow pace marching toward the front door. Stepping outside into the darkness, they could no longer find Guido.

"Where'd he go?" Michelle stammered. "He was here a moment ago."

"Behind you," Guido said out of the blackness. "Don't turn around. Walk to your left toward the small building near the end of the cathedral. Stop there."

"OK," Jack said.

"Wait at the entrance," Guido said.

The night air felt unusually brisk, but Jack kept their speed at an easy gait. When they reached the smaller building, Jack stopped.

Within a few moments, Guido emerged out of the shadows. "Go in," he whispered. "Look around like tourists until you know no one else is inside. I'll watch out here to make sure we are not followed."

"What is this place?" Michelle ask.

"The ancients built baptisteries apart from the actual church building. The baptistery for San Giovanni has stood on this spot for nearly two thousand years. You will find it most interesting."

Inside the heavy door, the interior revealed a large circular room with a substantial baptismal font in the center. The tranquil surface of the water stood motionless. The black stone had a chipped appearance and worn edges suggesting antiquity. Made to emulate candles, the electric lights around the walls cast long, dismal shadows across the room. Nothing disturbed the silence.

Jack looked up at the frescos decorating the ceiling and the walls. "Great paintings. This building hasn't had the bland changes that the main church has undergone. Interesting."

Guido walked in while Jack was talking. "My family has carefully followed the development of the baptistery through the years," Guido said. "You will notice the metal grates along the bottom of the walls. Look closely and you will see an opening exposing the smaller area beneath this floor."

Michelle bent to look. "Appears like another circular room is down there."

"That's the original level of this edifice," Guido said. "Go over to that door in the wall." He pointed across the baptistery. "You didn't notice it because it is so well hidden in the fresco." Guido walked around the stone font and pressed against the panel. A narrow door swung open. "You have to have the magic touch. Let's go down."

The narrow staircase wound in a semicircle as it dropped to the old ground level while only accommodating one person following another. Granite walls and stairs with rough edges gave the descent into the darkness an even more ominous feel. Michelle hesitantly planted her feet one after another climbing down the steps. Reaching out, she clung to the rough wall to maintain her balance.

A hint of dampness hung in the air, and it felt colder than above. The granite floor had been laid with slabs of rock set together to form triangular forms in a nondescript pattern. Smaller than the upstairs, the room remained circular. In the center stood a much smaller font. Against the back wall an ancient wooden altar emerged from the shadows. Paint had peeled and niches with scratches marred the surface.

"We are now on the original floor level of the baptistery when it was built by Constantine in the third century," Guido said. "While this church has been attacked by everything from the Vandals to earthquakes, this baptistery has prevailed. My family realized this fact long ago and decided that it would make an excellent hiding place for the original ending to Mark's Gospel. They concealed it down here."

Jack glanced at the stone walls. "In plain sight?"

"Not quite." Guido smiled. "They were too wise to simply put it out where someone might stumble onto the manuscript. It is much better concealed than simply tucking the document away."

"Where?" Michelle pressed.

"Watch," Guido said. "The altar has been rebuilt a number of times through many centuries, but because it was wooden no one took it seriously. No gold or precious frescos could be found here. When the attacks came, the marauders crashed in, but didn't stop for serious inspection. No one looked *under* the altar."

"I don't understand." Jack said.

"Help me move the altar" Guido answered and walked to the left side. "You get the other end and we'll swing it to one side."

Jack took hold of the side of the small altar and lifted. Carefully, they carried it around the side of the font. Guido knelt on the floor and slipped his fingers into a narrow crack in the wall. A cracking noise erupted from the wall. Slowly, a four-foot section of the wall swung forward.

"You'll have to stoop down to get inside. Remember you are the first people to walk down this tunnel in a thousand years," Guido said. "I would consider that to be an honor of the highest order."

"Indeed." Jack stared. "We would never have found this secret room."

Michelle said. "Never!"

"Let me go first," Guido said. "I will have to light the lamps that are supposed to be inside. This area was built long before anyone had a hint about electricity." He stooped low and worked his way through the small entry.

"We're about to realize one of our greatest dreams of a lifetime," Jack said. "After you, my dear."

Michelle hugged him. "By the grace of God, we have come a long, long way. Here we go." She inched her way down the tunnel.

Jack crawled in behind her. The noise of Guido flipping his lighter echoed through the stone entrance. Slowly candlelight began to flicker from different corners of the small room. The air smelled musty and stale, but the chamber didn't feel damp.

"My ancient relatives built this room behind the first rebuilding of the baptistery and constructed it carefully to preserve it's hidden character. With time, the street built up around the outside building and the new baptistery was rebuilt on a higher level, but no one touched this area down here. I have been told countless times that directly behind me is a loose stone that will slip out of the wall." He pointed to a piece of stone. "This is the moment to find out. You ready?"

"My heart's pounding like the blades on a helicopter," Jack said. "I don't think I would have noticed that piece of stone unless I was on an archaeological dig. We simply pull it out?"

"Time has probably mired the stone into the wall, but we should be able to work it loose. Let me try."

Guido began pushing and pulling on the rock, but the stone didn't move. Guido kept massaging the hunk back and forth without success.

"Got a screwdriver?" Jack asked.

"Yes. I keep one with me on excursions like this one."

"Let me try using the steel point like a wedge," Jack said. "Maybe it will help." He worked the point in between the stones and started prying.

"It's moving!" Michelle exclaimed. "Yes, it's starting to give."

"OK!" Guido said. "I think we're making progress."

Jack kept pushing the point back and forth while pulling on the bottom of the stone as it inched forward. Guido grabbed the stone and pulled it away. Dropping to one knee, he shined his small, high-intensity flashlight into the hole.

"There it is!" Guido gasped.

"What?" Jack hovered over his shoulder.

"They always told me the treasure was a flat stone box that had been sealed around the edges with pitch and gum to keep the contents from being affected by moisture. As the story was passed down from generation to generation, the details remained precisely the same. Probably back then no one realized air could be the greatest enemy, but the sealant should ensure nothing got inside." Guido reached into the dark hole to pull out the long slender container that was about a foot long. "Heavy." Guido dragged the rectangular stone object forward. "I've got to set it on the altar." He placed both hands underneath and slid the stone sarcophagus out. "Look at this! Astonishing!"

Jack stared at the roughly hewn container. "Looks like it was chiseled out of two pieces of rock that they must have hollowed out on the inside. Must have taken a considerable amount of time to cut this rock into a proper shape. Hard work." He ran his hand over the surface. "Feels like a piece of volcanic rock. That substance would have been easier to cut. I have no idea why they were afraid to share this document with the Christian community. Could be that some pope scared them to death. Probably their era was a time of attack and warfare. Maybe this seemed like the safest thing they could do. Perhaps they intended to retrieve it on a better day and never came back."

"Something like that," Guido said. "Nothing has happened in this hole for all these centuries until this moment. Let's take it outside where the light is better and see what we can find." Carefully he picked up the stone box.

"I'll get in front of you," Jack said. "You might need help in getting through the small exit then we can lay it out on the larger altar outside." He began backing into the tunnel with his hands extended to catch the container if Guido slipped.

Guido got down on his knees and inched his way forward. Michelle fell in behind him.

"Slowly," Jack said. "I've got my hands out to grab it if the container slips.

"No problem," Guido said. "We're just about out."

Jack backed into the ancient baptistery, keeping his eyes glued on the treasure. "Just about there." He straightened, but intensely watched the stone box.

Guido slowly emerged, never removing the object from his sight. Michelle came out at his heels and straightened up. Suddenly, she gasped and stiffened.

"Nice work," Dr. Albert Stein said from behind them. "We appreciate what you've accomplished for us."

Jack stumbled backward against the wall. Guido grabbed the stone object.

Klaus Burchel leveled his German-made 9 mm pistol at Jack's face. "I've been thinking about blowing your head off for a long time," he said. "If you even twitch, I'll do it *right now*."

52

Michelle's mouth went dry, and her heart pounded. She grabbed the wall behind her for fear of fainting. The goon pointing the pistol at her husband's face was the same creep who had been following her. At this close distance, she clearly recognized the depth of the scar on his cheek. Behind him stood Dr. Albert Stein, just as he looked the last time she saw him at the Translation Conference when Michelle thought a brawl would break out. She could hardly breathe.

"We made sure their was only one entrance in and out of the baptistery," Albert Stein said. "Of course, we knew you would come here to the church. We've been listening in our own special way. We just weren't sure *exactly* where you'd land."

"He-he followed me." Michelle pointed at the man holding the gun.

"Klaus can be a clever boy," Stein continued. "We were only making sure you showed up at the church. Once that was clear, it was only a matter of you leading us to this edifice. Your mistake was not making sure the panel wall door closed behind you. Once we saw that it was partially open, the rest proved simple."

"What are you after?" Jack asked with quiet intensity.

"I think we have it now." Stein pointed at the stone container. "You can scream all you wish, but history will record that I, Dr. Albert Stein, found it first." He jabbed his finger at Jack. "Not you, you worthless twit. This time I win big."

"You have three witnesses that will swear you stole the manuscript," Jack asserted forcefully. "We will prevail in a court fight, and you can count on the fact that there will be one."

Stein laughed. "I don't think so, and there won't be three witnesses."

"How dare you!" Michelle suddenly screamed defiantly. "You think you can frighten us? You don't scare me!" She shook her fist forcefully. "You want to take on a woman? Try me!"

"O-o-w," Stein mocked her. "I think we'll start with your husband and finish with you. How's that, my dear?" He turned to Klaus. "Blow Townsend's head off."

The shot roared through the small room with a deafening roar. Instantly, Klaus Burchel dropped to his knees and fell on his face. A man stepped out of the descending stairs and held a Beretta Modello pistol in front of him.

"What happened?" Michelle gasped.

"I think your boy got a little overextended," Tony Mattei said to Stein.

"Tony!" Jack exclaimed. "You've saved our lives."

"Only in a manner of speaking," the diamond merchant said. "Don't anybody move, and put that stone box on the altar." He motioned with his pistol. "Do it *now*."

"I don't understand." Jack held his hands out like he was greeting a friend.

"You just don't get it," Mattei groused. "I don't like Americans. In fact, I hate the American government, your capitalist system and everything it stands for."

"What are you talking about?" Jack said.

"I've only been playing along with you Yanks," Mattei said. "You were nothing but pawns in my game."

Michelle took a deep breath and stepped forward. "I'm not afraid of you either," she asserted defiantly. "I'm not going to sit back and allow you—"

"Shut your mouth!" Mattei shouted. "And keep it shut, or I'll finish what this punk on the floor started to do." He swung his pistol back and forth. "His body complicates matters because it will look like he was the killer and I can't have that. I want credit for what I do, not have this worthless stooge steal it from me."

"This doesn't make any sense," Michelle said.

"Tough, woman." Mattei turned his pistol directly on Stein. "You pick up that container and carry it upstairs. I'll be right behind you with this gun in your back. Got the picture?"

"Upstairs?" Albert Stein muttered.

"The rest of you get down on the floor with this corpse." Mattei kept moving the pistol back and forth between Jack, Michelle, and Guido. "Kneel and stick your arms straight out in front of you. NOW!"

Michelle dropped to her knees as she was told.

Jack stared across the floor into the lifeless eyes of Klaus Burchel. A haunting emptiness filled each pupil of his eyes and his expressionless face reflected only a void. Guido knelt beside Jack on the floor.

Mattei moved quickly behind the Townsends, feeling under their arms. "Well, well, you've come to the party armed." He reached under Michelle's light jacket and pulled her gun out. Without stopping, he did the same to Jack. Finally, he ran his hands down Guido's back. "Nothing here," he murmured. Walking to the wall, he dropped the Townsends' weapons in the hole.

"What are you trying to prove?" Stein hissed.

"How stupid you are," Mattei sneered.

"You can't get away with this, Tony," Jack said.

"But I already have. Start up the stairs," Mattei commanded Stein. "Listen, you German pig, I can drop you in an instant if you try anything cute. Just walk up the stairs carrying that stone box, and I'll tell you what to do next. Move it."

Stein picked up the stone container with both hands and glared at Mattei.

"Be glad I didn't put you down there on the floor with that houseboy of yours. If you didn't have a purpose, I'd still put a hole in your head. Now get moving."

From the floor, Michelle could see Albert Stein reluctantly carry the box and start up the stairs with Tony Mattei pressing his gun against Stein's back. Mattei turned and looked at the three figures on the floor.

"It's been interesting," Mattei said. "You Yankees proved helpful, but that was about it. I'm sure I'll be able to fetch a top dollar for whatever is in that container. You wouldn't have gone to so much trouble if this thing wasn't worth big bucks. Beyond that little exchange of the box for your lives, you ought to be thankful I haven't killed you."

Mattei disappeared up the stairs and silence settled over the room.

"God help us," Jack whispered. "We barely escaped."

Guido murmured. "I can't believe it."

The noise of a crash rolled down the stairs. It sounded like the stone box had been dropped on the floor. Another noise resounded like a person falling on the tile.

"Stop!" The command echoed down the stairs. "Don't go out that door!"

Another gunshot echoed through the baptistery.

The reverberation of the large front door slamming rang through the entire building.

Jack immediately sprang to his feet and rushed to the stairs. Flattening against the wall, he listened intently. Guido came right behind him.

"What's happening?" Michelle got up much more slowly.

"You can come on up," an entirely different sounding but not unfamiliar voice shouted down the stairs. "It's over."

Jack slowly moved up the stairs. Michelle rushed across the room to get behind Guido.

"Be cautious," Jack warned. "We don't know what's going on up there."

Michelle felt her heart pounding, but the paralyzing anxiety was gone. She crept forward much more confidently.

"What in the world?" Jack stepped out from the panel door. Guido and Michelle came out behind him.

Michelle stared at the floor. Tony Mattei lay unconscious, silently sprawled with his arms in front of him. Stein was gone, but Father Donald Blake stood with one foot on Mattei's gun hand and holding the jeweler's weapon in his other.

"Father Blake!" Michelle explained. "What w-what are you—"

"Everybody relax," Blake said. "And you can stop calling me Father. I've been after Stein and Mattei for weeks. I'm just surprised they both showed up tonight."

Jack stared uncomprehendingly at the priest in a clerical collar. "I don't get it."

Blake said. "I have international connections and have been chasing the terrorists since the subway bombing back at the first of September. Tony Mattei isn't just a local diamond merchant. You're looking at the general of The Scorpions. The stinger himself. This bad boy's been smuggling diamonds for years and selling them across Europe. Changing economic policies in America whacked his profits, and that set him in motion. The man's small potatoes from a terrorism point of view, but what he did had major repercussions. He's one dangerous maniac. One little bomber can blow a big hole in the street. That's how Mattei took on an importance that even exceeded his size. A small potato turned into a big watermelon.

"But Stein?" Michelle asked.

"I'm not sure what he was about. Seems to have a big hate on for you, Jack and Michelle. My guess is that Albert Stein is a sociopath at best and maybe on the psychopathic side. The man broke for the front door and by now is probably running down the street like a terrified hog. The police couldn't find him earlier. I imagine it will be even more difficult with his lackey lying dead down there on the floor."

"You've been an investigator all this time?" Michelle sounded baffled. "I would never have guessed it."

"Let's just say that your country pays better attention to its citizens than most people realize. We knew that Mattei was the big dog because I had an undercover connection with his small organization. Unfortunately, we simply didn't have enough evidence to take him to court yet. Obviously, we do now."

"But that crook downstairs?" Michelle ask.

"He was Stein's boy who apparently hated Americans as much as Tony Mattei did. Maybe more. Don't know his full story yet, but we'll immediately be after it. His actions make Stein a conspirator in murder for starters. For that reason, I'm sure Stein is heading out of the country as fast as his little legs will take him. Don't worry. The border police will be watching."

Guido pointed to the stone sarcophagus on the floor. "The receptacle belongs to my family. I would like to take it out of here tonight."

Blake looked at the box on the floor. "You know, I don't see a thing down there. If there's something around here that's

yours, I'd strongly suggest you take it with you right now without further explanation."

"Thank you!" Guido sighed. "Thank you so very much."

"That gunshot was muffled by the basement, but if anybody
was close, they might have called the police." Blake pulled a
cell phone from his pocket. "If they didn't, I'm about to sum-
mon the local constabulary. "Why don't you folks just hustle
on out of here? I can call you when you are needed. I'll tell the
cops that you left early to avoid the hassle during the second
part of this little drama. My hunch is that you need to get that
rock box out of here and somewhere in safe keeping. I don't
think you want your picture in the paper over this incident."

"That's for sure," Jack said.

"I want to call you Father," Michelle said. "You've been like
a spiritual overseer for us and have always been a caring person, but never as much as tonight. We can't thank you enough
for your concern and thoughtfulness.

"Oh, go on," Blake blushed. "Get that box and move it.
Go on now." He shooed them toward the door. "The clock is
ticking."

Michelle hugged him tightly. "Thanks, friend."

Blake grinned.

Jack grabbed her arm. "Give us a ring and we'll be there.
We're out of here."

The trio rushed through the front door and disappeared
into the night.

53

THE TAXI THAT PICKED UP THE THREESOME OUTSIDE SAN GIOVANNI IN Laterano sped through the dark streets at a good speed. Guido kept the stone box on his lap carefully concealed beneath his coat. The driver had been told to go to the Townsends' apartment. No one said much.

"I think we're going in the wrong direction," Jack finally spoke up.

"What do you mean?" Guido ask.

"I think we ought to go to Santa Maria Church. Our work began there. Now we've come up with a sort of sarcophagus. Since the church is filled with coffins, it seems like it would be a more appropriate place to open our own little coffin."

"Down there in that crypt?" Michelle shivered.

Jack smiled. "Why not? Santa Maria has its own history, and the priests have been good to us. Why not put our treasure on a table and let all those ghosts from the past gather around and watch?"

"I nearly got killed down there!"

"True, but you came out smelling like a rose," Jack said.

"It wasn't that easy."

319

"Michelle, I was also surprised that you came on so strong when that crackhead put a gun in my face. You didn't seem frightened."

"I had to fight to keep my emotions from erupting full blown. I may not be able to keep the attacks from coming back, but I think I've learned how to control and direct the energy the old memories generate. When I yelled at that thug, it dissipated the anxiety that turns me inside out. Even with all the difficult and terrible experiences we've faced, I've made progress. If I can't make the problem stop, I've learned something about controlling the results."

"Then I think you can take one more trip down to the crypt." Jack grinned slyly.

"Oh, brother!" Michelle said. "I talked myself into a corner."

"OK." Guido leaned over the seat. "Driver take us to Via Vittorio Veneto 27. We're going to the Santa Maria Church."

"Whatever you say," the driver replied. The cab sped up.

"I hope knocking that stone mummy case to the floor didn't damage the document," Jack said.

Guido nodded and looked grave. "Certainly."

Michelle settled back against the seat and watched her husband. Seldom had she seen Jack so nervous. He kept rubbing his fist against his palm and then folding his hands together before starting the rubbing all over again. His entire adult life had been spent chasing such documents. He had looked into everything from the *Secret Gospel of Mark* to *John of Damascus* as well as numerous classical and Hellenistic texts. She knew his grasp of Greek remained remarkable. This new find had to be the consummate moment in his research.

"I guess we can forget about someone watching or following the cab," Jack said. "Stein must be running for the border, and The Scorpion terrorist group is captured. We already ruled out the Vatican as bad guys. Maybe we can open this receptacle in the quiet peacefulness of the crypt under the sanctuary."

"*Peacefulness* is not exactly the word that I would use," Michelle said. "But if it makes you happy, I'll settle for it."

Jack winked at her. "That's a good girl."

The taxi pulled up to the curb in front of the old church where the austere exterior left no clues as to the extraordinary sights inside. The driver said nothing but held his palm up.

Jack reached over the seat and crammed several bills in the man's hand. "Keep the change."

"Thank you," the man said and prepared to drive away.

"Let's enter through the side door," Jack said. "I want to get downstairs as quickly as possible."

Darkness had covered the entire street in almost impenetrable shadows. Only one street light provided any light. The recessed side door had to be unlocked without the help of light.

When the wooden door opened, Michelle said, "I think I have a screw driver, a small hammer, and some other stuff we might need in our office. I'll get it."

"Good," Jack said and rushed forward.

Jack and Guido clomped down the stairs while Michelle hurried to her office. At the bottom, an old table held brochures, small religious medals, and a few holy cards.

"Let's lift the table over here," Jack said. "I want to carry the table under the electric light next to the skeleton still standing there in an ancient brown robe. That old guy ought to have a look at what we're doing."

Guido frowned. "You're kidding." He looked again. "You're not!"

Jack grabbed his end and Guido took the other. They walked the table over under the light by the remains of some long-dead monk. A biretta on the skull gave the figure a ghastly, haunted look; bones dangling out of the deteriorating sleeves hung lifelessly. Obviously, some now departed priest had given the corpse a few touch-ups probably intended to convey a warning message of some variety or the other.

"We've got everything in order," Jack said. "You ready, Guido?"

"I think it is time to start calling me Jonas De Lateran again. Generations and generations of my family are standing behind me in this effort. This is a moment that the centuries have waited to see."

Michelle came bounding down the stairs. "I've got 'em." She held up a screwdriver, pliers, tweezers, and a small hammer. "Let's start the operation."

"Jonas, you are the one who should open the box. Your hands are the right ones and have been conditioned by a long family history."

Jonas picked up the screwdriver and hammer. He bowed his head and closed his eyes. After a deep breath, he said. "I'm ready."

The screwdriver slipped between the edges in the middle of the pieces of volcanic rock. With gentle taps, Guido began prying the sections loose. A popping noise signaled movement. Finally, the rock lid broke open. Guido picked up the top and lifted the piece to one side.

"There it is!" Michelle shrieked.

Jack leaned over and stared at two portions of papyrus lying one on top of the other. "I can't believe my eyes." He reached in his pocket for a pair of rubber gloves. "I brought these up earlier in case we got this far. I can't believe I'm about to touch this priceless document."

Michelle handed him a pair of tweezers. "I had these in my desk drawer. You'll need them to lift the pieces out."

Jack smiled. "We're about to open the treasure of the ages."

54

THE DIMNESS OF THE CRYPT SETTLED AROUND THE ROOM WHILE LONG opaque shadows fell around the chamber. Jack leaned over the two sheets of ancient papyrus on the small table, studying them carefully. With the tweezers Michelle handed him, he pulled the fragile pieces apart and laid them side by side. Jonas De Lateran hovered over his shoulder watching carefully.

"The legend I picked up from my father was that some ancient ancestor named Plautius Laterani found this ending to the Gospel of Mark while pursuing the Apostle Peter," Jonas said. "When the male members of our family gathered in seclusion after each year's formal Easter services, they always shared such stories. Supposedly, the end had been torn off during Nero's persecution of the Christians. Of course, the centuries may have added to the stories, and this account may be nothing more than an old myth."

"Fascinating though," Michelle said. "It adds an aura to this moment. Come on, Jack. Keep looking."

"My father also said that Ambrogio di Laterani became alarmed during the Norman conquest of South Italy and Sicily in the last half of the eleventh century. His concern caused the ending to the Gospel to be hidden permanently. Ambrogio's fear precipitated the placement of the two portions behind the baptistery. Of course, none of these ancestors spoke or read ancient Greek so they had no idea what it said. Possibly, they even attributed magical powers to the text. Amazing story, isn't it?"

Jack bent closer. "The journey of these pieces of ancient parchment into the contemporary era is a big story unto itself. It will be an important part of the explanation we present when our translation work is done." He pulled the two pieces more directly into the light. "Let's see exactly what these lines say."

"As we all know, the New Testament was written in Koine Greek, which was the common language of the street," Jonas said. "The everyday folks made significant changes from the old Doric and Ionic dialects. The shifts produced a New Testament in the language of the common people."

"Yes," Michelle added. "We studied how the Ionic branch gave birth to the Attic dialect from which Koine sprang. Jack knows this subject well."

Townsend said nothing as his fingers moved quickly and adroitly across the lines of the manuscript. "The last lines that we have from Mark's Gospel say something like 'they went out and fled the tomb; for trembling and astonishment had come upon them; and they said nothing to any one, for they were afraid.' That's where this papyri should pick up the story."

"Does it?" Jonas pressed.

"Y-yes," Jack said slowly. "But it doesn't continue with a res- urrection account. It suggests that Jesus defeated evil through his resurrection and the final victory over death was his. It ends by saying 'we have been delivered from the present evil age.'"

"Everybody raise their hands slowly," Albert Stein's voice echoed out of the darkness.

"Stein!" Jack barely whispered.

"I've got this gun trained on you, and I'm more than prepared to shoot," Albert Stein said. "Now back away from the table."

"How did you get here?" Jonas growled.

"I thought you would come back to the church to open the little stone sarcophagus. It's how you think, Jack. You've got that little macabre twist in your personality, and you love the past. You're mired down in those ancient texts. I was correct."

"You're projecting your own draconian motivations onto me," Jack said, lifting his hands in the air.

"And the doors need better locks." Stein motioned with his gun. "Back up against the wall. All of you."

"Do what he says." Jack stepped back. "You know what he's capable of."

Michelle and Jonas lined up beside him and started stepping back.

"This time I will win, Jack," Stein said. "You were lucky back at the church, but there's no one here to save you." He reached out and picked up the tweezers. "I'm putting the document back in the stone box and will be leaving with it." Stein carefully lifted the parchment back into the stone container. "I should kill all of you, but I want you to be around when the story comes out in the paper describing how I found the original ending to Mark's Gospel in a church baptistery in Rome. I know there'll be poetic justice in your seeing my victory."

"You're crazy!" Michelle hissed.

"No, I'm the winner." Stein grinned. "Now if you'll excuse me. I must be on my way."

"You'll never get away with this," Jonas said.

"Oh, but I already have." Stein started backing to the stairs. "I have a tight schedule this evening and must be about my journey. Good evening, dearest friends." He quickly hustled up the stairs. Moments later the sound of the church door slamming echoed through the building.

"Stein's escaping!" Michelle screamed. "We've got to call the police!"

"It doesn't matter now," Jack said.

"What do you mean?" Guido gasped.

"I don't get it." Michelle pleaded.

Jack slumped back against the wall and looked at the skeleton hanging leisurely against the wall with a biretta on its head. "Seems we are in the appropriate place to celebrate a death, a demise of a great search. Unfortunately, the Greek in this document is in the language of Plutarch. By contrast, the language of the New Testament was strongly affected by Hebrew and Aramaic. The Semitic influence came from the business and street usage of Greek. It was the natural living lingo of everyday life. This document was written in the language of literature with a much more formal structure. My guess is it was written by a professional scribe of some sort."

"What are you saying?" Michelle asked.

"The biblical ending of Mark and these pieces of the manuscript are different. It's like reading *Don Quixote* in Castilian Spanish and then going to Texas and speaking Tex-Mex."

Jonas slumped. "The pieces don't fit?" His voice fell. "After all these centuries, I find out that this carefully concealed document was a fraud?"

"It has importance," Jack said. "Anything this old is significant. Most, most, most sadly, however, is that it's not the authentic ending."

"We've truly lost everything," Jonas groaned.

"No," Jack said. "Dr. Albert Stein has lost everything. He'll discover in time that the manuscript is only a fake. As he would say, 'that's poetic justice.'"

Deafening quietness settled over the crypt. A pained appearance washed over Jonas's face and his mouth dropped. "We've failed." Jonas looked like he was about to become ill.

"No!" Michelle suddenly interjected. "No, not at all! We haven't failed. Take a second look. We've written a new chapter in an ancient story. This isn't the end of the road."

"What do you mean?" Jonas asked.

"One of the most intriguing stories of all time is how the Scriptures have been preserved and handed down through countless difficulties. We have everything from Codex Vaticanus and Codex Sinaiticus to a host of textual fragments including the Hesychian or Egyptian type as well as Byzantine texts. There are more copies of this story than any other ancient document. These countless editions bare witness to the extraordinary value that the ancients placed on this story. What Jonas's ancestors did in hiding the two fragments is itself an astonishing story reflecting the value they placed on the New Testament."

She paused and took a deep breath. "No, we haven't lost," Michelle said. "We've simply found another example of the importance of our work. Don't miss the fact that we, the three of us, have already experienced the fulfillment of the message written in these two pages. This very night we have already been delivered from evil in this age. We have escaped death this evening. We simply didn't find exactly what we've been hunting."

Jonas nodded slowly and then shook his head more emphatically. "Yes, yes, I believe you are right."

Jack rubbed his chin and thought for a moment. "You're absolutely correct. Dear, I think you've remembered the most important truth of all. Regardless of the origins, the message on this ancient papyri remains true. It may not be Scripture, but its witness is true. By the grace of God, we've found our way through a multitude of skeletons in the world's oldest closet."

"I know we live in a complex time," Jonas said. "Still, it is amazing how events have turned out. Tony Mattei wanted to tyrannize and terrify by destroying his perceived and imaginary enemies, but even at this moment he's on the way to life behind bars. Albert Stein was willing to pay any price to gain prominence and fame, but he's running into the night to escape capture. A racist like Klaus Burchel ended up on the floor dead. And here we are. The survivors! It isn't what I expected either, but I am grateful. Yes, deeply grateful to be alive."

If nothing else, eventually Stein will have to turn the document over to other scholars for their examination if he wants any sort of credit for coming up with a fraud. If nothing else, he'll add another document for scholars to argue about. My hunch is that good ol' Albert is too arrogant to admit such a defeat."

"No," Michelle said. "We've done much more than circumvent an evil man. We have penetrated the darkness with an unquenchable light."

55

THE TYPICAL CONGESTION OF ROME'S STREET TRAFFIC CONTINUED AT ITS usual frantic pace down Vicolo del Bologna in front of the Dar Poeta sidewalk café. Luichi walked from table to table taking orders and swinging the silver coffeepot with his usual artistic flourishes. Even though it was late November, sitting outside with a sweater on felt exhilarating. Somewhere down some boulevard, the sirens of a fire engine signaled an emergency. No one slowed. Off in the distance, the top of the magnificent dome of St. Peter's Basilica towered above the surrounding buildings.

Jack and Michelle Townsend sat leisurely at one of the small tables eating breakfast. Now and then, Jack casually looked up and watched the endless parade of all shapes and sizes walking down the street.

"You really enjoy watching the sideshow," Michelle said.

"Really? Hmm. Perhaps." Jack grinned.

"Perhaps, nothing," she said. "Those artichokes cooked in the Roman-Jewish style are the only thing you like more than watching the marching army of the strange and beautiful go by."

"I believe you have made a profound point."

"There's no profundity there. It's simple observation made from watching you every chance you get to show up at the Dar Poeta."

Jack laughed. "I'm trapped. I have no defense. On the other hand, I brought you with me. See. That shows magnanimity."

"We haven't heard a word from Don Blake since we left last night," Michelle said. "I've called him Father so long that it's hard now not to keep from doing so."

"We'll get a call before long. Don't worry."

Silence fell between them again.

Finally Michelle said, "My thoughts keep returning to Dov Sharon. Our friend's death was pushed aside by the events we've lived through, but when I remember what happened, I am profoundly saddened. I'm ashamed that I had bad thoughts about him."

"Yes," Jack said. "Dov was our friend and such a compatriot. I wonder what he'd say if he knew how this pursuit has turned out?"

"Oh, he'd probably come up with one of his jokes. Maybe, he'd suggest that the ancient ending of Mark would now make good shelf paper. Something of that order."

"Dov knew how to push the pain of tragedy aside with a smile on his face." Perhaps, the struggles of his people taught him how to endure by using a grin as his friend."

"I suppose so," Michelle said. "I didn't tell you earlier but I did something yesterday that I felt I needed to do. The Jewish people believe that the soul lingers near the body for a period of months so I went to the Jewish cemetery and gave Dov a formal send off. A little best wishes from both of us."

"Nice," Jack said. "Thoughtful. You know, I've been thinking about that priest down there at the bottom level under the Vatican. Remember Father Donnello? The old priest tucked away in that basement where they are excavating the Circus of Caligula and Nero? Dov certainly touched that man's life. I was thinking of going back to see him today."

"Really?"

"Father Donnello has the answer to where *The Prologue of James* is hidden. I think another visit would be worthwhile for our next project."

"I know you haven't given up on finding the ending to Mark's Gospel, but this last failure has to be a let down since both of us came so close and then found our search to be futile."

Jack nodded. Michelle said, "It really threw Jonas De Lateran for a loop. The poor man had spent a lifetime waiting for this revelation only to discover it was a mistake. He kept a stiff upper lip though, but I know it was difficult."

"Certainly. To have a family secret kept through centuries of struggle disappear in a matter of seconds would be difficult for anyone to accept, but your words of encouragement helped him."

Michelle smiled. "I hope so. I really do believe in the meaning of what I told both of you last night. Those convictions came from the heart."

"You had a good word for us, dear." Jack pushed the empty plate back. "Oh, man! Those artichokes were good."

"I don't see how anyone could eat those greasy things for breakfast." Michelle's voice took on a cynical tone. "Really!"

"You know we're so close to the Amadeo bridge and the Borgo Santo Spirito street that runs into the Piazza San Pietro of the Vatican, I think I might run over there for a quick word with Father Donnello. What do you think?"

"Fine with me," Michelle said. "I've never been a big people watcher, but I can see how these street people held your attention. I think it might be fun to sit here and watch for a while, wondering about their struggles."

"You've got your cell phone. We can hook up without any problem."

"Sure."

Jack stood up. "I won't be long. Let's see what happens."

"Good luck," Michelle waved and watched him walk down the street.

During the next hour, she watched the endless parade of the unusual saunter past. One woman looked like she was over six feet tall with extremely long arms. Her smart miniskirt revealed slender but alluring legs. Probably a model, the young lady walked so straight she appeared to be reaching for another inch of height. An old woman with a scarf tied over her head came shuffling down the street. A simple silver cross hung around her neck over an old, hand-knitted sweater. Shrunken cheeks make it appear she had lost her teeth. The worn hands and recessed eyes reflected a hard life—just the opposite of the tall young lady.

Michelle took another sip of coffee. She'd often teased Jack about his incessant ogling of shoppers while dining at the Dar Poeta, but she enjoyed the variety of sights that drifted by on this cool November morning. Finally, she found the latest edition of the *Il Messaggero* newspaper and ran down the local stories.

The headlines screamed that detective Alfredo Pino made a significant catch in apprehending the terrorist Tony Mattei. She didn't remember Pino being within a hundred miles of the baptistery, but the nervous detective seemed to have a knack for showing up at the right time *after* the action was over. How could she ever forget the cop who thought they were up to something because Jack and she kept being the target of an attack? No mention of Don Blake anywhere. Their friend must have had his reasons for disappearing from the news story. The account concluded with the statement that Rome could sleep easy now that The Scorpion terrorist gang had been captured. No report of what became of the rest of the bad guys. How like Rome this story was.

She finished the paper and laid it on the table. For the next forty-five minutes, she watched the locals stroll by. Michelle concluded that the last three months had been like a lifetime crammed into a small box. Perhaps, one of the most profitable things that had happened to her was bringing her emotional problem under greater control. No longer did she fear the loud sirens or flinch when the unexpected happened. No small victory there.

Looking up the street, she saw Jack hustling down the sidewalk. Glancing at her watch, Michelle discovered that he had been gone for a shorter amount of time than she had expected. It should prove interesting to see what he'd come up with. He waved and picked up the pace.

"That didn't take long," Michelle said as Jack sat down.

"Father Donnello seemed absolutely delighted to see me. We drank a nice coffee and had a delightful conversation. I told him that he came to mind while we were discussing Dov Sharon. That remembrance particularly pleased him."

"And?" Michelle gestured with her hand for him to say more.

"I brought up *The Prologue of James* and asked if he'd come to a decision to tell me more."

"Yes?"

"The priest said he had." Jack stopped and smiled. "I think I know where the document won't be found."

"What?"

"The document is not in Rome."

Discussion Questions

1. Had you noticed that there are three endings to Mark's Gospel? Take a look. What would you make of these differences?

2. How might any one of these different endings affect the meaning of the entire Gospel?

3. How would you perceive the theological struggle between Gnostics (as represented by Stein) and the contemporary understanding of Christianity (represented by the Townsends)?

4. Can you explain why theological differences could make individuals angry enough to become dangerous? Where and how is that happening in our world today?

5. The story turns on issues of resentment and frustration that have become volatile enough to cause death and destruction. Where are similar boiling points exploding right now? Can they be disarmed?

6. We often identify with a particular character in a story. What character did you tie in with?

7. Would you have done anything differently from what this character did in the story? What?

8. The Church of Santa Maria della Concezione displays the bones of more than four thousand Capuchin monks. Why would the custodians of the church develop such a display? What kind of statement does it make to anyone today?

9. Have you ever imagined such a sight? How might bones and skulls hanging from the ceiling affect you?

10. Strange and unexpected sights may take us to distinct times in our own lives that could be difficult to deal with. Events around Michelle Townsend forced her to

fight post-traumatic stress symptoms. What would you do with such experiences? How can one successfully confront such issues?

11. We live in increasingly violent times. Do attacks, shootings, and explosions affect your sense of security? Do you find yourself being fearful of being out at night or in strange neighborhoods? How can we face such an environment?

12. What is a Christian approach to such fears?

Want to learn more about author
Robert L. Wise and check out other great fiction
from Abingdon Press?

Sign up for our fiction newsletter at
www.AbingdonPress.com/Fiction
to read interviews with your favorite authors, find tips
for starting a reading group, and stay posted on what
new titles are on the horizon. It's a place to connect
with other fiction readers or post a
comment about this book.

Be sure to visit Robert online!

www.robertwisebooks.com